Only one woman on earth had eyes the color of a winter sea, eyes that could burn a man's soul if she set her mind to it. And she was looking right at him.

Wil had to fight for breath as he called to her. "Elsa?"

Elise flinched at his use of her old name and contemplated the wisdom of dashing away. It couldn't be Wil Larsen staring at her. Fate wouldn't play this kind of trick on her.

Briefly she closed her eyes, willing him to disappear. When she opened them again, his gaze remained fixed on her. Under its scrutiny, she felt ten years of protective walls begin to crumble. She'd spent a very long time trying to put Wil Larsen—a man she'd once loved with a soul-consuming intensity—behind her.

So why, after all this time, did the mere sight of him threaten to tumble her into chaos?

Dear Reader,

Happy New Year! I hope this year brings you all your heart desires…and I hope you enjoy the many books coming your way this year from Silhouette Special Edition!

January features an extraspecial THAT SPECIAL WOMAN!—Myrna Temte's *A Lawman for Kelly*. Deputy U.S. Marshal Steve Anderson is back (remember him in Myrna's *Room for Annie?*), and he's looking for love in Montana. Don't miss this warm, wonderful story!

Then travel to England this month with *Mistaken Bride*, by Brittany Young—a compelling Gothic story featuring two identical twins with very different personalities…. Or stay at home with *Live-In Mom* by Laurie Paige, a tender story about a little matchmaker determined to bring his stubborn dad to the altar with the right woman! And don't miss *Mr. Fix-It* by Jo Ann Algermissen. A man who is good around the house is great to find anytime during the year!

This month also brings you *The Lone Ranger*, the initial story in Sharon De Vita's winsome new series, SILVER CREEK COUNTY. Falling in love is all in a day's work in this charming Texas town. And watch for the first book by a wonderful writer who is new to Silhouette Special Edition—Neesa Hart. Her book, *Almost to the Altar*, is sure to win many new fans.

I hope this New Year shapes up to be the best year ever! Enjoy this book, and all the books to come!

Sincerely

Tara Gavin
Senior Editor

Please address questions and book requests to:
Silhouette Reader Service
U.S.: 3010 Walden Ave., P.O. Box 1325, Buffalo, NY 14269
Canadian: P.O. Box 609, Fort Erie, Ont. L2A 5X3

NEESA HART
ALMOST TO THE ALTAR

Silhouette ®

TM

SPECIAL EDITION®

Published by Silhouette Books
America's Publisher of Contemporary Romance

To Joyce Flaherty, for sharing the dream; to
Denise Little for sharing the vision; to Deb Dixon,
for sharing her wisdom;
to Mom, who fixed everything and…
To the grease-covered heroes at Ferry Farm
Automotive who made sure I got everywhere I needed
to go—and who *never* charge $50 to screw in a
light bulb.

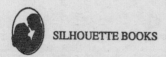 SILHOUETTE BOOKS

ISBN 0-373-24080-5

ALMOST TO THE ALTAR

Copyright © 1997 by Neesa Hart

This edition published by arrangement with Harlequin Books S.A.

® and TM are trademarks of Harlequin Books S.A., used under license.
Trademarks indicated with ® are registered in the United States Patent
and Trademark Office, the Canadian Trade Marks Office and in other
countries.

Printed in U.S.A.

NEESA HART,

who writes contemporary romances under her own name, and historical romances as Mandalyn Kaye, lives outside Washington, D.C., where, she says, "Truth really is stranger than fiction."

An avid romance fan for years, she got hooked while majoring in international affairs and geography in college. "Romances," she said, "were always more fun, more informative and more relaxing than anything I was supposed to be reading for class." After a brief political career, including a Senate-confirmed appointment to the President's Council on Women's Educational Programs, Neesa abandoned the hectic world of politics to pursue her dream as a full-time author. "Nothing," she says, "could be better than telling stories for a living."

Her interests, other than writing and reading, include volunteering at her church, collecting Barbie dolls, and playing the banjo. One day, she hopes to learn to pick "Oh, Susannah."

Neesa loves to hear from her readers. You can write to her at: 101 E. Holly Avenue, St. 3, Sterling, VA 20164.

Chapter One

Mud and a wet woman, he decided, had to be one of the sexiest combinations on earth.

As Wil Larsen splashed through the convenience-store parking lot, he studied the bedraggled woman awaiting him by the pay phone. In the two months since she'd hired him for a major restoration of twenty vintage automobiles, Wil hadn't actually spoken to her. He'd cursed her plenty of times, but he'd left the person-to-person contact up to his father, his business partner. Her law firm was handling the auction of the vehicles as part of an estate liquidation, and she'd driven his father crazy with her demands for constant invoicing, supervision and status reports. If the job hadn't been so big, and if her business hadn't mattered quite so much to their business, Wil would have told her to take a flying leap a long time ago.

His father, Jan, had insisted, however, that he could handle her, that her excruciating addiction to detail, her obsession with minutiae, merely reflected an appreciation of the rare cars' value. Wil had an entirely different spin on the situation but, heretofore, had managed to keep his not-so-kind opinion to himself.

The restoration project was enormous, and as he and his father were continuing to build a reputation in auto refurbishment, Jan had wisely advised that they'd be foolish to turn it down simply because the inimitable Ms. Christopher was a royal pain in the butt. To keep peace, Jan had even agreed to handle all the contacts with her himself, the only saving grace in the situation.

This very afternoon, in the pouring-down rain, his seventy-two-year-old father was out scrounging in a junkyard, looking for a part that Ms. Christopher had insisted must be original. It didn't matter that a perfectly usable fabrication was available for half the price and a tenth of the effort, nor did it matter that the fabrication would in no way lessen the resale value of the car. Elise Christopher wanted it done one way and one way only.

The mere thought made Wil furious. His father had no business being out in weather like this, but despite Wil's considerable efforts to volunteer for the errand himself, Jan had insisted he would do the search. As it turned out, providence must have played a hand in the old man's stubbornness. Elise Christopher needed a tow, and Wil needed to let off steam. He was about to accomplish both ends.

The curtain of rain blurred her figure where she huddled in the shallow phone booth. He didn't need to see her face to know she was miserable. A pathetic excuse for an umbrella made a valiant attempt to shield her from the rain. Water dripped from her hair. Mud caked her navy trench coat.

Latent frustration still pumped through him when he thought of the hours of unnecessary aggravation this woman had caused them. At times he could picture her, subdued, sophisticated, aloof, phoning their garage from her high-rise office in the heart of Chicago to issue her latest unreasonable edict. He'd known plenty of women just like her, knew how they operated, how they thought. Elise Christopher was just one more professional broad who thought herself too good for the rest of them.

This morning's long walk in the rain to the pay phone had probably wounded her pride more than her body. The thought should have satisfied him. But it didn't.

He raked another glance over her disheveled appearance. It didn't satisfy him at all.

It turned him on.

Maybe it was the feeling of revenge, or the simple male satisfaction of seeing her, a woman with as much tact as Attila the Hun, in such a predicament. He wasn't sure. He just knew that the sight of her set his nerve endings on fire. The thought made him chastise himself for his lack of civility. For the past two months, he'd been cursing her to high heaven, but that didn't seem to stop him from ogling her like a hormone-driven teenager.

With a brief shake of his head, he guided his white tow truck through the obstacle course of potholes. If she knew what he was thinking, she'd probably deck him. At the thought of telling her she looked sexy with her stockings caked in mud and her clothes pasted to her body, he almost laughed out loud. Granted, most women—hell, most men—in her predicament wouldn't find the matter very laughable, but there was something extrasweet about seeing Elise Christopher meet the real world.

As he neared her position by the pay phone, he almost allowed himself to feel a twinge of sympathy. Up close, she looked more like a drowned cat and less like a temptation. His gaze slid to her mud-splattered legs. Not much less, true, but less. Rolling his truck to a stop five feet from the phone booth, he lowered the passenger window with a press of a button. "Elise Christopher?" he asked.

She dropped the umbrella enough to meet his gaze. At the wide-eyed look of stunned horror she gave him, a look in eyes that were unmistakably familiar, unmistakably known to him, the breath left his lungs in a *whoosh*. Only one woman on earth had eyes the color of a winter sea; eyes that could burn a man's soul if she set her mind to it. And she was looking right at him. The impact of that gaze began to stir a long-dormant tempest, like a storm coming to life. Wil had to fight for breath as he mentally subdued the first wave of undiluted panic.

"Elsa?"

She flinched. "Wil?"

Elise was contemplating the wisdom of dashing away into the rainstorm. It couldn't be Wil Larsen staring at her from the warm haven of that truck. Fate wouldn't play this kind of trick on her.

Briefly she closed her eyes, willing him to disappear. When she opened them again, his fog-colored gaze remained fixed on hers. Under its scrutiny, she felt ten years of protective walls begin to crumble. She'd spent a very long time trying to put Wil Larsen—a man she'd once loved with a soul-consuming intensity—behind her. Her life was different now, together, ordered. So why did the mere sight of him, after all this time, threaten to tumble her into chaos?

Of all the things in the world she wasn't prepared to deal with this afternoon, a confrontation with Wil Larsen topped the list. Why, oh, why hadn't his father come to fetch her? What was he doing here in Valdona, instead of in Chicago, where he belonged? And how the hell was she supposed to avoid getting into that truck with him?

"Are you getting in?" he asked, his tone harsh, almost as if he wished she'd say no.

Despite the very real possibility that she might drown if she refused, Elise considered telling him she'd changed her mind about the tow. But the warm breeze from the truck's heater beckoned like a tropical sea, and before her courage could desert her, she mentally braced herself, then climbed into the truck. She refused to give him the small victory of knowing he'd scared her away. She was an adult. She'd act like one.

Shaking the water from her umbrella, she studiously avoided his gaze. "I— Thanks so much for coming to get me," she told him. "This storm is horrible."

"You didn't look very pleased to see me."

Shocked had been more like it. "I was expecting your father."

His scrutiny seemed to bore into her. She had to force herself not to squirm. He'd always had an uncanny ability to make her feel awkward. Summoning up years of self-discipline, she said, "I'm sorry you had to come out in this rain."

"I'm not the only one out in this mess. My father," he told her, his voice harsh, "is scrounging around in a junk-yard for a Diana radiator cap."

"Oh." She gave him a stricken look. "I didn't mean for him to go today. Stevenson would have held it for him until Monday."

"Funny, Pop didn't see it that way."

Elise frowned. She didn't like the thought of Jan Larsen out in this downpour. He'd always been susceptible to damp weather. "I wish I'd made that more clear. I just thought he'd like to know that I'd found an original part."

"It's our job to find the parts." Disapproval dripped from his tone, making the atmosphere inside the cab as damp as the afternoon.

Elise mentally counted to three. She refused to let him goad her into an argument. They'd done all the arguing she could stand the day he threw her out of his life. "I know that," she said, in much the same tone she used to pacify irate judges and irrational clients. "I just happened to stumble on this. Still, I hadn't meant for Jan to make the trip today." The dreary sky seemed to close in on them. "No one should be out in this."

She was looking at her drenched hair and mud-splattered clothes. "Especially not you," he said.

She refused to consider what he might have meant by the comment. Wil, she knew, felt any number of things about her, and none of them were good. He'd made that clear enough the day he broke off their relationship. Shivering, she wrapped her arms around her middle. The best she could do was try to make light of the situation. The sooner they got her car towed and on the road, the sooner she could be away from this infuriating, frustrating man. "This whole thing wouldn't have been so bad," she continued, hoping her voice sounded at least partially normal, "if this place had been open." With a flick of her wrist, she indicated the closed convenience store. "If I'd known the owner's daughter was getting married this weekend, I'd have picked a different place for my car to break down."

The joke fell flat. An impassive expression remained firmly in place as he continued to watch her. Since she'd last seen him, his face had hardened. His thick blond hair should have lessened the severity of his determined features, but a quick glance at his face dispelled any hope she had that years had lessened the impact of his expression. It was still as hard as granite, as welcoming as a stone barricade.

When his gaze caught hers and refused to let go, she felt the umbrella slip from her cold fingers. It tumbled to the floor mat with a dull thud. She wondered if her imagination was playing tricks on her, or if the expression in his eyes really did cause the windows to fog.

Instinctively her fingers gripped the worn leather pocket calendar she still clutched in her hand. Besides the umbrella, she'd carried nothing else with her from the car on the long trek to the pay phone. Jan's number was scrawled in the back of the small organizer. Elise ran her fingers over the carved leather cover, finding a strange solace in the familiar feel of it. The cover had been a high school graduation gift from Wil, almost twenty years ago. It was one of the few links she kept to a time long past. If his hard expression was any indication, the time was not just past, it was forgotten.

"Elise Christopher," he said again, as if testing the sound of her name. She'd never heard it carry so much anger. Instinctively she leaned as far from him as possible, not because she feared him physically, but because the hardness in his voice threatened to hurt her emotionally. Her arm pressed into the door. If he noticed, he ignored her discomfort. "Were you and Pop planning to tell me, or was I going to get strung along for two more months?"

"Tell you what?" At the question, his firm mouth pressed into a thin line, and the sight made her stomach quiver. She mentally berated herself for being ridiculous. Wil might be angry, but she had no reason to be afraid of him. He'd hurt her as much as he ever could ten years ago.

"Nobody thought that maybe I should know that the Elise Christopher who's been driving us crazy for the past eight weeks is really the Elsa Krestyanov who drove me crazy ten years ago?"

Stunned by the accusation in his voice, she frowned. "It never occurred to me that you didn't know."

His eyebrows lifted a fraction. "You've been issuing orders to Pop left and right. Didn't you think I'd find out sooner or later?"

Pushing her damp bangs off her forehead, she said, "Wil, I—well, I really don't know why you think you should have been involved in this."

"Involved?"

"Yes. I mean, my business with your father is just that— business. I had a job that needed to be done. Your father was competent and available. I knew he'd been servicing the cars for my client for years, and it simply made sense to get him to complete the restoration for the auction. I was very glad I could give him the business, but it never occurred to me that you might get involved."

His gaze narrowed to an edge so sharp she felt impaled against the window. "Great plan, Elsa," he told her, then jammed the truck into gear. "Which way's your car?"

Evidently he wanted the encounter over as much as she did. Seeing no reason to argue, she pointed south. "Back that way. About a mile, I think."

Without looking at her again, Wil shoved the heater button to the defrost position, then headed for the deserted stretch of highway. For several long seconds, the only sound in the cab came from the heater fan and the steady drone of the windshield wipers.

Elise drew four or five calming breaths, while mentally chiding herself for not realizing the risk she'd taken by calling Jan Larsen for a tow. When she phoned his garage, it had never occurred to her that the man barking at her through the receiver would be Wil. She should have realized that he might be home for the weekend, that no one else would be manning the shop while Jan was out.

She slid her sodden penny loafers off to wriggle her toes in the comforting heat along the floorboards. Yes, she'd been a fool not to anticipate this possible confrontation. Worse, she'd underestimated the effect he'd have on her. Ten years should have been enough to diminish the way his presence sharpened her awareness, the way he made her flesh feel sensitive beneath her clothes, the way her blood ran hot and the pulse pounded in her throat at the sight of him. But it hadn't. The sensations were just as acute as she remembered, and, judging from the way his knuckles had turned white from his grip on the steering wheel, he wasn't exactly immune to her, either.

She found satisfaction in that, but the more she considered his attitude, the more she allowed aggravation to help conquer the unsettling experience of seeing him again. No matter what his opinion of her, Wil Larsen had no right to treat her as if she had the plague. His disapproval crowded in on her like a palpable thing in the close confines of the truck. It was no surprise that she found she resented it as much today as she had ten years before. So why did the sight of his muscled thighs encased in grease-stained jeans raise unwanted goose bumps on her forearms?

Frustrated with herself for reacting to him, she jerked the elastic band from her thick braid, so that she could work the tangles from her hair. She'd put Wil, and his memory, behind her, where they belonged. If she kept her head about it, once she made it through today, she could again close the door on that part of her life.

Wil stared at the road as his mind raced in a thousand different directions. His father must have known. He had to have known. Despite the fact that Jan hadn't met with her face-to-face in the two months since she'd hired them, there was simply no way he hadn't been aware of who she was. His father might be getting older, but he was sharper than most men half his age.

She continued to play with her hair. Wil resisted the urge to watch as her fingers combed through the dark waves. He was concentrating so hard on not looking at her that his heart nearly skipped a beat when her arm brushed the sleeve of his flannel shirt.

Nothing, it seemed, had changed. As always, the merest touch from her heated his blood.

No woman on earth had ever had the power to affect him like Elsa. When he was a teenager, all he'd had to do was look at her and his pulse would shoot to the moon. By the time childish infatuation evolved into teenage lust, any-thing—a whiff of her perfume, a note stuck in his cap, even a thought of her—had made him rock-hard. For years, he'd waited for Elsa to quit looking at him as her older broth-er's best friend—to see him, and not a substitute for Maks. Elsa was three years younger than he. It had taken longer for her teenage crush to blossom into the kind of very adult emotions he craved from her.

To the day he died, he'd never forget the moment when he'd first seen the recognition in her eyes. She'd been twenty, home from college. He'd been twenty-three, ready to leave for graduate school in Boston. She'd been sitting on the fender of his Mustang, handing him tools as he tuned the engine. He'd requested a quarter-inch socket wrench. When she placed it in his hand, he'd glanced at her, only to find himself mesmerized by the way her storm-blue eyes were studying his hand. Breathless seconds had passed as he waited for her to meet his gaze. When she finally lifted her eyes to his, the look in them had all but sent him to his knees. Desire, mingled with a heart-stopping wonder, had chased away her childhood, and left in its place a woman's wants, a woman's needs.

He'd waited too long, spent too many sleepless nights, waiting for that look. On impact, hunger had seized him. Nothing in the world could have prevented him from making love to Elsa that night. Warning bells had screamed in his brain, cautioning him that it was too soon for her, her awareness was too new, her desire too untested. His mind had known he should give her time, not rush her into accepting the feverish passion between them, but a searing urgency had forced every consideration aside. At that moment, he'd have sworn that he'd die if he didn't have her.

Elsa had fallen into his arms with an eagerness that lessened the guilt he felt for rushing her. With equal fervor, she'd torn at his clothes, pressed hot, needful kisses to his skin. The feel of her had fulfilled every fantasy he'd ever had, and awakened some he hadn't even known existed. That night, she'd become the center of his world. When he was inside of her, he'd finally found the meaning of *forever*. Without her, he'd known, he'd never be complete again.

And he'd spent years paying the price for losing control that night.

With his body and his actions, he'd promised Elsa forever. When he made love to her, he'd given her a piece of himself, and taken a piece of her in return. Even if he wanted to, he could no more give her back what he possessed than he could claim what she now owned of him. It didn't matter that he'd intended to marry her, didn't matter that he'd told her he loved her. He'd made a commitment to her that night that had never been kept.

And he'd spent ten years trying to pretend it didn't matter.

Unbidden, those images from the past skittered across his mind, creating a deep sense of panic as he struggled to find his balance in the face of her sudden reappearance in his life. He wasn't ready to face Elsa, might never be ready, but fate, and what he suspected was his father's interference, had tossed him over the threshold. Whether he liked it or not, he couldn't run from the past any longer.

Despite his better judgment, he stole a look at her. With her head bent, her damp hair trailing over her shoulder as she combed it with her fingers, she looked more than a little vulnerable. For ten years he'd fed his sense of betrayal by cultivating an image of Elsa as an invincible, self-centered snob. That image was a hell of a lot safer for his peace of mind than the one she presented now. The woman who sat in his truck bore an unsettling resemblance to the one he'd been ready to sell his soul to possess.

With a mental shake, he dragged his mind back to the present. Jan had known, all right, he decided, but not Elsa. He could feel her trembling beside him, knew she'd been as disconcerted as he when he met her in the parking lot. Evidently he wasn't the only one who'd been kept in the dark. If she hadn't known he'd gone back into business with his father, she probably didn't know why. That thought calmed him. He clung to it as the storm of panic began to abate. If he could get through the afternoon without having to explain himself to her, he might just survive.

The delicate scent of her perfume carried on the dry, heated air, effectively destroying his efforts to ignore her. Damn her to hell. Unless he missed his guess, she knew exactly what she was doing to him as she sat there and unmatted her hair. Unbidden, his gaze slid to her feet. As he'd expected, he found them bare, wet, and far too appealing. Elsa never had liked wearing shoes. It didn't surprise him that she'd shed her loafers, but as long as he lived, he'd never know what was so sexy about a woman's ankle. And hers were better than most.

Those ankles were the first thing he'd noticed about her when he stopped seeing her as the pesky kid sister of his best friend. The day he finally realized that what he felt for her didn't have a damned thing to do with brotherly love had been the beginning of the end for him. If his present reaction to her, the way his blood was running hot and his gut had tightened into an uncomfortable knot, was any indication, she hadn't lost her touch. His wayward gaze found the spot where her skirt lay against her damp thigh. Soon, he promised himself, it would be over.

Blissfully he saw the dark shape of a car just ahead on the highway. "That it?" he asked. He knew his voice sounded harsh, but couldn't seem to help it. He was getting desperate to put some distance between them.

Elsa nodded. "Yes."

He whipped the truck in a sharp U, then backed it quickly into position. "You want me to try and fix it here, or tow it?"

"I don't think you can fix it here. I think it needs a new fuel pump. Besides, I don't think you should mess with it out in this storm. Why don't we just take it somewhere dry?"

He didn't question her diagnosis of the car. When things were different, he'd taught her all about engines. If she said it was the fuel pump, it probably was. "Fine." He put the truck in park and fled into the rain, where finally he felt the air refilling his lungs, his heart began to beat a normal rhythm, and he could force the image of her—cold, trembling and tempting—from his mind. She reminded him of the mythical sirens who'd lured men to their death with the sound of their voices. All she had to do to lure him to destruction was climb into his truck, damp and smelling like violets.

Elise huddled in the cab, mentally estimating how much more of this nightmare remained. With any luck, Wil would get the car to his father's shop, she'd call Parker to come get her and she could be back on the road, back to her life, in less than an hour. She clung to that thought as if it were a lifeline.

In the rearview mirror, she watched as he struggled in the rain to secure the car. There'd been a time when the sight of him, the warmth of his smile, the light in his eyes, was enough to send shivers of longing down her spine. Evidently things hadn't changed as much as she'd thought. When she climbed into the truck, she'd been trembling from the cold. The chill that now left goose bumps on her skin had nothing to do with the temperature.

Determined to think of anything but how the feel of him next to her in the truck had made her skin tingle, she found a clean-looking hand towel behind his seat. She used it to wring the bulk of the water from her hair, relying on the mundane task to take her mind from his troubling presence.

By the time he climbed back into the truck, her hair was almost dry. He was soaked. Somehow, that gave her an added measure of confidence. With the dampened towel lying in her lap, she felt more in control than before. Even the cool look he gave her failed to elicit another round of shivers.

"That's an expensive car you're driving these days," he told her.

She recognized the condemnation in his voice, contemplated not answering, then changed her mind. She'd done nothing wrong, and she saw no reason to let him bait her. "It's not mine. It belongs to my fiancé."

She felt his gaze slide to her left hand. "I see."

Tension began to crowd in on her, knot her muscles and churn her stomach. "Wil, I don't think we should talk about this."

The look he gave her could have frozen lava. He ignored her quiet plea. "You're engaged to a man who drives an eighty-thousand-dollar sports car, you're wearing a disgustingly enormous engagement ring, and you've been deceiving me for the last two months. Seems like ten years hasn't changed you a whole lot."

At the snide taunt, she bristled. "I don't know what you think you have to be so angry about, Wil, but I really don't want to listen to this. I haven't been deceiving anyone." He slammed on the brakes so suddenly, she pitched forward in her seat. "What are you doing?"

He jerked the tow truck back onto the shoulder and shoved the gear lever into park before turning to stare at her. With his arm stretched along the back of the seat, she felt pinned, caged, between him and the car door. "We might as well hash this out now, Elsa—or is it Elise, now?" When she didn't answer, he leaned closer. "I don't know what you're up to, or what game my father is playing—"

"There isn't any game."

He ignored her. "But I don't like being lied to, and I sure as hell don't like being manipulated."

"What are you talking about?"

"If Pop decided this was a good idea—"

Tired of feeling intimidated, she held up her hand. "Stop it. Whatever you think is going on here, your father had nothing to do with it."

"Then why don't you explain it to me?"

"I just don't think it's going to do either of us any good to have another argument."

"We're not going anywhere until you tell me just what the hell you're doing here."

She glanced at the car attached to the back of the truck. Her long trek through the rain had been more than a little exhausting. She was perilously close to losing her temper. "You know what I'm doing here."

"Don't split hairs with me, Elsa. That's not what I mean, and you know it."

"Wil—"

"Since you seem to be having trouble grasping the concept, let me spell it out for you. I want to know why you've decided to drop back into our lives after ten years of not giving any of us the time of day."

The angry charge caught her off guard. "Drop back—?" she bit off the sentence with the self-reminder that she owed this man nothing. "That's not what happened at all."

"No? When was the last time you spoke to your parents?"

"Wil—"

"Did you know your mother slipped on the ice over the winter and broke her hip? You didn't, did you?"

"I did. Nikki told me."

He ignored the reference to her brother. "Did you know your father's business is growing so fast he had to add extra help? Did you happen to hear that when Nick got his promotion to detective they had a block party in his honor, at which you were conspicuously absent? Maybe you were so busy getting yourself engaged you missed the fact that your parents celebrated their forty-fifth wedding anniversary without you."

When the tirade seemed to have ended, Elise straightened in her seat. No matter what he thought, she didn't have to take this from him. "You don't know what you're talking about. I can't believe you haven't discussed this with my parents, with your father.''

''What were they going to tell me that I didn't already know?''

''You don't know anything. All you know is what you've concocted in your mind.''

''Is that a fact?''

''Yes, it's a fact. You were never willing to listen to my side of this, so I just quit trying.''

''Your side?'' His eyes widened in disbelief. ''You don't have a side.''

Stung, Elise struggled for control. From almost the day her relationship with her father ended, Wil had turned on her. At the time, it had hurt unbearably. Losing his love, on top of her father's rejection, had been like a double wound. She'd loved him, and when he cast her aside, she'd been devastated. But she'd had ten years to come to terms with his rejection. And ten years to resent him for it. ''Who the hell do you think you are?''

He frowned at her. ''I'm the guy that used to care about you, remember? I'm one of the people you left in the dust when you decided you couldn't stand being Elsa Krestyanov, the Russian kid from the ethnic neighborhood.''

The anger in his voice stung her. Time had obviously done little to lessen his rage. Years ago, she'd tried to make him understand, tried to explain the situation to him, but he'd refused to listen then, and she knew from his palpable anger that he'd refuse now. ''You've made a lot of decisions about me, and most of them are wrong. And if you want to know the truth, I just don't have the energy to try and correct them.''

When he leaned close enough to envelop her with his heat, she felt the familiar, unwanted quickening of her pulse. ''Then let's get one thing straight right now,'' he said, his voice a lethal whisper. "I don't know what you think you're doing by involving my father in this, but you've hurt a lot of people, my people. Last time you breezed through our lives, I let sex get in the way of my better judgment. It's not going to happen again. I'm not going to let you off as easily the second time."

The bitter accusation laid bare an old wound. "You have it all figured out, don't you?" she asked, horrified when she heard the thready note of tears, dangerously close to the surface, in her voice. She would not cry in front of him.

"All I know is that you left some pretty heavy-duty destruction in your wake. I didn't know any better then, but I do now, and I'm not letting you get away with it."

"I didn't do anything," she told him.

She saw a flash of anger in his eyes. "You did a hell of a lot more than you think."

Staring at him, she felt the full measure of his bitterness, like a weight against her heart. How could decisions made in the innocence of youth lead to such turmoil? All she'd ever wanted was to build a better life, to have the kind of security her parents had never enjoyed. Once, she'd believed that Wil shared that vision, but he, too, had turned on her. When she was cast out of the inner circle of her family's warmth, he'd been one of the first to lock the gates.

Seeing him now, she wondered how the tender love they'd once shared could have become so tainted. There'd been a time when she would have given five years of her life for each moment with him, but his choices were made, as were hers, and the only thing left to do was face the consequences.

With a heavy sigh, she turned to stare out the window, afraid he'd see the tears that lurked behind her eyes if she continued to hold his gaze. "Just tow the car, Wil," she told him. "That's all I want from you."

An hour later, Wil slammed shut the hood of the black Jaguar and met Elsa's gaze across the roof of the car. "Yep," he said. "Fuel pump."

A frown marred her forehead. Dry now, she looked less bedraggled, but no less unsettling, standing amid the relative clutter of the garage he operated with his father. She hadn't spoken to him again since their argument in the truck, but had watched while he examined the car. Still, her soft hands, and soft hair and soft scent, worked their way into his consciousness. Too many unwanted memories crowded in at the feel of Elsa standing so close to his shoulder. Twice he'd turned his head and caught her staring at him. After the second time, she'd moved away from him to study the cream-colored 1928 Stutz he'd been restoring when she called.

Now she looked at the black sports car as if it had somehow betrayed her trust by landing her in this position. "And you don't have one in stock, do you?" she asked.

He shook his head. "It's a specialty part."

Jan had returned from his errand at the salvage yard shortly after Wil left to fetch Elsa in the rain. When they towed her car into the garage, Elsa had fled to Jan's welcoming smile. Unlike Wil, his father had greeted her with a warm embrace and a noticeable lack of antagonism, a fact that merely served to heighten Wil's growing frustration. Now Jan came out of the back room. His blond hair, so like Wil's own, had begun to thin on top, but even that didn't hide the definitively youthful twinkle in his eyes, or the spring in his step.

Jan had spent a full ten minutes exclaiming over Elsa when they reached the shop. After pumping her full of coffee, and hugging her so many times Wil was fairly certain she'd have bruises on her shoulder blades, he'd finally scurried off to the office with some imaginary excuse designed to let him leave them alone. "You can't fix it, Wilem?" he asked in his accented voice. Jan Larsen had never lost his Swedish accent, despite spending more years in Illinois than he had in Helsinki.

"No, Pop. No part."

"How long will it take to get one?" Elsa asked. At the soft question, Edsel, the obscenely overweight tomcat who'd taken up residence in the garage, seemed to take interest in the conversation. He uncurled from his favorite spot, inside an old tire, to plod across the concrete floor. Wil watched, envious and irritated all at the same time, as Edsel twined between Elsa's legs. She gave the monstrous tabby a surprised look, then scooped him up in her arms. As if the fat beast knew precisely what Wil was thinking, he squirmed against Elsa's full breasts, purring in rapture as she scratched the sensitive spot between his ears.

Wil cleared his throat. "The part may be hard to get. I can tow the car into the city for you and leave it with a dealer, or I can have the pump sent out. Either way, probably about three days."

"All right." She continued to stroke Edsel's fur with her elegant hands. "Parker's coming to pick me up. I'm sure he'll just want to leave it here to be fixed." Her gaze slid to the Stutz. "If you have time."

Jan nodded. "Yah. Of course we have time. Not a problem. We are cleaning the engine of the Stutz now, and won't be able to start on the Suiza until I find a few more parts. We can fix your friend's car between jobs. Done?"

Elsa didn't look at Wil. "Done. Thank you, Jan."

Jan chuckled. Wil frowned at him. With a twinkle in his eyes, his father turned a full smile on Elsa. "Glad we were here," he told her.

Wil grunted, then walked to the Stutz, whose still-open hood beckoned him like a safe haven. The famed "straight-eight" engine he'd been working on when she called seemed to smile at him as he picked up a wrench and went to work on the adjustments it needed.

From the corner of his eye, he saw Elsa set Edsel on the floor. When the cat whined, Wil glared at him. Elsa picked up her navy trench coat from the workbench and shrugged into it. "If you don't mind, Jan," she said, "I'd appreciate it if you could call me Monday or Tuesday and give me your final estimate on those parts for the restoration. I know all this paperwork is a pain, but I need to brief Mr. Philpott on the progress for this auto auction."

Jan laughed. "Tell me, Elsa—how does a lawyer like you end up with a project like this auction?"

With a tight smile, she looped the belt of her coat around her narrow waist. "If an associate at Philpott, Philpott and Drake wants to make partner, she handles whatever cases Roger Philpott dumps on her desk, even if it is something as mundane as Chester Collingham's estate liquidation." Shrugging, she added, "At least I get to work with the cars. There have to be some advantages to this."

Giving Wil a meaningful look, Jan patted her on the back. "I want to thank you again for thinking of us. I hope everything has been pleasing to you."

Wil felt, rather than saw, the way her eyes rested on his face. His gaze remained stubbornly fixed on the Stutz engine.

"It has," Elsa told Jan. "So far, I've been very pleased—"

The low hum of an auto engine interrupted her comment. Wanting to faint with relief, Elise watched as Parker pulled into the garage. His handsome face and concerned eyes had never looked better to her. He hurried from the car to her side.

"Elise, honey, are you all right? I got here as quickly as I could."

She almost sagged against him when he bent to drop a perfunctory kiss on her cheek. "I'm fine, Parker," she told him. "Tired and wet, but fine."

He rubbed his hands on the sleeves of her coat. "I'm so sorry about this. I should have left you the cell phone."

"You couldn't have known," she told him reassuringly. "I'm just glad you got here so quickly." With unusual affection, she wrapped her arms around his waist as she leaned against him. Parker generally didn't approve of public displays of warmth, but at the moment, she needed his solid strength.

If he objected, he didn't let on, merely extended his hand to Jan. "You must be Jan Larsen."

"Yah," Jan told him, giving his hand a firm shake.

"I'm Parker Conrad, Elise's fiancé. She's told me a lot about you."

Jan pursed his lips as he studied Parker. "Has she, now?"

"This auction is driving her crazy," Parker continued, making light conversation, despite Elise's insistent pressure on his waist. She wanted him to shut up and drive her home, anything to get away from the feel of Wil's gaze boring into the back of her head. "More than once she's told me how glad she is that you're handling the auto restoration. That's one set of details she doesn't have to worry about."

"I'm glad to hear it," Jan told him. "We're enjoying the work."

Elise reached for Parker's hand. "Parker, I'm sure your parents are waiting for us."

He lifted their entwined hands to press a brief kiss to the back of hers. "Of course. You must be exhausted." With a friendly smile for Jan, he said, "I assume there won't be any problem fixing my car."

"No, no problem." Jan glanced at Wil. "My son, Wilem, will order the part. We should have it done in a few days."

Parker flashed Wil a million-dollar smile. "Nice to meet you."

Wil grunted what might have been "hello," though Elise doubted it. Parker seemed unaware of the tension in the garage. "I was sure Elise would know how to handle it," he told Jan. "She knows three times as much about the thing as I do."

Jan shot Wil a contemplative look. "I've always been impressed with Elsa," Jan said.

Wil forced himself to concentrate on the Stutz's engine until the sound of Parker's departing car faded into the distant rain.

Chapter Two

"Damn it." Wil swore when he banged his knuckles for the third time on the new fuel pump. From his position on the fender, Edsel gave him a knowing look.

His father handed him a towel. "Here. Let me do it, before you break your hand."

"I'm not going to break my hand."

"Hmm... The part, then."

"Funny, Pop."

Jan gave him an amused look. "You've been cranky, like a bear, since Friday. It wouldn't have anything to do with Elsa?"

"No. It wouldn't." He hoped the succinct answer would end the conversation.

He should have known better. "I didn't think so," Jan said as he picked up a socket wrench. "You wouldn't let a woman get to you that way." He lowered himself to the dolly so that he could roll beneath the car. "It was good to have her back here, no?'' he continued once he was positioned beneath the chassis. "You still like this one.''

"Sure. The same way I like oral surgery.'' Edsel momentarily stopped licking his paw to give Wil a sleepy-eyed look. Wil glared at the obese cat and mouthed a succinct curse.

"No, no.'' Jan's voice came from beneath the car. "This one you like. You've always liked her. She bothers you.''

"She bothers me, all right.''

"It's a good bothers. I know you.''

Wil shot him a disparaging look. "Knock it off, Pop. What happened between me and Elsa was over a long time ago. She's changed, and I've changed. She's not my type.''

"Bah! Your type. At the rate you're going, you'll be dead before you find your type.''

"My type isn't a society lady from Chicago. I tried that, remember?''

"Celine.'' His father had always been able to make his ex-fiancée's name sound like a four-letter word. "A baccaruda, that's what she is.''

Wil suppressed a smile at his father's mispronunciation of the word. "*Bar-ra*-cuda. Like the car.''

"Whatever. This one—'' he rolled out from under the Jag to give Wil a meaningful look "—this one is no Celine.''

"What makes you think that?''

"She knew it was the fuel pump, didn't she?''

"I hate to break this to you, but just because a woman knows her car has a faulty fuel pump, that doesn't mean she's a high-caliber dame.''

Jan smiled. "There was a time when you thought so.''

"Any eighteen-year-old boy would be turned on by a pretty girl who knew her way around an engine.''

"Still, I don't see Celine sticking her head under the hood of a car with you."

Wil shook his head with a brief laugh. "Celine's idea of hard work was a hotel with bad room service."

"This one, you like," Jan insisted, then rolled back beneath the car.

"I haven't spoken to her for the last ten years." He scooped up a grease rag from the workbench and began wiping the oil from the accumulated tools. "She didn't look any happier to see me than I was to see her."

"You were surprised, that's all."

"Pop?" he said, finally broaching the subject he'd studiously avoided all weekend. "Why didn't you tell me that the Elise Christopher you've been grumbling about for two weeks is Elsa?"

After a long pause, Jan rolled out from beneath the car. "I wasn't sure what you'd say. It's a good job, Wilem. Elsa is paying well for the work."

"I wouldn't have turned down the job."

"I'm not so sure." He waved the socket wrench. "The air between you, it was thicker than ice, yes?"

"Yes."

"You resent her. Am I right?"

"I resent what she did to her family, to our family."

"You don't necessarily know all you think you know, Wilem."

"Stop talking in riddles."

"There's more to Elsa than meets the eye. You were quick to believe Andrei when he told you Elsa had betrayed him."

"She did betray him."

"Is that so?"

"Of course. Elsa decided she didn't want to be the kid of a Russian-speaking butcher and a German-speaking mother anymore, so she packed herself off to Chicago, where she could ignore her past. Look at her—she's even engaged to that Conrad character."

"Interesting theory."

Like a thermostat, Wil's temper kicked his blood temperature up a couple of notches. "Look, Pop. I don't know exactly what happened between Elsa and Andrei, I admit, but I know he was devastated when she left. So was Anna. Elsa's even calling herself by a different name now. Isn't that enough to show you something's wrong?"

"Perhaps. I've been on this earth a good while longer than you, Wilem. I've learned things aren't always as they seem."

"This is."

"You sound sure."

"I'm sure."

Jan gave him a speculative look, then sat up on the dolly. "Sometimes, our life is dictated by the choices we make. It's true. But no one said we couldn't change our choices."

"I'm not in the mood for a philosophy lesson," Wil said, deliberately keeping his voice calm. "What happened between me and Elsa is over and done. End of story."

"Still, you're not going to stand there and tell me you haven't been thinking about her all weekend. I saw the way you looked at her when her boyfriend..."

"Her *fiancé*," Wil corrected.

Jan ignored him. "...picked her up on Friday afternoon. That woman is under your skin."

"You're making something from nothing. It had been a long time since I'd seen her. Things were tense the last time we spoke." He paused. "She seemed as surprised to see me as I was to see her."

Jan tipped his head to one side. "Perhaps she was."

"You hadn't told her I work here with you, had you?"

"No."

"Why not?"

"She didn't ask about you."

"You didn't want to tell her." Frustrated, Wil studied the spoked wheels of the cream-colored Stutz. Over the weekend, he'd all but finished what minor restorations were needed to bring the car to showroom quality—a remarkable achievement, considering that he hadn't been able to stop thinking about Elsa since she'd left the garage.

He didn't even want to consider the implications of the long hours he'd spent staring at the leather-bound pocket calendar she'd left behind in his truck. He remembered giving it to her, remembered how she'd gushed over it as if it were a diamond necklace. The fact that she still carried it disconcerted him. Perhaps that explained why he'd taken such pains on Saturday to find a part and replace the faulty catch for her.

"Wilem," Jan said, prompting him, "stop fighting your heart. It'll attack you again."

Despite his sour mood, Wil smiled. When he suffered a stress-induced heart attack at thirty-six, he'd made plenty of radical adjustments in his life. One had been to leave his high-pressure job as a commodities broker in favor of the slower, more contented life he enjoyed sharing his father's business. The other had been a conscious decision to cope with stress as it happened, rather than allow it to eat him alive. Since Elsa had crawled into his truck on Friday afternoon, he'd forgotten rule number two. No wonder Edsel had spent the weekend frowning at him. He drew a deep, calming breath. "So what do you think I should do about it?"

Edsel had taken a sudden interest in the conversation, and by some miracle of gravity defiance he managed to leap into Jan's lap. Studying the cat's orange fur, Jan said, "I think after ten years, perhaps you should listen to Elise's side of the story before you make up your mind."

"All we'd do is argue."

"Hmm..." he muttered.

"What's that supposed to mean?"

"I knew your mother ten minutes, and I knew I would marry her."

"That's not the way she told it."

"That's because she remembered arguing with me that afternoon about what was wrong with her bicycle. That's how I knew. The good ones, you argue with." He set Edsel aside, then reached for a rag to wipe the grease from his hands. "The car. It is fixed. You promised to tow it into the city."

"*You* promised."

"I think you should take it."

"You think I should see Elsa."

"This one," Jan insisted, "she is good for you."

"This one irritates me."

"It's good irritation."

"Pop..."

"Wilem, I think you should do this."

"I'm too busy."

"Busy," Jan scoffed. "There's nothing here I can't handle."

"It's a two-hour drive into the city."

"An hour and a half."

"Damn it—"

"Ah," Jan said, giving Wil a triumphant look. "I was right."

"Right about what?"

"If you didn't want to see her, you wouldn't be swearing."

"That's ridiculous."

"Is it?"

"Yes."

"Then you will take the car to prove me wrong."

Wil studied his father for several long seconds, then released a frustrated sigh. He didn't want to see her again, didn't want to reopen old wounds, but a part of him knew they'd taken an irrevocable step forward on Friday. If he didn't work Elsa out of his system, she'd haunt him for another ten years. Best to get it over with, he decided, reaching for his truck keys.

"Hook up the car, Pop," he told his father.

"Elise, stop pulling at your dress," Parker told her as they stepped from the elevator into the Art Institute of Chicago. "You look fine."

She squelched the burst of irritation she felt at his condescending tone. Parker had a tendency to treat her like a sixteen-year-old debutante. Normally she ignored it, but after the long and somewhat harrowing weekend she'd spent with his parents, it grated on her nerves more than usual. "I'm not pulling on it. I'm just making sure my slip's not showing." She gave her red silk chemise a dubious look. She'd purchased the dress on a whim, and she hadn't realized until later that it revealed more than she would have liked. "It isn't, is it?"

Parker dismissed her question with a brief shake of his head, as if he'd considered the topic, made a decision and dispatched it. "It looks fine."

"Of course," she mumbled, and just barely refrained from telling him that "fine" was hardly glowing praise. With a weary sigh, she concentrated on the task at hand. After the weekend in Wilmette, the last thing she wanted was to be on display at this black-tie event. Business, however, was business. Alex Devonshire was one of her primary clients, and nothing short of a death in her family—preferably her own death—could have excused her from his company's annual charity bash at the Art Institute. "Do you see Alex?" she asked, already weary. She'd slept little over the weekend.

Parker, looking a little too perfect in his tailored tuxedo, scanned the room. Elise tried not to resent the way he assessed the occupants, mentally estimated their value to him, then dismissed them or calculated the importance of his approach.

Normally she valued his insight into the politics of society. She'd never had much stomach for it, and Parker had proved to be an important tutor in the intricacies of playing the game. In many ways, she owed Alex Devonshire's business, and its positive effect on her career, to Parker's wizardry. Tonight, however, after having spent an entire weekend under the disapproving scrutiny of his parents, she loathed the thought of working the crowd.

"I don't see him yet, darling," Parker said. "He must be out of the room."

"Must be."

"I do see Gleason Archer, however," he said. She didn't like the predatory look in his eyes when he pressed his hand to the small of her back. "Come along, I want you to meet him."

With the obligatory smile firmly in place, she allowed Parker to guide her through the room. He stopped along the way to charm, to intimidate, to cajole—whatever he felt necessary. The effortless way he played the crowd failed to impress her tonight. Tonight, she found it strangely oppressive. And artificial.

"Elise!" She glanced up to find Alex Devonshire bearing down on her. "So glad you came." He pressed a glass of champagne into her hand. "Parker, my boy, good to see you."

Parker shook Alex's hand with a warmth that failed to reach his eyes. "Hello, Alex."

It wasn't, Elise knew, that Parker disliked Alex Devonshire, it was merely that he considered the older man to have little use to him. Parker rarely bothered with people like that. The bitter thought surprised her. Parker wasn't a calculating man. She knew that. He merely knew what he wanted, determined the best way to get it and allowed little to stand in his way. With a stern reminder that she'd never thought less of him for that—had, in fact, admired it—she slipped her hand through the bend of his elbow.

Telling herself that her sour mood was merely a hangover from the unsettling encounter with Wil on Friday, and the even more unsettling way it had affected her weekend, she gave Alex a deliberately bright smile. "Thank you so much for inviting us, Alex. You seem to have a great turnout this year."

His round face lit up. "We do. We do. With Congress threatening to pull the plug on arts funding, it's become all the thing. Our attendance is up nearly fifteen percent over last year. I think we'll be able to make our heftiest contribution ever, and that's got to be good PR."

"How fortunate," Parker drawled.

The comment made Elise cringe, but Alex seemed oblivious of Parker's sarcasm. "Do you mind if I steal Elise for a while, Parker?" he asked. "There are several people here I want her to meet."

Without waiting for Parker's permission—primarily because she didn't need it, or want it—she took Alex's arm. "Parker can function quite well on his own, can't you?" she said.

His scrutiny told her he hadn't missed the slight irritation in her tone. "Of course. I was on my way to talk to Gleason," he told Alex. "Just make sure she saves the first dance for me." Without waiting for a response, he strode away.

Elise made a mental effort to shrug off her bad mood. Things had been strained between them since they'd left Wilmette the previous afternoon. Parker had quickly grown irritated with her insistence that his parents disapproved of her, but Elise had known the instant she walked into their home, from the way Cornelia Conrad inspected her mud-splattered clothes, that they considered her in the same vein Parker considered Alex Devonshire: not particularly distasteful, but certainly of little value. The fact that she'd been unable to tear her thoughts from Wil Larsen for the better part of the weekend had only exacerbated the problem.

"Well, Alex," she said, forcing aside her grim mood, "tell me how things are going with the SYNTEC merger."

The next half hour passed uneventfully, with the usual blur of names and faces. The band was good enough to put people in a dancing mood, and after four partners her feet hurt, her head was pounding and she'd had more than her fill of the crowd. She was scanning the room for a glimpse of Parker, contemplating her chances of coaxing him to take her home, when a prickling sensation at her nape arrested her attention. Slowly, almost afraid to look, she turned her head.

Fog-colored eyes met her gaze from across the room.

Her fingers tightened on her champagne glass. Wil, clad in an elegant tuxedo, captured her gaze with a look so compelling, she felt her heart miss a beat. If she'd thought him disarming in jeans and a sweatshirt on Friday, there were simply no words to describe what he looked like in his tuxedo. Most men, including Parker, looked elegant, sophisticated, in evening dress. The way Wil's double-breasted jacket hung casually on his broad shoulders, the way his full trousers emphasized his narrow waist, had nothing to do with sophistication. He looked dangerous.

In the look he gave her were a wealth of emotions: resentment, frustration, desire, and something else, something that she couldn't read but that sent tiny bursts of electricity skittering down her spine. As if he'd said the words, his gaze told her that he'd come for her.

She nearly fainted in relief when Alex Devonshire appeared at Wil's side, capturing his attention. Feeling more than a little panicky, Elise set her glass on a passing waiter's tray, and slowly began to pick her way toward Parker. She'd finally spotted him at the far end of the room, standing just beyond the dance floor. With any luck, she could slip through the crowd before Wil confronted her.

She managed to curl her fingers onto Parker's arm seconds before Wil reached her.

"Hello," Wil said. "Good to see you again, Elsa."

Elise swallowed. Parker, who'd been talking idly with a young man whose name she didn't recall, glanced at her in surprise when her fingers tightened on his forearm. He frowned briefly, then looked at Wil and his companion. Elise finally managed to drag her gaze from Wil's eyes long enough to notice the attractive woman. Parker's ready smile was already in place.

"Shelley Castelbrooke," he said, his tone charming, caressing, in a way Elise recognized. Whoever Shelley Castelbrooke was, Parker thought her useful. "How long has it been?"

"At least five years," she said. Giving Elise a bright smile that lacked the artifice she'd expected, she added, "and I'm sure I don't look a day older."

Parker laughed. "Of course not. Elise, this is Shelley Castelbrooke, a very good friend of the family. Shelley, this is my fiancée, Elise Christopher."

Elise met the knowing look in the other woman's eyes. "How nice to meet you," she said, holding out her hand.

Shelley smiled again, as if some private joke were keeping her amused. "Nice to meet you, too," she said. Either she actually meant it, or she could act at least twice as well as Parker. "I believe you already know Wil Larsen."

Ah, Elise thought, so that's it. She glared at Wil. He'd evidently already given Shelley an earful. "Yes. We've met."

"You have?" Parker asked.

That he couldn't imagine the possibility added to Elise's irritation. In a flash of insight, she realized that for the two years they'd dated, he'd controlled their social life. Her friends were his friends. While he had associates she'd never met, the same didn't hold true for her. The thought made her uncomfortably aware of Wil's piercing look. "You remember Wil," she told him. The urge to retaliate against Wil for making her the brunt of the joke between him and Shelley was too strong to resist. "He's fixing your car." Never mind that he was one of the most talented commodities brokers in the city. Never mind that just two years ago he'd been widely touted as the hottest broker on the Merc. Tonight, she'd let him experience the full force of Parker's dismissal.

"Oh, the mechanic," Parker said. Elise almost laughed out loud at the way he tried to mask his surprise. "Of course."

To her frustration, amusement sparkled in Wil's eyes. His lips twitched as he studied Elise's face. "Of course," he drawled. "We didn't actually meet on Friday, I don't believe."

"No, no," Parker said, still clearly flustered. Elise could just imagine how rapidly his brain was trying to assimilate why Shelley Castelbrooke was in the company of a mechanic. Since Wil hadn't bothered to enlighten him, neither did she. Parker snapped his fingers in sudden recollection. "You were working on that white car—"

"The Stutz," Wil supplied.

"Yes, that's right. You were working on the Stutz when I arrived at the garage."

"Hmm." Wil nodded. "Elise must have forgotten to introduce us." He slid his hands into his trouser pockets with a detached air that belied the current of energy she felt beneath the surface of his cool façade. "You'll be happy to know," he told Parker, "that your car's fixed. I towed it into the city and left it at the office building, per Elise's instructions." He produced the keys from his pocket, then pressed them into Parker's palm. "All yours."

Parker stared at the keys. "What was wrong with it?" he asked.

When Wil's gaze found hers again, Elise forced herself not to look away. The heat of his body seemed to reach her across the short space. How, she wondered, could Parker be unaware of it?

"The fuel pump was bad," Wil said. His gaze slid slowly, in an insolent inspection, down the length of her body. "You had nothing driving the stroke."

Elise swallowed.

"The stroke?" Parker asked.

Wil shifted his pelvis forward ever so slightly, just enough to make her palms go damp. "The stroke," he explained. "The pump supplies power to the pistons." The sultry tone in his voice told her he wasn't even remotely concerned with Parker's car. "Without it, the stroke is too short." He raised one hand to his face to skim the line of his mouth with a fingertip. "Without power, a short stroke causes premature ignition."

Elise coughed. Parker, evidently oblivious of the innuendo, continued to stare blankly at Wil. Wil's heated gaze remained firmly riveted to Elise's face. She thought about telling him that public mortification was a considerably worse fate than premature ignition.

Fortunately, Shelley came to her rescue. With a genuine laugh that reminded Elise of the soft sound of rustling leaves, she told him, "Enough, Wil. Can't you see you've lost poor Parker? He doesn't know his piston from his crankshaft."

"I'll bet," Wil drawled.

Shelley glanced at Elise. "Boys," she told her, in a conspiratorial voice that made Elise warm to her. She abruptly changed the subject. "Wil tells me you're handling the Collingham auction."

Elise seized on the verbal olive branch. "That's right."

"You know, I'm very interested in the inlaid armoire. I've always admired it. I wondered if you'd let me put in an advance bid."

"Of course," she told her, trying to concentrate on the conversation, instead of on the way her flesh felt tingly and damp. "I'm preselling most of the estate by silent bid. If you'll let me know which piece interests you, I'll be happy to send you the specs."

"Are you sure it wouldn't be too much trouble?"

Elise laughed. "No. I already handle fifty pages of paperwork a day for this thing. One more set is more or less a moot point." When Shelley still seemed to hesitate, Elise continued, "Really. I don't mind at all. Actually, the more I presell, the less work I'll have to do at auction time."

Shelley's gaze slid to Parker, then back to Elise. "I'll do that, then. Perhaps I could come by your office and talk with you one day next week."

"That would be great. Why don't you call me Monday or Tuesday and we'll set up a time?"

Parker nodded enthusiastically. "Wonderful idea. I'm sure Shelley could be a great help to you, darling."

Elise's spine stiffened. Before she could retort, Shelley gave Parker a look that would have withered most men. "Don't be obtuse, Parker. Elise doesn't need any help. I want her to do me a favor."

His face flushed. "That's not what I meant."

Shelley rolled her eyes. "You never did master tact as a social skill." With a knowing look at Elise, she reached for Parker's arm. "You won't mind if I steal him for a dance, will you? I see he still has some manners to learn."

Before Elise could protest, Shelley led Parker away. Elise felt a sinking sense of dread at being left alone with Wil. The moment Shelley had guided Parker to a safe distance, Wil's fingers clamped on to her elbow, preventing her planned flight. "I want to talk to you," he told her.

Dear God, the last thing she wanted to do was talk to him. All she wanted was to get away from him, somewhere, anywhere, away from his overwhelming presence. "What are you doing here?" she asked him.

"Looking for you."

"For me?"

He reached into his jacket pocket and produced her leather-bound calendar. With a surprised gasp, Elise snatched it from his hand. "You found it."

"You lost it."

"You fixed it."

He pointed to the clasp. "I put a new clasp on it. The old one was worn out."

"I—" She made herself meet his gaze. All weekend she'd worried that she'd lost the calender. Now she hesitated to let him know how much its return meant to her. It seemed too revealing, too intimate. "Thank you," she said. "Thank you. I thought I'd lost it."

"You left it lying on the seat of my truck. That's how I knew you'd be here tonight."

"Here?"

"I checked your schedule."

She glanced from him to the calendar, then back again. "You read this?"

"I wanted to see you again. I knew I'd find you here."

"You're here because of me?"

"Because of you."

She stared at him for long seconds. "But, Shelley..."

"Shelley's an old friend. When I called and asked her if she'd been invited to this thing, she agreed to let me come along."

"I see."

"I doubt it." He placed a firm hand at her back. "Will you dance with me, Elsa? I need to talk to you."

Unbidden, the thoughts that had haunted her over the weekend swept through her, potent and overwhelming. She finally understood why she'd been unable to shake the uneasy feeling that had plagued her since she'd last seen him, on Friday. Without realizing it, she'd allowed his memory to strike at her most secret fear. Deep in her heart, where only she knew it existed, lay a kernel of doubt about her relationship with Parker Conrad. More than she needed to breathe, she needed to expunge that doubt. Time and again she'd reminded herself that Parker was everything she'd ever wanted in a husband. He loved her. He valued her.

But their relationship lacked passion.

The kind she'd felt only for Wil.

She respected and admired Parker, cared for him very deeply, but not once in the time she'd known him had she ever felt the consuming fire she'd once felt for Wil Larsen. With time, she'd managed to convince herself that those feelings were merely the memories of youth, that her relationship with Parker was built on more concrete things than mere physical chemistry.

She'd almost believed it, until she saw Wil again on Friday. Maybe, she told herself, just maybe, Wil had already talked himself out of what had occurred between them that afternoon. If he had convinced himself, perhaps he could convince her, too. Reluctantly she agreed. "One dance."

She felt the tension drain out of him as he led her to the dance floor. When he turned her into his arms, she was immediately assailed by the certain knowledge that this had not been a good idea. The feel of his body pressed to hers awakened too many memories.

Worse, dancing with Wil was an incredibly erotic experience. His scent, slightly musky and all male, enveloped her. Beneath her fingers, the crisp fabric of his jacket seemed to ask for her touch. With his hard, sinewy body fitted to hers, she felt a warm feeling begin to flow through her blood, start to wend its way down through her system until her stomach flipped over.

His large hand settled in the small of her back, and Elise willed herself not to melt into the floor. "What—what do you want?"

He bent his head so that his cheek rested against the top of her head. When his thighs moved against hers, a coil of heat formed in her stomach.

They moved for several moments before he answered her. "I haven't been able to stop thinking about you since Friday."

The soft rumble of his voice gave her goose bumps. She tried to concentrate on following his lead, instead of on the way his fingers were rubbing circles at the small of her back.

"When I saw you that afternoon," he continued, "it was like laying open an old wound." He tipped her slightly away so that he could meet her gaze. "I never wanted to hurt you."

"I never meant to hurt you, either," she told him. "We were—friends."

"And lovers."

"And lovers," she conceded.

"I never stopped wanting you, Elsa."

She pushed aside an angry retort. His final words to her had seemed more like disgust than desire. "It just wasn't meant to be."

He gave her an odd look. "Is that what you think?"

When she didn't answer, he pulled her back against his chest. "You were my best friend's little sister. When Maks died—" he shrugged, as if reliving the memory of her older brother's death were too great a burden "—things changed. Everything changed."

"Things changed for all of us. I know how much you cared for Maks."

Wil shook his head. "It's not just about Maks, and you know it. It stopped being about Maks a long time ago. Friday, I could see it in your eyes. You were afraid of me. I've been haunted by that for four days."

"I wasn't afraid of you."

"No? Then what put that hunted look in your eyes?"

A tight band seemed to be squeezing out her breath. She had to concentrate on her breathing for several seconds. "I wasn't prepared to see you again. I already told you I was expecting your father."

"Fine. I was surprised, too. But that doesn't explain why you were afraid of me."

"I wasn't afraid of you," she insisted.

"What, then?"

She took a deep breath. "I couldn't stop thinking about what we'd done to each other the last time we were together. I don't want us to tear each other apart again."

He missed a step. "Elsa—"

She didn't let him continue. "I think we'd both be better off if we just forgot what happened on Friday."

"Can you do that?" he asked as he began to move with her once more. "Can you put it out of your mind?"

"Of course."

"Then you're a better person than I am, because I'm consumed with it."

She shuddered. She had to make him understand. Had to. Across the floor, she saw Parker laughing with Shelley. "Please, Wil," she said, her voice just above a whisper. "Please understand. For the first time in my life, I have what I want. I don't want anything to jeopardize that."

"Look me in the eye and tell me that seeing me again didn't give you serious doubts about marrying Parker Conrad, and I'll do what you want," he told her.

As usual, he'd cut to the heart of the matter, without all the polite preliminaries. Deep inside her, where she'd carefully locked away her doubts and fears, her memories and longings, the lock threatened to give way. Wil's challenge lay before her like a thrown gauntlet. Impaled on the intensity of eyes the color of a midnight fog, she couldn't find the words. "Please..." was all she could say.

He brought his face closer. "How many times this weekend did you look across the table at Parker and think of me?"

"None," she lied.

"You want to know how many times I thought of you?"

She did. "No."

"Every time I breathed."

Elise's stomach flipped over. "This isn't right."

"What's not right about it?"

"You. Here. This." She knew she sounded inane, and didn't particularly care. He had to leave her alone.

"Oh, it's right, all right." He leaned even closer, and her nostrils flared when she caught his scent. "Admit it. It affected you just like it affected me."

She shook her head in mute denial.

Wil's lips curved into a knowing smile. "Then let me see you again."

"What?"

"If you're not affected by what's going on, let me see you again."

She hedged. "I'm very busy right now. Perhaps after the auction."

"Tomorrow."

Her stomach clenched. "Tomorrow?"

"Have lunch with me tomorrow."

"I can't."

"Why not?"

"I have an appointment."

"There's nothing on your calendar."

"It's on the one I keep at work."

Wil moved his body against hers in a suggestive rhythm that made the blood sing in her ears. "I don't think so. Come on, Elsa, see me tomorrow. Say yes."

She couldn't bring herself to say no, so she asked, "Why are you doing this to me?"

"Because you're complex, and full of contradictions, and I've never forgotten what it was like to care for you."

"Did you try?"

"For ten years."

At the slightly vulnerable admission, her resolve began to crumble. As usual, she found herself powerless to resist his persuasion. Wil had a sorcerer's power over her. She'd never been able to deny him. "I don't want to do this."

"I know."

"But you're not going to walk away, are you?"

"Not this time."

She hesitated, still torn. "Not even if I begged you."

"No."

With a shuddering sense of resignation, she asked, "Just lunch?"

For the first time that evening, his mouth relaxed into an easy grin that chased away the haunted look in his eyes. "Just lunch."

Chapter Three

"Elise, you know I'm counting on you to see this thing through with no complications."

Elise gritted her teeth as she studied the man across her desk. Roger Philpott, senior partner at her law firm, held her career future in his hands. In three months, the voting members of the firm would elect one of the three eligible associates as a partner. There wasn't a chance in hell that mere coincidence had prompted Roger to dump the mundane, if monstrous, responsibility of Chester Collingham's will on her shoulders at a time when she needed the added edge of being able to show her talent in the courtroom. As far as he was concerned, the earth would end before a woman would become a partner at his grandfather's law firm.

"Of course, Roger," she told him. "Everything's under control. The largest portion of the estate to be auctioned is the collection of antique cars. The restorations and certifications are being handled by a very reputable firm just outside the city."

She refused to let it fluster her that her mind was consumed with thoughts of that very reputable firm. All morning, her gaze had strayed relentlessly to the clock on her desk. Wil had left her last night without a time for their lunch date. As noon came and went, the anxiety of waiting had begun to give her a queasy feeling in her stomach. It was now a quarter to one. Perhaps he'd gotten tied up on the floor of the Merc. Maybe he'd forgotten their informal lunch date. If she was lucky, he would have considered it and changed his mind. She tried to be glad.

Roger's beady gaze rested on the reproduction Pierce-Arrow hood ornament she kept on her desk. "I suppose you realize the value of the collection."

"I estimate it at about three million dollars," she told him, dragging her thoughts back to the present. "The firm I'm using is doing excellent work for us."

"And the rest of the collection?" he asked.

Briefly she thought about the odd assortment of art, antiques and vintage items that comprised the Collingham estate. Except for the bizarre assortment of clothing, including a set of seven wedding dresses dated between 1825 and 1950, she'd found museums to purchase most of the antiques. Only the cars, the costumes and a few odds and ends would have to be sold at auction in order to complete the liquidation and pass the profits on to Chester's heirs. "I have everything under control," she assured him.

"I hope so," he said. "Chester Collingham and his family have been among this firm's biggest clients."

"I'm aware of that. I—" The buzz of her intercom nearly sent her through the roof. With a sinking sense of dread, she punched the button. "Yes, Carrie?"

"There's a gentleman here to see you," her assistant told her. "His name is Wil Larsen. Said you were expecting him."

Elise felt the color drain from her face. "Oh."

"Larsen?" Roger said. "Isn't that the firm handling the automobile restoration for us?"

Elise shook her head. "Actually, his father is doing the work. Wil and I are having lunch."

"Well, this is opportune. I'd like to ask the fellow what's costing so much."

"Roger—"

"Have Carrie send him in. By all means." Roger moved his large frame out of the chair, giving the points of his vest a tug to settle it more firmly over his rounded belly.

With her stomach twisting into knots, Elise asked her assistant to bring Wil into her office. When he appeared in her doorway, her hard-won calm withered in the resulting heat wave that spiked up the temperature. "Hello, Wil," she said, proud of herself for managing to stand behind her desk without her knees giving way. "I'd like you to meet Roger Philpott."

Wil slanted a glance at her boss, then extended his hand. "Philpott," he said. "Nice to meet you."

Roger seemed taken aback by Wil's steady confidence. He couldn't have been prepared, she realized, for a man who'd made a reputation for himself as one of the most ruthless, and successful, commodities brokers in Chicago. Roger had expected the son of a mechanic, and come face-to-face with two hundred and twenty pounds of solid masculine power. She almost smiled.

Roger cleared his throat. "So, Larsen, is it?" Wil nodded. Roger fiddled with the buttons on his vest. "Larsen, I understand Elise is quite pleased with the work your father is doing for the firm."

Wil gave her a speculative look. Why, she wondered, couldn't Roger feel the sudden, too-stuffy tension in the room? She forced herself not to shuck her blue pinstripe jacket.

"Is that so?" he asked.

"I told you it was," she said, hoping Roger wouldn't notice the sharp note in her voice. Wil looked no less attractive, no less dangerous, today than he had last night at the party. He wore a pair of faded jeans that did nothing to disguise the firm, muscled contours of long legs. A Harvard University sweatshirt that might, at one time in its life, have been a shade of blue emphasized wide shoulders and a narrow torso, and his presence filled her office with the subtlety of a tornado ripping through the roof.

To her acute mortification, he appeared to notice her discomfort. His lips twitched in the barest hint of a smile. "I hope I'm not interrupting anything important," he said, his voice even less sincere than a greeting card.

"No, no," Roger insisted. "We were just discussing you."

"Oh?"

She hated the way his mouth twitched at the question. He'd always been too sure of himself, too secure, too certain. "I was telling Roger how well everything is coming along," she explained, carefully keeping her tone impassive, "and how I don't anticipate us having any problem finishing the restorations in time for the auction."

"No," he said. "I don't think it will be a problem."

Roger coughed. "I must admit, though, Larsen, I'm a bit distressed at the cost of this. I was led to believe that Chester Collingham's collection was in excellent condition."

"It is," Wil assured him, "but to auction vintage autos at book price, they have to be showroom quality. That kind of work requires precision parts, and quality time. It's not cheap, but it'll pay off in the long run."

Elise felt a wave of irritation as Roger readily accepted from Wil the same explanation she'd been trying to give him for the past eight weeks. "I suppose that makes sense," he said. He gave Elise a tight smile. "Just see that you keep up with the paperwork."

Elise forced a cool reply. "I will."

He nodded briefly at Wil. "Nice meeting you, Larsen."

Wil regarded Roger for several tense seconds. "You too."

"Don't forget to have that report on my desk by this afternoon, Elise," Roger added, as he exited her office.

Without waiting for her invitation, Wil dropped into the seat Roger had recently vacated. "What a jerk," he said.

Elise fought a desperate battle for self-control before taking her seat. She ignored his comment about Roger. "I guess you're ready to go," she said, still holding out hope that he'd changed his mind.

"Are you?"

"Of course." She rummaged through her desk for her leather pocket calendar. On business days, when she didn't wish to carry a purse, it doubled as a wallet. She found it, slipped it into her pocket, then faced him once more. With a sweep of her hand, she indicated his casual clothes. "I expected you to be back at work today."

"I am," he told her.

"Is that what they're wearing on the floor of the Merc these days?"

He merely shrugged as he studied the plush interior of her office. The environment that had once seemed comforting to her now made her feel uneasy as she watched Wil scrutinize the mauve carpet, burgundy leather furniture and dove-gray walls. When his gaze found the collection of polished hood ornaments on her credenza, his mouth pressed into a narrow line. "Nice office," he said conversationally.

She refused to rise to the bait. "Yes," she said with controlled calm, "It's also busy. How long do you think it will take us to eat lunch?"

He ignored her not-too-subtle warning as he continued to scrutinize her desk. Finally his gaze rested on the Pierce-Arrow hood ornament she used as a paperweight. Elise felt exposed as he studied the chrome archer. "You still have that," he said.

She had to fight the urge to snatch the incriminating object from sight. On her twenty-first birthday, Wil had presented her with the chrome archer and a corny note about how she could pierce a man's heart one day. It might have been corny, but she couldn't have been more impressed with Shakespeare. In the bottom of her cedar chest, buried in a box of memories, she still had the note. "Of course." She tried to keep her voice even.

"I'm glad."

He was deliberately taunting her, and she knew it. He seemed to find her discomfort vastly amusing. Elise decided not to allow him the edge. In the long run, things would be easier if she simply cleared the air between them, no matter how unpleasant the prospect seemed. "Look, Wil, I don't want to play games with you. Both of us would be better off if we just left the past alone." She swallowed. "I know you don't like me, and it wasn't easy for me to spend that much time with you on Friday. I was expecting your father. When you showed up, I was surprised. That's all."

Whatever she'd expected, it hadn't been the shock that registered on his face. "I don't dislike you."

"No? You could have fooled me."

"Elsa—"

"Really," she said, interrupting him. "I thought it was a foregone conclusion. I seem to recall something being said ten years ago about me being a selfish little girl who cared more about myself than the people around me; about how I didn't care who I hurt, and whose life I destroyed as long as I got my own way. Did I get it right, or did I forget something?"

He scrubbed a hand over his whiskered chin. "That was ten years ago, Carina."

At the childhood nickname, she flinched. In Swedish, it translated as "little heroine." For years Wil had taunted her with the name. When he used it now, it brought back a painful memory of a time when the nickname had changed to an endearment. 'Aina' he'd called her. With a twinge of regret she realized she'd never asked him what it meant. "Don't call me that," she said softly.

He studied her for several long seconds. "I'm sorry. Not for the nickname. For all of it."

She stared at him, wide-eyed. He'd never said that before. "You are?"

"I am. I didn't want things to turn out this way."

The soft tone in his voice made some of her convictions teeter precariously on a ledge of indecision. "Wil—"

He held up his hand. "Before you say anything else, I'd like to apologize for Friday. I think you should know that Pop hasn't exactly been honest with you."

"Honest about what?"

"I wasn't just home for the weekend," he told her. "I work there. At the garage."

She stared at him for several long seconds. "You work there?"

"Full-time."

"But—" quickly she shuffled mental puzzle pieces in her mind, trying to make that piece of information fit into what she knew "—the Merc. What about your job at the Merc?"

"I quit."

"You quit?"

"Two years ago. I guess no one told you."

"I— No. No one."

He nodded. "I didn't want the stress anymore."

"Stress? You were on your way to the top, Wil. I remember reading that article about you in the *Tribune*. You were close to making partner at your firm."

He shrugged. "One day I decided there were more important things in life than a seven-figure salary."

"One day?"

He paused for long, tense seconds. "The day I had a heart attack on the floor and nearly died before they got me to the hospital."

Elise gasped. "Wil!" she said. "Oh, my God!"

"I see you didn't know."

"Of course I didn't know." She sank back in her chair, stunned. "If I'd known, I would have—"

"What? Come to see me? Commiserated?"

"I don't know. Something. How could you think I would have just ignored something like that? Not after— Well, I wouldn't have."

He shrugged. "Had the roles been reversed, I probably would have."

Stung, Elise swallowed. "Oh."

"Sorry," he said. "That sounded more blunt that I intended."

"At least you were honest."

"Maybe."

Elise drew a shaky breath. "Are you all right? Now, I mean."

Wil nodded. "I'm fine."

"I can't believe Nikki didn't tell me," she said, referring to her brother. "Surely he knew."

"He knew."

"Why didn't he say anything?"

"I don't know. Maybe for the same reason he didn't tell me you were engaged and using a different name now. I guess he figured it was easier to be my friend if we didn't talk about you."

At the comment, Elise frowned. Her family had always been close to Wil and his father. She'd merely assumed that he knew the whole story of how her relationship with her father had gone sour. Evidently he, too, had been kept in the dark about many things. Briefly she thought about the way he'd consumed her thoughts for the better part of the weekend. The fact that she'd been unable to exorcise Wil from her mind was one of the major reasons her weekend at Parker's parents' home had been so stressful.

For ten years, she'd managed to keep the bitter hurt of her father's rejection at bay by refusing to think about it. For ten years, she'd tried to pretend that losing Wil's love hadn't stolen an irreplaceable piece of her soul. Seeing Wil again had brought the painful memories back to the fore. The day she told her father that she'd legally changed her name from Elsa Krestyanov to Elise Christopher because she felt her legal career would benefit from the "Americanized" version, he'd accused her of being ashamed of who she was, of turning her back on her family.

Her father's anger had hurt, deeply, but at some level she'd been able to understand that their relationship had always been strained. Both too stubborn and too willful for their own good, she and her father had struggled for years. The argument that ended their relationship had been merely a catalyst, not a cause. A proud man, he'd spurned every effort she made to reconcile with him. After five years, she'd quit trying.

But she'd had nothing, no emotional armor, to protect her when Wil rejected her as well. She'd given him everything she had to give, her heart, her body, her soul. With Wil, everything was supposed to be forever. His bitterness had shocked her, wounded her. The man she'd thought she knew had disappeared. In his place had stood a man with a haunted look in his eyes that chilled her soul. And she'd walked out of his garage and never looked back.

Until Friday.

By the time Parker arrived at the garage, her nerves had been shot. It hadn't helped that his only reaction to her rescue by Adonis the mechanic had been a solicitous concern for her well-being and a generous offer to pay Wil for his time. If she'd been threatened by Wil's presence, by the obvious energy that crackled between them, certainly Parker should have been. Even last night, after the encounter at the Devonshire event, Parker had been aglow from his renewed acquaintance with Shelley, whose father, Elise had learned, was in a position to give Parker a seven-figure contract. He'd failed to notice her agitation.

Nervously her gaze flicked to the strip of tanned flesh where the crew neck of Wil's sweatshirt rested against the corded strength of his neck. A tiny drop of perspiration worked its way down her spine. "Why are you really here?" she asked him, and wondered if he heard the thready note of panic in her voice.

Wil surged to his feet and began pacing her office. A barely checked energy pulsed beneath the surface of his taut body. She felt it all the way across the room. The afternoon sun turned his blond hair to a coppery gold, and Elise watched him with something akin to dread as he roamed the thick Persian carpet. "Good question," he told her.

"All weekend I kept telling myself it was just a fluke. Seeing you again had been unsettling. That had to be the reason it affected me so deeply."

"Affected you?"

"That's putting it mildly." The look he gave her made her stomach flutter. "I haven't been able to think of anything but what it would feel like to touch you since you slid into my truck on Friday afternoon."

"I don't think—"

He shook his head. "After last night, it just got worse."

Bleakly she thought of the cold shower she'd taken before going to bed. It hadn't stopped the sweats that kept her up most of the night. "Worse?"

"Yeah. And don't try to tell me you didn't feel it. I could feel the energy in you, Elsa. I could practically smell it on you."

Her nerve endings screamed a warning. She supposed she should have been insulted by the statement, but instead it made the soles of her feet tingle. "I don't know what to say," she admitted.

"Tell me you felt it, too."

After several breathless seconds, she nodded. "I did."

His rigid posture relaxed. "Thank you for telling me that."

"So what are we going to do about it?"

"Do about it?"

Elise nodded. "This can't go on, Wil. We're different people now. We can't let this consume us."

"I'm already consumed."

"No. Both of us are overreacting. I'm sure that's all it is."

"I'm glad you're sure," he said, though his expression told her he didn't believe it.

Feeling suddenly weary, Elise stood. "I think we should just go to lunch and get this over with. I haven't slept well in days."

"Neither have I."

With a brief nod, she preceded him out the door.

"So," she asked him fifteen minutes later as she studied him across a plate of onion rings and tried not to feel nervous, "what do you want to talk about?"

He glanced at her as he took a bite of his grilled chicken sandwich. "What do you think I want to talk about?"

"Did you come here today just to argue with me?"

"No."

"Then stop being a pain." Searching for a neutral topic, she settled on his career change. "Tell me how you like working with your dad."

"You mean as opposed to trying to kill myself on the Merc trading floor for some guy who wants to corner the market on pork bellies?"

Elise frowned. "You don't have to get defensive," she told him. "This was your idea, you know."

He nodded. "Sorry." After a long drink of his ice water, he set the glass down with measured precision. "I love working with Pop. You know how much I've always loved working with the cars."

As his fingers rubbed slow, mesmerizing circles on his water glass, Elise felt her skin grow warm. The way her body seemed attuned to his every movement was beginning to eat away at her sanity, like the slow, consistent drip of a faucet, or a splinter beneath the skin. She had only to think of him, to see him, to wonder what it would feel like to have him touch her, to touch him in return. Forcibly she dragged her thoughts back to neutral ground. "You know,

I'm surprised you never got married," she told him, tearing her gaze from his hand.

"You are?"

"Sure. You always seemed like the big-family type. You used to talk about how you wanted at least half a dozen kids."

"Until two years ago, I was too busy trying to get rich to worry about anything as important as family."

"You don't miss it at all, do you?" Despite herself, she couldn't keep the surprise from her voice. Wil had once been full of ambition, eager to make his mark in the financial community. Now he seemed as content as she'd ever seen him, perhaps more so.

"I really don't," he told her. "Why should I? I'm doing something I always loved."

"But you were so talented. You were on your way to being one of the top brokers in the city, in the country, even."

"I'm pretty talented with a socket wrench, too, Elsa," he told her.

"Oh, damn. Why do you keep insisting on twisting around everything I say? I'm not trying to find fault, I just feel like I don't know you anymore."

The tension visibly ebbed out of him. "It's a lot more fun watching a car come back to life after restoration than gambling with billions of dollars on the trading floor. So I'm happier—" he waved the chicken sandwich at her "—and healthier."

"I'm really glad."

"I'm glad you're glad. So how do you like being a corporate lawyer?"

"You mean as opposed to doing something really meaningful, like being a snake-oil salesman?" The afternoon had grown warm, and she slowly unknotted the white silk scarf at her throat.

To her immense satisfaction, he laughed. She'd forgotten how much she liked the sound of his rich baritone rumble. She was startled to realize, perhaps for the first time, that most of the men she now knew rarely laughed at all. Certainly they didn't do it naturally, and when they did, it was generally at someone else's expense. And their laughter never, ever, sent tingles racing down her spine the way Wil's laugh did.

"I should have known," he said. "I imagine there are just as many people who insult lawyers as there are people who insult mechanics."

"More. You know," she said, idly twirling her straw in her glass, "I looked into your father's references in the field before I gave you this restoration job."

"I should hope so. Three million in merchandise isn't something you want to play around with."

"Your shop has developed quite a reputation. Some say you can compete with the best in the country."

"We've won a couple awards," he acknowledged. "Nothing really serious, but it's mostly a hobby, anyway."

"Wouldn't you rather do the restorations full-time?"

"Sure." He polished off his ice water. "The regular repairs pay the bills, though. There are a lot more people driving sedans with bad plug wires than there are antique cars on the road."

Elise finished her lunch, then tossed her napkin on the table. "Why did Jan decide to move the shop from West Chicago out to Valdona?"

"More space and cheaper rent. We need more room to do the restorations."

"Is the work you're doing for us the largest job you've ever done?"

He nodded. "Definitely. Elsa?"

"What?"

"Why are we talking about cars?"

She swallowed. "What do you want to talk about?"

"Us."

"There is no 'us.'"

His eyebrows rose a fraction. "Is that so?"

"Of course. I told you. It's been a long time, we didn't part on the best of terms, and it was only natural that we would both feel somewhat uneasy about seeing one another again."

"Oh, really?"

"Yes, really. It was good to see you. I'm glad to know you're doing well, and now we'll just forget the whole thing ever happened. I'll go back to my office, you'll go back to Valdona, and we'll continue with what has become the status quo."

His laugh was a rich burble that made her hair tingle. "I'll bet you're hell on wheels in the courtroom."

"I'm very serious about this."

"So am I. I can't remember the last time I was more serious about anything."

"Then why don't you act it?"

"Just because I'm not trying to explain it away, that doesn't mean I'm not serious about it."

"We don't even like each other," she insisted.

"That hasn't got a damned thing to do with what's going on here, and you know it. Every time I look at you, I want to touch you. I can't stop thinking about what it felt like to have my hands on you while we danced. I can't stop remembering what it used to feel like when I could touch you, make love to you." The look he gave her threatened to wilt her eyelashes. "Tell me, did you have to take a cold shower before you went to bed last night? I did."

She glanced quickly around, relieved to find no one watching them. "Have you forgotten that I'm engaged?"

His gaze slid to her ring, then back to her face. "Are you engaged, or are you hiding?"

Frustrated, she pushed her chair back from the table. "Stop it, Wil."

"Too close to the mark?"

She stood. "Too rude." Without waiting for him, she turned to leave.

Muttering a soft curse, he tossed some bills on the table. Once again, she'd left the leather-bound calendar behind. He stuffed it into his back pocket, then hurried after her. She was waiting at the crosswalk when he caught up with her. Grabbing her elbow, he pulled her from the stream of pedestrian traffic into the empty doorway of a high rise. "Listen to me."

"I want to go back to work."

When she would have looked away, he grabbed her chin with his fingers. This wasn't going at all the way he'd planned, yet, somehow, he was powerless to stop himself. Something about her always did this to him, destroyed his concentration, ruined his better intentions. With her, and only with her, he was a man of passion, not the calculated decision-maker he could trust to do the right thing. That passion scared him, but just as before, he was helpless to do anything about it. "Listen to me," he said again. "I don't like this any more than you do. I want you to know that, but just because I don't like it, that doesn't mean I can stop it from happening. I feel things for you. I can't turn them off anymore than I can stop the earth from spinning."

"You can just leave."

"And you think if I leave it'll go away, don't you?"

"Of course it will."

He brought his mouth within inches of hers, so close he felt her breath fan across her lips. "It won't. Once, I tried to ignore it, but it didn't work then, either. I don't know about you, but I was miserable.''

Elise pulled in a weak breath. The trapped look in her eyes held him immobile. The sight of her full mouth, so close to his, threatened to send him crumpling to the pavement.

"We can't do this," she said, sounding desperate. "I don't want to do this."

He ignored the plea in her voice. "Did it go away over the weekend?" At the question, her eyelids fluttered shut, but too late to disguise the revealing spark in her eyes. "It didn't, did it?"

When she didn't answer, Wil narrowed the space between them, until the weight of his body pressed her against the cold concrete of the office building. "What about last night? When you left that party, could you still feel my hands on you? Could you stop thinking about what it was like to be close to me? It's not going away, Elsa. Trust me on this. I waited ten years, and it didn't go away." His gaze lowered to her mouth. "Just because we want things, that doesn't make them so."

And right there, amid the skyscrapers and afternoon traffic, heedless of the surging lunch crowd on the sidewalk, oblivious of the consequences, reckless and impassioned, he captured her mouth in a kiss that sent shivers to the soles of her feet.

Chapter Four

"Right there in the middle of the sidewalk? Right in front of everybody?" LuAnne, Elise's hairstylist and close friend, stared at her in the mirror as she busily styled Elise's hair the following Wednesday.

Elise met her friend's gaze. With her singsong Jamaican accent, impossibly big hair and even bigger heart, LuAnne had become one of Elise's favorite people on the planet the day she first walked into her shop. "Right in the middle of everybody," Elise confessed. Wil had left messages with her secretary twice in the days that followed, but Elise had studiously avoided returning his calls. She was trying, hard, to convince herself that time would ease the twinge of awareness that seemed to have permanently worked itself under her skin.

It wasn't working. To make matters worse, Parker had left the country on business, and she'd had nothing but time to think about the way her body had responded to the feel of Wil Larsen.

"Um-hmm..." LuAnne shook her head, then clipped another piece of Elise's hair. "So you tell me, what did it feel like?"

"I don't know. It felt like a kiss, more or less."

"*More* like a kiss, or less?"

Elise ignored the leading question. "It's not that big of a deal, LuAnne. I've known the man for years." She glanced around the small beauty shop. "I was in love with him. We used to be lovers. He just provoked me. That's all."

"No, no." LuAnne dropped her scissors in their holder. Reaching for her hair dryer, she said, "I mean, what did it *feel* like? Was it good, was it bad?" She paused. "Did the earth move?"

Elise tried not to squirm. The earth had moved, all right. They'd hit about a nine on the Richter scale of emotional experiences. "I was surprised. I wasn't paying that much attention."

"It was good, wasn't it?"

"I don't know. I haven't thought about it."

LuAnne gave her a look that spoke volumes. "Sure you haven't." She flipped on the hair dryer. "It was good. You wouldn't be telling me otherwise if it wasn't."

"I didn't say it was good."

LuAnne made a comment that Elise couldn't hear over the buzz of the hair dryer. So she thought about what it had felt like to kiss Wil, to have him kiss her. Was it good? Somehow the word seemed inadequate. It couldn't begin to describe the current of emotion that had surrounded them. Champagne and chocolate-covered strawberries and sunny afternoons and weepy movies were good. This...this had nothing to do with life's lesser delights. This was more like a cataclysmic experience. Good like she'd never imagined it could be. Good, she admitted, like it had never been with Parker.

"So—" LuAnne switched off the hair dryer "—you gonna tell Parker?"

"What?"

"You know, your fiancé? The tall guy with the dark hair?" LuAnne met her gaze in the mirror. "You gonna tell him you kissed this guy?"

"I didn't kiss him. He kissed me."

"Sure about that?"

"Of course I'm sure."

"I see. So then, what you got to be so upset about?"

"I'm not upset."

LuAnne removed the all-but-shredded magazine from Elise's lap. "That's why you in here tearing up my stuff?"

"I'm not—"

"Elise." LuAnne pivoted the chair so Elise faced her. "I know you a long time. You and me, we been friends, what—six years?"

"Seven."

"Seven years. I know some things about you nobody else knows. I know you got worries about marrying Parker Conrad."

Against her will, Elise remembered Wil's questions. He, too, had pressed her about her relationship with Parker Conrad. "That's not true. Parker is exactly what I've always wanted."

"Maybe, but that don't mean you in love with him."

Elise stared at her friend for several long seconds, then drew a quick breath. "You're being ridiculous."

"I don't think so, and if you smart, you gonna tell Parker you got doubts."

"I can't do that."

"You better. He's a nice man, Parker Conrad. Dull, but nice. His mother, now there is another story, but Parker, he don't deserve what you're doing to him."

"I'm not doing anything to him."

"You kissing other men on the sidewalk while Parker's in Bangkok on business. That's what you doing."

"I already told you—"

"I know, he kissed you. You listen to me, Elise. You got two and a half weeks to make up your mind. Then Parker's coming back from Bangkok, and you got to tell him. You the only one what knows who was kissing who on that sidewalk."

"I don't think you understand, Lu. Wil's an old friend, and we parted on bad terms. Of course I was off balance when I saw him again."

"Of course."

"You don't believe me, do you?"

"What do I know? I'm just your stylist."

"And my best friend. And the person who's supposed to be my maid of honor."

"Provided Parker tells his mama it's none of her business."

Elise frowned. Parker's mother had made her dislike of Elise's choice of maid of honor abundantly clear. "He will," she said firmly. "You will be in my wedding."

"If you and Parker ever pick a date. You gonna do that soon?"

Again Elise tried not to squirm. "Soon. You know how things have been for me, with this auction coming up."

"Sure. I also know that all six times I was engaged, we picked a date."

"You were engaged six times, and married zero. That's not exactly the world's best track record."

LuAnne shrugged. "So I was smart enough to know they weren't the right one. Maybe you should try that."

In spite of herself, Elise laughed. "All right, all right," she said, holding up her hands in surrender. "I promise I'll think about it. Now, are you going to do my hair or not?"

LuAnne grinned at her. "Of course. I'm not going to have you walking around with this gray showing. People might start to talk." She paused as she reached for the hair dryer again. "And you still haven't told me if he kisses good."

Elise spun her chair around so that she faced the mirror. "I do *not* have gray," she insisted. The familiar joke calmed her nerves. She and LuAnne had been sharing this same conversation about coloring her hair for the past three years. Once a month LuAnne put a color wash in Elise's hair to hide the gray, and once a month Elise denied it. The familiarity seemed to anchor her thoughts back in the present, where they belonged. "And yes," she added, "he's good."

At seven o'clock Saturday morning, her phone rang. Elise awoke through several layers of fog. For days she'd been wrestling with her reaction to Wil, and the mental turmoil had taken its physical toll. She'd planned to sleep in that morning, before making a Saturday trip, necessitated by the details of the Collingham auction, to the office. At the jarring ring, she squinted at the clock with a low groan.

It had to be Parker. With the time difference between Chicago and Bangkok, he called at strange hours. She reached for the phone with a weary sigh. Grappling for a moment with the receiver, she finally managed to juggle it to her ear.

"Hello?"

"Elsa?" The heavily accented voice momentarily confused her.

"Hello?"

"Elsa, this is Jan Larsen."

She frowned. "Jan?"

"I woke you, no?"

The fact that he sounded more amused than contrite heightened her irritation. "Yes. Is something wrong?"

"Yah. We got a problem with the Packard."

Instantly she came awake. Elise sat up in the bed, clutching the receiver. "Problem?"

"Yah. I found rust inside the body."

"Rust? How much?"

"Bad. Painted over. Collingham might not have known."

This, Elise knew, was a potentially serious problem. The cars had to be ready for sale, and certifiably restored, in less than two weeks. A problem like this could mean weeklong delays in finding replacement parts and restoring the vehicle. Expenses would rise, and if Jan spent too much time working on the Packard, the refurbishment of the other cars might suffer in the meantime. Roger Philpott was not going to like this.

Elise quickly considered the options. "The whole body, or just several parts?"

"Mostly the rear quarter panel. The rest, I think I can grind and putty."

"Can you get a new part in time?"

"This is the thing," he told her. "I have found the part, but I need it today. Rob McKitrick has one, but he will be gone, on vacation, after tomorrow. If I don't get it today, we will not have it until too late."

"Fine. Great. Whatever you need."

"Not so easy," Jan said. "This part, it is expensive. I didn't know before, so it's not part of our original estimate."

"Not a problem. I'll authorize the extra expense, and fire you out the paperwork on Monday."

"No. Won't work. I can't get the part without credit authorization from you."

A sinking sensation settled in the pit of her stomach. "From me?"

"Yah. As I say. It's expensive. McKitrick wants to know your firm will pay. I will need the paperwork."

"I can fax it to you this afternoon."

"I have to have an original signature. That's part of the contract we signed with your firm."

Frustrated, she mentally cursed Roger Philpott to hell. He'd insisted on the unwieldy contract, and now they were stuck with its terms. "Do you need it this morning?"

"Yah. It's a two-hour drive to McKitrick's."

"Oh, all right." There didn't seem to be a choice. She glanced at the clock. "I'll be there in thirty minutes."

By the time she reached the garage, her nerves were ready to split her in two. From the moment she hung up the phone, she'd begun a silent vigil of prayer that Wil would have the good sense not to be at the garage when she arrived. She needed another confrontation with him like she needed a hole in her head. She still hadn't recovered from the last one.

In the days since she'd seen him, she'd done all she could to put him out of her thoughts, but memories had intruded on her peace of mind like berry seeds stuck between her teeth. If only she could find a way to spit him out, she thought wryly, she could get on with her life.

Between arguing with Roger all week about the details of the auction, crushing down the overwhelming feeling of panic she'd experienced both times Parker phoned her from Bangkok and trying not to ponder all the reasons why she was allowing the havoc Wil caused in her life, she'd worked herself into a first-class case of neurosis.

The last time Parker called, she'd told him she wanted to be married in September. He'd hedged, telling her he didn't think six months gave her adequate time to plan the wedding, but Elise had insisted. She felt better, more in control, knowing the date was on the calendar. At the moment, control was at a premium, and she'd take whatever she could get.

Scanning the quiet garage for signs of Wil, she killed the engine with a sigh of relief. He didn't appear to be on the premises.

"Jan?" she called as she entered the service bay. "You in here?" Silence greeted her. Only Edsel appeared to be tending the shop. She stopped to scratch his ears. "Morning, Edsel. Where is everybody?"

The tomcat purred in rapture, then flopped onto his back so that she could scratch his stomach. With a soft laugh, Elise rubbed his wide belly. "You lazy thing," she told him. "It's no wonder you're so fat."

"Well, he gets more action than I do, that's for sure." The humor in Wil's deep voice startled her.

Abruptly she stood. Edsel gave Wil an irate look for having interrupted her stroking. Elise felt a strange sense of relief at seeing him again. Somehow, the conversation they'd had had drained the pressure from their relationship. For the first time, she felt as though she were facing him on equal footing. "Wil."

"Morning, Elsa."

"I—I wasn't expecting you."

"I figured you probably weren't."

She forced herself not to fidget. "Jan said he had something for me to sign."

"Uh-huh. Are you ready to go?"

"Go?" He leaned against the door frame of the small office, looking just as sexy, and just as lethal, as always.

He wore a white collarless shirt, its billowy fit offset by an unbuttoned suede vest the color of melted chocolate. Somehow, the loose-fitting shirt made his shoulders seem even broader than she remembered. Jeans with the faded look of an old friend rode low on his hips, and the morning light found golden accents in his hair. Vividly she remembered the feel of that silky hair beneath her fingers, the weight of him pressing her to the building. She had to stifle the urge to take a hasty step back from the door.

"Go," he said. "It's a long drive. Almost all the way to Milwaukee." His voice was steady, in stark contrast to her nerves.

"Milwaukee?" She had the vague idea that she sounded like a fool, but somehow she'd missed an important part of the discussion. Fiddling with the top button of her royal-blue cardigan, she continued to stare at him.

He advanced the final paces across the garage to where she stood. Capturing her fingers, he gently pried them away from the button of her sweater. "McKitrick's shop," he clarified. "It's over two hours away, and if we're going to get there before noon, we'd better go."

The feel of his fingers on hers broke the spell long enough for his words to sink in. "Oh." She edged away from him, pulling her fingers free of his grasp. "I'm not going with you. I'm just here to sign the papers."

Wil frowned. "Pop didn't tell you, did he?"

"Tell me what?" His scent, warm and musky, like leather and soap and pleasantly natural, wrapped around her, a seductive cocoon.

"Damn it," he muttered.

"Tell me what?" Elise insisted, fighting a growing surge of panic.

"You have to go with me."

She stared at him, wide-eyed, then slowly shook her head. "I'm not—"

"You have to." He rubbed a hand over his face. "He planned this, the coot."

"What are you talking about?"

Frustration showed in his gaze. "Pop knew you wouldn't come if he told you you'd have to go up there with me."

"He was right about that."

"But you've got to sign the credit forms. I can't do it, and I can't take your signature. It's a premium part, and McKitrick doesn't trust lawyers. He wants the real thing, in person."

"Well, then, he'll just have to—"

"Look, if you want this car done in time for your auction, we have to get the part today." He paused. "Before noon."

"Why can't Jan go with me?"

"He left."

"Left?"

"Left. He went after some varnish for the Suiza."

"He could have sent you for the varnish."

"Yeah, he could have. But he didn't. He also didn't tell me that you hadn't agreed to go."

Despite herself, Elise couldn't quite prevent a smile at the ludicrous situation. "So here we are, right back where we started."

He seemed slightly taken aback by her odd mood. "I guess we are."

With a shake of her head, she muttered. "Crafty man, your father."

"Devious, too."

Elise glanced out through the open service bay of the garage. The weather promised a clear day, the kind made for long drives. Jan had deftly outmaneuvered them. The only way around the situation would be for them to take separate cars, which seemed both ridiculous and childish. A part of her suspected that Jan probably could have found a quarter panel closer to Chicago, and less difficult to obtain; but another part, the part that prided itself on besting a legal colleague, or developing a particularly effective strategy, had to admire the old man's cunning. With a brief smile, she said, "Okay, look. You're an adult, I'm an adult, we should be able to handle this."

"He set us up, you know."

"Sure, I know. Your father's playing matchmaker. So what else is new?" Deliberately she calmed the flutters in her stomach.

"We'll have to be together all morning."

"I can promise to get through one day without arguing, if you can. We used to be friends. How hard can it be?"

His eyes narrowed. "Elsa?"

"What?"

"Do I make you nervous?"

The flutters returned with a vengeance. "Nervous? Of course not."

"Hmm. You make me nervous."

Her eyes widened. "I do?"

He crossed the garage to stand directly in front of her. "Sure. You make me nervous as hell."

At his quiet admission, what remained of her anxiety ebbed away, like air through a punctured balloon. This was Wil, once her closest friend. Once her lover. She had no reason to fear him. "All right, maybe I am a little nervous."

Wil paused to tuck an errant lock of hair behind her ea The feel of his fingers on her skin was like a summer breez warm and gentle. "So let's make a deal," he said.

"Last time you wanted to make a deal with me," she to him, remembering that he'd offered to leave her alone their lunch date failed, "I lost."

The spark in his eyes told her that he remembered it, to "So you did."

"I'm a smart person, a lawyer, for God's sake. I shou know better than to cut deals with a guy who used to tra several million dollars a day at the Merc."

His laugh warmed her. "You probably should, Cou selor."

"So why do I keep falling into this trap?"

"Because I figure you have to be at least as curious as am about why things combusted between us on Tuesday.

"What's going on is a simple case of chemical attracti and overblown memories."

"If you say so."

"It is. I told you, if we ignore it, it'll go away."

"Just like that?" He waved his hands in front of hir "Poof."

"Poof."

"So why are you nervous?"

He'd neatly maneuvered her into a corner. The only wa clear was a bluff. "I don't know. The last time I saw yo we ended up having yet another argument." With a bri shrug, she tried to ignore the tantalizing way his scent tic led her nose. "It's not exactly a promising precedent for pleasant morning."

"Have I ever told you," he asked, with a grin that ma the soles of her feet tingle, "how much it turns me on wh you speak lawyer?"

At the quip, Elise frowned at him. It was past time she exerted her own rules in this little game he was playing. "I want you to stop baiting me," she told him. "And if you don't, I'm not going."

"I'm not trying to bait you."

"You are, too. I've known you a long time, Wil, and I know just what you're up to. The only way this is going to work is if you quit trying to get under my skin. Absolutely no conversations about pistons, premature ignition, or Parker Conrad."

"What *will* we talk about?"

"You figure it out."

"That brings me to the deal I want to make with you."

"It does?"

"It does." He took another step forward, and if she hadn't been so distracted by wondering how one man could possibly generate so much heat, she might have resented the intimidation tactic. Wil took her hand in his and laid it on his chest. "Today, can we just forget everything that's happened in the past, and see what's happening now?"

A tiny sliver of fear worked its way down her spine. That, she knew, could be dangerous. Without the past to divide them, she could fall hard for this man as she had once before. Only a fool would accept a bargain like that. "It's impossible."

"Of course it isn't. We'll just find something else to talk about. Today, it'll just be you and me, like two normal people. No secrets, no regrets, no hang-ups."

"Everyone has hang-ups. If they didn't talk about their hang-ups, they'd have nothing to say."

"Maybe we'll consider getting to hang-ups around three o'clock this afternoon."

Elise hedged. "Then what?"

The twinkle in his eyes taunted her. "You afraid?"

"Maybe."

"Me too."

"There's only one way I'm going to agree to go with you today."

"Name it."

"If, after today, we find out we've got nothing in common anymore, I want you to leave me alone."

"I will."

Elise drew a resigned breath. His concession gave her the edge she needed. "Then we have a deal."

As if the sun had suddenly found its way through the clouds, Wil felt a pall lift from the prospect of the day with Elise's concession. His mood eased into one of lazy contentment as he considered spending an entire day learning what made Elise Christopher just so tempting. "Okay," he told her, flashing her a brilliant smile as he dug into the pocket of his jeans. "Want to drive?"

Chapter Five

Five minutes later, they stood behind the garage while Elsa inspected his red Stingray. With what could only be called a loving caress, she dragged her fingers along the sleek lines of the driver's-side fender. Wil felt a familiar tightening in his lower body as he watched her slowly examine the car. If he knew one thing about Elsa, it was that she was one of a rare breed of women who truly appreciated the artistic value of a fine automobile, something that had always managed to keep his hormones in an uproar.

Evidently, he decided, when her hand rubbed the hood emblem, age hadn't lessened the effect. As he watched her stroke his car, he knew with a primitive surge of satisfaction why car shows inevitably featured gorgeous women draped over the hoods of expensive automobiles.

"Where did you find this?" she asked him.

"You want the truth?"

She stopped to check the polish on the grill as she rounded the hood. "Um-hmm."

"I picked it up for twelve hundred dollars at a junkyard where I was scrounging for parts. It was in horrible condition."

She gave him a look of shared outrage. "How could somebody let that happen to a car like this?"

"My thoughts exactly," he told her. "It took me almost two years to get it restored to the way I wanted it. There are still a couple of parts I'm trying to find originals for, but they're minor."

The look she gave him was pure feminine delight. "You're *sure* I get to drive this?"

He laughed. "I wouldn't tease about something like that, although I confess, when I taught you to drive that clunky sedan, I never imagined I'd be letting you behind the wheel of something like this."

"How are we going to bring the part back?"

"We'll tie it down. Pop's got the truck."

"Yet another well-laid plan, I guess."

"Probably. I doubt he counted on my letting you drive, though."

She wrinkled her nose at him. "I drive very well, thank you."

He opened the driver's-side door for her, and waited until she'd settled herself in the luxurious leather bucket seat before he rounded the car to the passenger side. "I don't doubt it," he said as he eased into his seat. "I just recall that you really liked speed."

She flashed him a brief smile. The engine roared to life with a turn of the key. The feeling of power and energy hummed through the vehicle. It seemed a particularly appropriate backdrop, he decided, for the energy he felt pulsing from Elsa to him. "You know," she said, "I think, aesthetically speaking, I've always preferred 1930s-model cars for sedans, but nobody—'' she revved the engine ''—no body did sports cars like the fifties.''

As she shot away from the curve, he had the sensation of being on an emotional roller coaster. Whatever happened today, it had the potential to be exciting, adventurous, and more than a little terrifying.

Late that evening, Wil rubbed his thumb on the top of her hand, where it lay nestled against his thigh. Elsa had deftly managed to keep him scrambling for verbal and mental balance for the better part of the day. By mutual consent, they hadn't discussed what had occurred between them. Neither of them had agreed to let the morning lengthen into afternoon, and then become evening, but neither had seemed ready to end the day. When she drifted off to sleep, almost as soon as they'd left the city, he'd been grateful for the silence, his first opportunity to sort through the day's events.

Being with Elsa again had been even more potent than he expected. Her ready laugh, the way his heart missed a beat when she smiled at him, laughed at him. In a few short hours, she'd reawakened feelings in him that he'd long since suppressed. Before today, he'd convinced himself that his life was complete. He didn't need or want the chaos that Elsa would bring back into his world.

But he craved it. Like a man addicted to a deadly substance, he hungered for her. And he was fooling himself if he thought he could dismiss the feeling as anything so mundane as physical attraction. Even the sexually charged atmosphere that had him aching to touch her probably wouldn't have destroyed his mind so thoroughly if it wasn't so easy to enjoy her company.

After procuring the part, they'd driven out to the Brooks Stevens Automotive Museum to see the impressive collection of racing cars. They'd spent hours debating the merits of the various technological innovations and aerodynamic designs. When their conversation developed into a friendly argument about the year Chrysler introduced champagne blue into its paint selection, Elsa had been the one to lead the charge to a nearby library, where a 1946 edition of *The Saturday Evening Post* had proved her correct. Laughing the kind of laugh that made his nerve endings tingle and his palms sweat, she'd made him buy her dinner in exchange for losing the argument.

Dinner, he decided, had been his worst mistake. By seven o'clock, he'd started to feel more than a little desperate. Urgently he'd needed an edge. That was why he'd chosen Annalina's.

Like a fool, he'd convinced himself that if he could see her in a familiar backdrop, one that would remind her, and him, of home, he could remember all the things that had torn them apart. So he'd taken her to Annalina's, the Swedish diner his father frequented when business or pleasure brought them into the city. Seconds after he had them settled in the booth, he began to feel a strange discomfort seeping through his blood.

If he expected, hoped, that Elsa would be out of place amid the boisterous atmosphere, the too-friendly staff, the music and food that were a painful reminder of the past, he'd grossly miscalculated.

She'd been enchanted. She'd settled readily into the spirit of the restaurant, unconsciously tapping her fingers to the music, digging into a plate of buttered noodles and Swedish sausage with a gusto that made his blood pump faster. He'd watched her nibble and lick her way through a piece

of raspberry *krydderi* until his insides threatened to spon-
taneously combust.

By the time he gratefully paid the bill and hurried Elsa
from the restaurant, sweat had pooled at the base of his
spine, and the thundering pace of his heart had had nothing to do with anxiety and everything to do with raw sexual hunger.

Beneath his fingers, her hand felt soft, warm, welcoming. His own hand had trembled as he enfolded hers. At the
feel of Parker Conrad's diamond pressed against his palm,
Wil had gritted his teeth. Once again, he wanted the woman
he couldn't have, a woman who wanted something he
couldn't, wouldn't give her. With startling clarity, he'd realized that, before he even recognized the signs, the emotional storm had engulfed him. No false moves required—
he was in the middle of it, fighting for his life.

With a deep, shuddering sense of defeat, he eased his car
into a parking space near her apartment. After waiting
several long, calming moments for the demons to subside,
he tapped her on the shoulder. "Aina, we're home."

The sooty curtain of her lashes drifted slowly open.
"Hmm?"

"Your apartment. We're here." He couldn't make himself remove his hand from her shoulder. The nubby feel of
her cardigan proved too much of a temptation to his palm.

She continued to watch him through half-closed eyes.
"Did I fall asleep?" she muttered.

His fingers found the spot where her sweater gave way to
the worn cotton of her T-shirt. "Almost as soon as we left
the city." He ran his fingertip along the ribbed collar.
"Must have been the *krydderi.*"

"Must have been." When she yawned, her head rubbed
against the back of her seat.

Wil's fingers slid the final fraction of an inch to touch the warm skin of her neck. He felt, rather than saw, the crackling awareness that flooded away what remained of her languor. "Wil—"

He didn't wait for her to voice the doubt. If he did, she'd talk him out of kissing her. All day he'd needed to kiss her. The driving, insistent throb of desire had, at times, seemed to consume him. Now he needed the feel of her more than he needed his next breath.

Like a man too long denied, he slanted his lips over hers, delving, devouring what she'd give him, tempted to take what she wouldn't give. Everything about her confused him. Only this, only touching her, seemed to clear the conflict in his mind.

This was right. This belonged.

When he felt the cool pressure of Elsa's hand curved around his neck, his heart slammed into an erratic rhythm. His sanity fled, and with it, what remained of his self-control. "God, Aina," he muttered as he levered her back against the seat. "You're tearing me apart."

She, too, seemed to lose herself in the heat of the kiss. When he opened his lips over hers, she moaned against his mouth, then sucked his tongue between her lips. Fumbling, Wil found the hem of her cardigan. He had a desperate need to touch her flesh, to feel her warm and smooth beneath his hands.

The T-shirt slipped from her waistband. Wil shoved his hands beneath. Her skin felt like hot silk as it flexed and shivered against his hands. When he cupped her full breasts through the soft lace of her bra, she arched into him. At the feel of her, warm and welcoming, he groaned, a ragged, needful groan, born of a deep, ravaging want. Finally, *finally,* he had her where she belonged. No woman had ever inflamed him like Elsa. Never had he needed so urgently to give pleasure, to cherish.

Her lips yielded beneath his, soft and moist, as he ran his tongue along the line of her teeth. Elsa's hands clutched at his neck, holding him to her with a strength that answered his passion. When his lungs screamed for air, he tore his mouth from hers. "Aina," he murmured, raining a line of kisses along the curve of her jaw. "Aina, I want you." His fingers flexed against her breasts. "I want you."

Elsa's body shuddered. Through her bra, he felt her nipples bead into taut peaks. The exquisite sensation sent blood surging to his already aching groin. He found the lobe of her ear and nipped it with his teeth.

"Wil—"

"Don't be afraid of me," he urged, although he doubted she could possibly fear him as much as he feared the sudden flood of emotion that was clouding his judgment. He'd be a fool not to walk away from her. He knew that, but the feel of her shivering beneath his hands, arching toward his touch, beckoned him like a siren's call. "I need you."

Her breath fanned across his face in a gentle gust as he pressed his mouth to the curve of her neck. "Wil—"

"Shh." He rubbed his lips against hers. "I won't hurt you," he muttered. "I swear, I won't hurt you."

The tension seemed to drain out of her. Elsa relaxed against her seat. Sensing her surrender, Wil wasted no time claiming her. "Aina," he whispered, "what have you done to me?"

Pressing her into her seat, he ran his hands over her skin in a fevered frenzy as he sought, then found, the front clasp of her bra. The catch gave way with a light *snick*. Wil dragged his mouth from hers. With hands that suddenly seemed too large and too clumsy, he shoved her T-shirt over her lush breasts, so that he could see them, taste them.

When he pressed his mouth to one swollen peak, she gasped. Her fingers threaded into his hair to hold him to her. "Ah, Wil . . ."

"Hold me," he muttered against her breast. "Hold on to me."

Elsa's breath was coming in fits and starts. He kissed the throbbing pulse at the base of her throat. Filling his palms with her breasts, he moved to kiss her once more. "I love the taste of you."

Elsa kissed him with equal passion, pulling at his mouth, sucking at his tongue. He couldn't seem to get close enough, near enough, to satisfy her. She pulled at his shoulders, pressed herself against the hard length of his body.

A shudder ran through him when he felt the heat of her against his groin. "Aina . . ." He tore his mouth from hers. "Aina, I can't . . ." She arched against him. "Ah . . . don't . . ."

Elsa shuddered. "Don't stop, Wil."

He fought a desperate battle for control. Desire raged like a fever as he looked at her flushed face, lips swollen and wet. "Aina—"

Her fingers moved from the column of his neck to the plane of his chest. He felt the slight pressure and yielded, levering his body far enough from hers to see her face in the yellow glow of the streetlight. "Don't stop."

For a moment, the temptation nearly overwhelmed him. But he knew that if he took her now, she'd resent him for it. A part of him suspected that she knew it, too. It would be too easy for her to withdraw from him again if he yielded to the clawing feeling of need that was slowly eating away at his insides.

Gently he moved away from her. "Elsa—"

The jarring whistle of a police siren interrupted him. A halogen light's bright, intrusive glare broke the sensual spell in the car. Wil reared his head in the direction of the light, feeling a certain predatory antagonism toward the intruder. Parked behind them, a dark vehicle, with a flashing red light, had its searchlight trained on Wil's car. "Damn it." The horrified expression on Elsa's face might have been funny if he hadn't been so irritated, so aroused. "Take it easy," he told her. "We're not two teenagers caught necking."

"No," she muttered as she struggled with her clothes, "we're two adults caught necking. That's worse." She pulled at her bra, her T-shirt. "Move your hand." Pushing him away, she yanked the cardigan into place.

From the police car's loudspeaker came an ominous "Please wait in your vehicle."

With a groan, she dropped her head into her hands. "Oh, God."

Wil combed his fingers through his rumpled hair. "I'll get us out of this."

"You better."

"Hey, you're the crackerjack lawyer. Isn't this some kind of—" At the sharp rap of knuckles on his window, Wil bit off the sentence with a curse. "Never mind." He rolled down the window, trying not to feel too irritated that the officer's flashlight shone directly in his eyes. "Evening, Officer."

"Well, well, well." The light zoomed closer. "If it isn't—" Before the man could finish the statement, Elise's breath came out in a sharp hiss. "Nikki! You fiend!" She dived for the handle of her door, leaped from the car and quickly rounded it. When the policeman dropped the light from Wil's face, Wil recognized Nikolai Krestyanov, Elsa's brother and a Chicago Police Department detective.

Elsa launched herself at her brother in a flying leap that had him laughing as he fended off halfhearted blows to his chest. "Hey, hey, cut it out."

Elsa landed a well-aimed punch to his gut. "Moron! You scared us to death."

Nikolai laughed harder. "How was I supposed to know I'd stumbled on the scandal of the decade?" His gaze shifted from his irate sister to Wil. "How ya doing, Wil?"

Wil eased himself from the car. "Fine, Detective." Two years had passed since he'd last seen Nikolai. In the years since he'd left Chicago, he'd gradually lost touch with the friends from his former life. The younger man's once youthful looks had matured, Wil realized, probably owing a good deal to the realities of his job. City detectives tended to grow up fast, and at thirty, Nikolai already looked toughened. Wil regretted the loss of innocence for his friend. "What brings you here?" he asked.

In a quick move, Nikolai captured Elsa's wrists, wrapped her arms around her body and held her fast, with her back against his chest. "There," he said, "be a good girl, and hold still." Elsa muttered something in Russian that made her brother laugh. If her irate expression gave any indication, the abrupt word needed no translation.

"None of that," Nikolai told her. "I'd let you go, but you'd hit me again." With a grin at Wil, he told him, "I had to interview a potential witness out in Mendota. I was hoping I could get Elise to let me crash on her couch tonight, although—" he slanted a look at his still-struggling sister "—if you had other plans—"

With the flat of her foot, she kicked him in the shin. "You big jerk," she said. "I should let you sleep on the sidewalk."

With a final laugh, Nikolai freed her. "Go inside and make us some coffee, *Knyìeza,* I want to talk to Wil."

"He was just leaving," she told him.

"I was not." Wil leaned back against the side of his car. "I didn't have any intention of leaving."

The glare Elsa shot him could have wilted a lesser man. "Just once, do you think it would be too much to ask for you to agree with me?"

He wondered what she'd do if he told her how attractive she looked with her hair still mussed, her lips still swollen and moist. He decided to err on the side of caution. "This time it would."

With an irritated huff, Elsa glanced at her brother. "Then make your own damned coffee," she said. With a brush of her hands, she freed herself from his light hold, then stalked toward the door of her apartment building.

Wil waited until she'd disappeared into the building before he shared a laugh with Nikolai. "Well," he said, offering the other man his hand, "it's good to see you again."

Nikolai shook his hand. "Even under the circumstances?"

"Your timing could have been better."

"I bet Parker Conrad wouldn't think so."

Wil released Nikolai's hand. "Probably not."

Nikolai continued to study him in the dim light from the street lamp. "So," he said after several nerve-racking seconds, "are you going to tell me what you were doing with my sister in that car, or do I have to pound it out of you?"

"I'd think what I was doing should have been pretty obvious."

"You know what I mean."

Wil nodded. "I know. We were—" he paused, not sure how to answer the question "—getting reacquainted."

"So I noticed."

Wil scrubbed a hand over his whiskered chin. "Look, what's between me and Elsa is complicated. There's no way

I can explain it to you, when I'm not even sure I understand it myself."

After a brief pause, Nikolai gave Wil a slight nod. "Don't hurt her again, Larsen. You did enough damage in the first round."

"The feeling was mutual."

At the soft admission, the younger man seemed to relent. He clapped Wil on the shoulder with a strong hand. "I'll bet you a dollar Elsa made coffee anyway," he said.

Elise gave Wil a glacial look as she shoved a mug into his hand. "Coffee's in the kitchen. I hope you choke on it." Nikki's warm chuckle only served to irritate her further. She sank down onto one of the overstuffed chairs in her living room.

She heard them laughing in the kitchen, enjoying each other's company. Once again, she felt like the outsider. Evidently Nikki and Wil had managed to maintain an easy camaraderie over the past ten years. Only she had been tossed out of the circle of warmth. She couldn't stop the bitter resentment that rose in the wake of the realization.

Nikki must have noticed her sour expression when he joined her in the living room. "You been sucking on a persimmon?" he quipped.

"Very funny."

"You look madder than hell, Elise. What's with you?"

"Oh, I don't know," she drawled. "Could it be that you two are having a good laugh at my expense?"

"We're not laughing at you."

Wil strolled into the room, cradling a mug of coffee in his large hand. "I assure you. I'm not laughing."

Nikki gave him a dry look. "If I were half the brother I should be, you ought to be sprawled on the pavement outside licking your wounds."

Elise snorted. "Well, that's mature."

"Careful." Nikki eased his jacket off, then quipped, "I carry a gun." He removed the weapon from the rear waistband of his jeans so that he could set it on the end table. "Don't fool with me."

Elise glanced from her brother to Wil, then back again. They both gave every impression of settling in for the night. Neither seemed to have given any thought to her presence, her obvious discomfort or the unsettling scene Nikki had witnessed in the parking lot. Wil seemed to have completely recovered, and it peeved her that he managed to enjoy an easy camaraderie with Nikki while her own equilibrium was still in a tailspin.

Deliberately she tamped down her growing irritation. It would only make her look foolish if she lost her temper. The best thing she could do was assert her territorial claims to her apartment. This day, she now realized, had been a terrible mistake. She couldn't remember the last time she'd spent an agendaless day with Parker. It had been too easy to enjoy Wil's company, too easy to relax in the warmth of his smile and the bond of their remembered friendship. Around three that afternoon, she'd begun to notice something that felt suspiciously like a yearning begin to grow and flourish in her soul. Now it threatened to overwhelm her. Best close the lid on it before it soared out of control.

"If neither of you minds," she said as she stood, "I'm going to leave you to your male bonding and go to bed. I've got to go to work tomorrow."

Wil frowned at her. "Tomorrow's Sunday."

"And I have a meeting with Edgar Collingham's attorney."

"On Sunday?" Nikki asked.

"He wants a complete rundown of all the costs associated with the auction. I don't have time to do it next week, and he wanted the figures as soon as possible. Tomorrow worked best for both of us."

"What's Edgar's problem?" Nikki asked.

"He thinks his stepmother is getting a disproportionate share of the estate."

"Because," Wil guessed, "he thinks you're hiding costs in the expenses associated with the auction."

"Something like that."

"Mostly the cars," he said.

She hesitated. "All right. Mostly with the cars. Edgar doesn't understand what's involved in the restorations, and the expenses look inflated to a person whose only opinion of his father's collection is that it was a frivolous waste of money. I plan to meet Rich Proliss—"

"*The* Rich Proliss?" Wil asked, evidently recognizing the prominent attorney's name.

"That's the one. He's Edgar's attorney. I plan to meet him at the Collingham estate to visually inspect the cars. He'll want to see the work you've done so far, and it'll be easier for me to explain what's been happening, and what expenses are involved, if I show him. Besides, Brandy Collingham plans to be present, and I liked the idea of meeting with Rich on her territory. I thought it gave her more leverage. Especially if Edgar happens to tag along."

Nikki snorted. "What a yutz. Just because his father married a hot-looking woman a third his age, poor little Edgar is convinced that he's being cheated out of his due."

Elise shrugged. "It's fairly common in families like this. People who think money solves everything should spend a day or two with the Collinghams."

"Well, hell," Wil said, "how long have you known about this meeting?"

"Since Wednesday."

"Then why didn't you call me? Pop can run the numbers for you straight from the computer. You should see him on that thing. He looks like a mad scientist with a new toy."

Elise wasn't ready to admit that she'd deliberately avoided calling him. "I have copies of all the invoices. I ran the report I needed myself."

"But we already have them computerized. We can sort the data two or three ways, and give you a projection analysis. If you're dealing with Rich Proliss, you can't be too prepared."

"He's got a point there, Els."

Elise resisted the urge to ask her brother just whose side he was on. Instead, she shook her head. "Well, it doesn't matter now. I've already got what I need. Thanks for the offer, though."

"Look." Wil evidently wasn't going to be deterred. "Why don't I meet you at the estate tomorrow? Pop and I have been shuttling the cars out to the garage one or two at a time, so everything we've completed is housed at the Collingham place. I can show Rich and Edgar exactly what we've been doing, and give him a more detailed analysis of what costs are involved. That way, I get to take the heat, and you can concentrate on protecting Brandy."

Elise felt the trap closing in. It was her job to do whatever was in the best interest of Chester Collingham's estate and his widow, even if it meant sacrificing her own sanity in the process. Still, she hedged, seeking blindly for a way out. "I don't know . . ."

"It makes perfect sense," Wil insisted. "You've got to pick up your car tomorrow anyway. So have Nick drop you at the garage, then you can meet me at the Collingham's. I'll head over early to get things ready."

Nikki nodded. "That works great."

Oh, sure, she thought, just great. She grasped at the first straw she could find. "I need to go by the office first and pick up the report. I brought my file home, but I left the data report to run on the computer overnight on Friday. I'll need it tomorrow for Rich."

"No need," Wil said. "I'll have Pop run whatever numbers you need on the computer. It'll save you the trip into town."

Nikki nodded. "I don't like the thought of you driving in and out of the city by yourself at weird hours, anyway. This is much better."

Irritated, Elise sent him a sharp look. "I'm thirty-five years old, Nikki. I know how to take care of myself."

"Yeah, well, thirty-five-year-old women can be just as vulnerable as younger ones. I don't like it."

Wil pointed to her door. "And you need better locks."

Nikki's gaze darted to her door, then back to her. "You don't even have a dead bolt."

At their tag-team approach to controlling her, Elise's temper snapped. "Will you two kindly cut it out?" she said. "I'm not a child, and if I want a security lesson, I'll ask for it. If you want to do this tomorrow, then fine. It probably will make it easier on Brandy. That's what matters. But this doesn't mean I'm giving the two of you permission to take over my life all of a sudden."

Nikki's expression turned suddenly serious. "Take it easy, Els. We're just concerned."

She drew several breaths. A part of her knew she was acting irrationally, but they'd pushed her too hard. Damn Wil, she thought. He'd done this to her. In a matter of days, he'd unraveled most of what it had taken her ten years to build. With a mental effort at self-control, she gathered the threads of her dignity around her like a sheltering blanket. "I'm sorry. I'm not trying to be so cranky. I'm just tired. Roger is driving me crazy at work. This auction is sucking up all my time. This is the third weekend in a row I've had to work exclusively on details. If that's not enough, I'm about to have the Collingham family feud on my hands." She gave Wil a shrewd look. "I don't need any more pressure right now."

Nikki either didn't notice or ignored the undercurrent. "Understood. Look, I'm really beat. Otherwise, I wouldn't have insisted that you invite me in. I know when to keep my nose where it belongs."

At his explanation, Elise felt a twinge of guilt. She'd been concentrating so hard on her reaction to Wil, she hadn't taken time to notice Nikki's fatigue. She should have spotted the dark circles under his eyes, the way his face was drawn taut, the stark outline of the needle-thin white scar on his chin that he'd received years before from a suspect's switchblade. "You know you are always welcome here."

His gaze slid to Wil. "Not always."

"Always," Elise insisted.

Wil set his mug down on the coffee table. "On that note, I really am leaving." He glanced at Elise. "What time tomorrow?"

"I told Rich I'd meet him at the Collinghams' at ten."

"Fine." She refused to be intimidated by the slightly predatory look he gave her. "Tomorrow, I'll make sure you get whatever you need."

She didn't start shivering until he'd closed the door behind him.

Chapter Six

A steady rain was pounding against her window when she awakened to the sound of rattling in her kitchen on Sunday morning. Her first thought was that if she failed to beat Nikki to the percolator, the coffee would taste like sludge. Her second was a panicky feeling that she'd be trapped with Wil inside the confines of the Collingham garage for the better part of the day. With a groan, she pulled her covers over her head.

"Elise?" Nikki bellowed from the kitchen.

"What?" she asked without lowering the sheets.

"You up?"

"I am now."

"Good." The proximity of his voice told her he'd entered her bedroom. Seconds later, she was practically catapulted from the bed when he tumbled onto it. "What are you making me for breakfast?"

She lowered the covers to glower at him. In spite of his shadowy beard growth, he looked rested and recovered from the night before. It felt good to have him here, she realized. With the pressures of his job, and hers, they didn't see each other as much as she would have liked. "I'm not."

"What kind of way is that to treat a guest?"

She glanced at the clock beyond his shoulder. "It's seven o'clock in the morning. I'm not ready to get up yet, and you're not a guest."

"I know, but I'm going to run down to the hardware store to buy you a dead bolt. Since you didn't have any eggs in your refrigerator, I figured I'd ask if you wanted me to stop and get something."

Despite herself, Elise felt a smile tug at the corners of her mouth. "You're determined to fix my life, aren't you?"

"Right now, I'm just worried about your locks."

"Are you still going to drag me off to Wil's today?"

"Yep."

"Then you're worried about more than my locks."

Nikki didn't answer for a long time. "Elise, are you in love with Parker Conrad?"

"Of course."

"You're sure?"

"Of course I'm sure."

"Then what was going on last night when I pulled into the parking lot?"

She snuggled deeper beneath the comforting warmth of the blankets. "I thought you were going to keep your nose where it belongs."

"That was last night. This is this morning."

"Then trust me to know my own mind, Nikki. Especially in the light of day."

He rolled onto his side so that he could prop his head on his hand and study her face. "When did you get so good at arguing?"

"About the time you kept stealing my dolls and holding them hostage. I didn't have a prayer of beating them out of you, so I had to learn to negotiate. Besides, I'm a lawyer. It's my job."

"Yeah, well, I'm a brother. Torment is my job."

"Stick to protection. You'll get a lot farther with me."

"Does that mean shut up and go get the locks?"

"Yep."

"All right." He rolled to his feet. "I'll leave it alone for now. But I'm watching you."

She turned her back to him. "And pick up a dozen eggs on your way home."

Three hours later, from the tiny window inside the garage where Chester Collingham's collection was housed, Wil watched Elsa approach the large building. He knew her well enough to suspect that she planned to use the trio of people accompanying her as a kind of armor against him. But Brandy Collingham, looking gorgeous as ever in a figure-hugging black dress—the kind that had probably had a lot to do with the persistent nature of Chester Collingham's high blood pressure during the latter part of his life—her stepson, Edgar, predictably attired in khaki trousers and a navy-blue blazer, and a white-haired man Wil identified as Rich Proliss, wearing a severe three-piece suit; looked more like a circus act than sentries.

Elsa, he figured, would give her right arm to avoid a confrontation with him. The last thing in the world she wanted was to know why she'd responded to him the way she had last night. He'd spent the better part of four hours trying to wind down from the encounter. She probably didn't have the first idea of how hard it had been for him to walk away from her, and unless he missed his guess, she didn't want to think about it. Elsa found things easier to deal with if she ignored them. This time, he'd vowed during the long, sleepless hours of the previous night, things would be different.

With a measured control, Wil tossed a grease rag over his shoulder and headed for the door. If she thought her little entourage was going to make him retreat, she was about to learn, the hard way, that he didn't let anybody manipulate him.

He leaned against the doorjamb, studying her with pure masculine appreciation as she picked her way along the gravel walk. If she'd thought to diffuse some of the sexual energy that seemed to pulse between them by dressing in a tailored black suit and red shawl-collared blouse, it hadn't worked. His gaze skimmed the slim line of her legs, encased in sheer panty hose, the spot where her skirt ended at midthigh, the loose ponytail caught at her nape. His body kicked into overdrive. One of these days, somebody was going to have to tell her that the sight of a woman with a seemingly impenetrable façade was one of the biggest turn-ons in the world.

Armed with a computer printout and a grease rag, he prepared to do battle.

"Hello, Wil," Elsa said when she stepped inside the garage a few seconds later.

"Hi." He allowed himself several seconds to absorb the impact of seeing her again, then flicked his gaze to Brandy. He'd met her several times before, and he'd always liked her. Despite the odd circumstances of her marriage, he found her charming, guileless and genuinely entertaining. The slightly pained look in her eyes told him too clearly that she found this encounter difficult, at best, and he mentally cursed Edgar's selfishness in putting her through the ordeal. "Morning, Brandy."

She gave him a watery smile. "Hello, Wil."

Edgar's beady eyes narrowed. "You two have met?"

Brandy flicked away a tear with a black-gloved hand. Wil gave Edgar a glacial look. "It was my pleasure to service these cars for your father during his lifetime. I've met your stepmother several times."

Elsa coughed. "That's one of the reasons I chose Wil's firm to handle the restorations. I knew that he and his father were already familiar with the cars."

Edgar frowned. "If you serviced them while my father was alive, why do they need additional work now?"

"That's what we're here today to find out," Elsa said smoothly, before glancing at Wil once more. "Wil, I'd like you to meet Edgar Collingham, and Rich Proliss, his attorney."

Wil took his time wiping his hand on the grease rag before he extended his hand to Rich. "Is that so?"

"Yes." Rich's grip was solid. Wil knew from the calculating look in his eyes why Elsa was wary of this man. His protective instincts began to rumble. Rich's gaze swept over the neat row of automobiles in the well-lit garage. "I'm here to ensure that my client's interests are well protected."

"And make sure Philpott, Philpott and Drake isn't slipping money under the table to Chester's widow."

Brandy gasped. Elsa gave him a censorious look. "Wil."

"Let me ask you something," Wil said to Rich, ignoring the warning note in Elsa's voice. "How many times did dear old Edgar go visit his father in the last five years of his life?"

"It's not my business to know," Rich said, his tone sharp.

"Well, I happen to know," Wil told him. He gave Brandy an encouraging look. "I happen to know that Edgar hadn't set foot on this estate since Chester married Brandy."

"Edgar didn't approve of his father's marriage," Rich said.

"That's right," Edgar chimed in, eyeing Brandy with obvious dislike. "I knew all she wanted was his money. I didn't see the point in condoning his marriage by agreeing to visit while she was in the house."

At Brandy's soft whimper, Wil took a step in her direction. When he slipped a supporting arm around her waist, she leaned into him. "I also happen to know," Wil continued, "that he hadn't been to see him for two years before the marriage, either."

"Mr. Larsen." Rich's expression turned predatory. "I don't make it a point to get involved in my clients' private lives. I make it a point to ensure that their interests are protected."

"All I'm saying is, the way I see it, Edgar lost interest in anything that happened here about seven or eight years ago. Brandy was the one who took care of Chester while he was dying. She was the one who kept him company, and made sure he got fed. Hell, toward the end, she was more nurse-maid than wife. If you ask me, she ought to get every red cent out of this estate."

"But nobody asked you, did they?" Rich's voice was so condescending, Wil almost laughed out loud.

"Nope," he said, slanting Elsa a knowing look. "Nobody asked me. After all, I'm just a dumb mechanic. I couldn't possibly know anything about something as complex as family loyalty and compassion. That's a little out of my league."

Elsa frowned at him. "Wil, please."

Rich's expression held an unmistakable challenge. "Frankly, I really don't care, Mr. Larsen. My concern is that my client receives everything he's entitled to under the law. Before today, I had some reason to suspect that your firm's hand in the restoration of these automobiles was less than honest." His gaze flicked to the spot where Wil's hand rested at Brandy's waist. "Now, I know it. I will need a complete inventory of what work has been done on the cars, as well as a justification for that work, and a projection of what you anticipate will be future costs. I warn you, if your calculations are off by a half cent, I'll recommend that my client conduct a complete audit of the accounts."

"While you, no doubt, charge him two hundred dollars an hour," Wil replied.

Elsa groaned. Rich's lips twitched in a self-satisfied smile. "Don't tell me you've never charged a fifty-dollar labor fee to install a twenty-cent brake-light bulb."

"As a matter of fact, I haven't."

"Well, then, let's hope you're a better mechanic than you are a businessman." Rich held out his hand. "The accounts, please."

Wil dropped the four-inch computer printout into his hand. "Knock yourself out," he told him, then forced himself to walk away. He'd been working on the 1938 Alvis when he heard Elsa's car on the gravel driveway. The Alvis had always been Chester's favorite to drive, and its engine needed the most cleaning. He scrubbed at the chrome plating on the radiator grille with a wire brush while he waited for Rich Proliss to admit that he couldn't make heads or tails of the numbers and figures on the printout.

He felt, rather than saw, Elsa approach him. "Smooth move, Einstein," she muttered as she reached his elbow. "Next thing you know, you'll have him siccing the IRS on you."

"Yeah, well—" he rubbed more polish on the grille "—good thing I know a great lawyer."

"You're nuts if you think I'd defend you."

He slanted her a wry look. "You're nuts if you think you wouldn't."

Elsa frowned at him. "Why do you have to make everything so hard?"

"It's easier that way." He turned his attention back to the Alvis. "Besides, I give Mr. Two-Thousand-Dollar Loafers about ten more seconds before he cries uncle. There's no way he understands that report."

"Try to cooperate, Wil," she said. "We can get this over with a lot quicker."

"Elise." Without either of them noticing, Brandy had joined them at the side of the car. "Do I really need to be present for this?"

Elise shook her head. "Not if you don't want to. I just thought you might be interested in knowing what was said."

The other woman brushed a lock of her strawberry-blond hair off her forehead. "I don't care what's said. I don't care if you give every cent of Chester's money to Edgar. I just want this finished."

Elsa cast a hasty glance at Rich and Edgar. While she understood Brandy's distress at the messy way the estate liquidation was proceeding, she wasn't about to let the woman sell her future just to appease Chester's irresponsible son. Reaching out, she squeezed Brandy's hand. "I know, Brandy. I'm sorry it had to be this way. Why don't you go on back to the house? If you trust me to handle the details, there's no reason you need to stay for this."

With a sigh of relief, Brandy glanced at Wil. "Thank you. I'm so tired of all of it."

"I know," Elsa said.

"Wil, why don't you come by and see me one afternoon? I'd really like to visit with you."

He gave her one of his lopsided smiles. "I'll do that. How's Thursday?"

"Thursday's great. Can you come for lunch?"

"Sure."

"And bring your father," she added. "I could use the company."

"I'll see if he's free."

Brandy looked at Elsa once more. "Thank you again, Elise. In case I haven't said it recently, I really appreciate everything you're doing."

"It's my job, Brandy."

"No, it's not. It's your job to liquidate Chester's estate. Being thoughtful doesn't necessarily come with the territory."

Without waiting for a response, Brandy left the garage. Elsa frowned at the way Edgar's gaze followed his stepmother's progress from the building.

"Nick's right," Wil said near her ear. "He's a yutz."

"Yes." She watched as Rich continued to study the reports. "A yutz with a very good lawyer."

Rich was approaching the car, with the computer printout in his hands. "I have some questions here."

Elsa gave Wil a final warning look, then squared her jaw. "What's the problem, Rich?"

"I was under the impression that all these cars were in working order when Chester died."

"That's right," she said.

"Then I'd like to know why this—" he scanned the report "—this engine redress on the '37 Cord was a necessary expense." He glanced at Wil. "And why it cost seven hundred and fifty dollars."

"Yeah," Edgar said, sauntering over to join them. With his hands in his pants pockets, he looked more like a recalcitrant child than an adult. "Why does it cost over seven hundred bucks to clean some chrome?"

Elsa stifled a groan. They were talking about nearly three million dollars in merchandise, and Proliss wanted an explanation on a seven-hundred-and-fifty-dollar invoice. It was going to be a very long day.

"I can answer that," Wil said. He indicated the Cord with a wave of his hand. "A lot of these cars Chester drove on a regular basis. He had definite favorites, like the Alvis. Some, though, he didn't like so much, and they sat for long periods of time. Older engines weren't designed for that. If a car wasn't cranked every so often, the oil ran out into the splash pan, and dry lock could set in."

Rich blinked. "Dry lock."

"Hmm." Wil tilted his head in the direction of the Cord. "I guess I'll have to explain it to you."

Elsa punched him in the back. He ignored her as he strolled to the Cord. When he lifted the hood, the newly cleaned and polished eight-cylinder engine gleamed in the artificial light. Elise leaned on one of the pontoon fenders and peered into the car with a look of pure delight. Wil's body tightened at that look. Nothing had ever turned him on like the way Elsa appreciated an engine.

"Here," he said, pointing to the gleaming engine. "That's a redressed engine."

Rich laid the printout down on the fender opposite Elsa, then leaned in to look at the car. "The object here, as I understood it, Mr. Larsen, was salability. Not cosmetics. If I'm supposed to be impressed by how shiny the parts are, I am. If I'm supposed to see the need for spit and polish—" he gave him a dry look "—you've lost me."

Wil glanced from Rich to Elsa. Her eyes sparkled as she rubbed one finger along the wraparound exhaust pipe. "It's gorgeous," she said, her voice a breathy whisper.

His gaze remained focused on the butterfly touch of her finger on the chrome. "It's about lubrication," he told Rich, deliberately emphasizing the last word. Elsa was wreaking havoc on his nerve endings, and as far as he was concerned, turnabout was fair play.

"Lubrication?" Edgar frowned at him.

"Um-hmm." He rubbed his hand on the oil cap. "In an engine like this, the oil is force-fed. It only works if the engine is running."

"Or dry lock?"

"Or dry lock." His gaze met Elsa's in the engine's reflection. He saw her tongue dart out to wet full lips turned apparently dry. Sensing victory, he leaned closer to her, letting her feel his heat. "The oil leaves the pump," he continued, still speaking to Rich, "and divides into two streams. The first stream goes through the shaft to the large connecting rods."

He saw Elsa's knuckles turn white where they gripped the side of the fender. Deliberately he ran his hand along the exhaust pipe. "The second stream," he drawled, enjoying the way the color began to rise in her face, "runs through the camshaft. When the engine is in good condition—" he traced his hand along the line of the fender "—the oil can slip through slowly. Everything gets properly lubricated."

"I see," Rich said.

"I don't," Edgar added.

No doubt, Wil thought.

Elsa looked as if she were about to faint. Wil caught her gaze and held it. "But if the bearings are loose, or the oil is cold and sluggish, the system has insufficient pressure. That can deprive some parts of the necessary lubrication for proper function.'' He wet his lips, and didn't think he imagined the way Elsa swayed toward him. "The oil also travels from the camshaft to a hollow member which supports the valve rocker—''

Elsa coughed. "Really, this is all very technical." She gave Wil a quelling look. "Edgar, you and Rich can't possibly find this interesting.''

Edgar gave her a dull look that said he'd been lost since Wil had begun the explanation. Rich seemed oblivious of the undercurrents. "I can see I'm going to have to have an expert run over these invoices." He straightened his vest points with a sharp tug. "Which I will.''

"Oh, please do," Wil drawled.

Rich's mouth curved into an unpleasant expression. "Don't worry. I shall.''

Elsa hastily stepped between the two men. "I know you wanted to do a visual inspection of the autos, Rich, but as I already explained to you and Edgar, the upgrades are necessary to bring them to showroom quality." Her expression brooked no argument. "If you think you've seen enough here, we can probably finish the rest of this at my office.''

"Let's go," Edgar said. "I've seen more than enough.''

Rich seemed to hesitate. "I suppose—''

Before the other man could finish, Wil interrupted. "I need to speak to you for a minute before you leave," he told Elsa. "About the billing.''

Her head moved in an almost imperceptible denial. "Can't it wait?''

"It'll only take a minute.''

From the corner of his vision, he saw her hands fist at her sides. "I will call you on Monday.''

"Now would be better.''

"I'm busy.''

He crossed his arms over his chest. "So am I. I need to settle this before I can finish up the work on the Suiza next week."

"What's the problem?"

He glanced at Edgar. "I'd rather discuss it with you alone." She looked ready to protest, so Wil held up his hand. "I think you'd have to agree it's not a good idea for us to discuss finances in front of an audience." Wil jerked his head toward the small room at the far end of the garage. "Now works for me," he told her.

He'd trapped her. He knew she couldn't discuss business in front of Edgar and Rich, and if she refused him, she'd look childish and irresponsible. At all costs, Rich Proliss had to know that she'd handled every detail of the estate liquidation with nothing but professional detachment. She didn't doubt for a minute that Wil was doing this because of what had happened last night. Trust him to deliberately put her on the spot with a client. Once again, nothing was as important as what he wanted, when he wanted it. It didn't matter that she was the one under pressure, or that he was putting her in an impossible situation. He had to have his way, and he'd go to any lengths to get it.

With an irate look, she stalked past him. If she hadn't known better, she'd have sworn he winked at her.

Once inside the confines of the narrow room at the end of the garage, Elise wrestled with her temper. Shelves lined the dingy room. Oil bottles, gas cans, plug wires, assorted bulbs and parts, littered the available space. The glorified closet was cramped, and when Wil entered it behind her, then shut the door, she immediately felt closed in.

The feeling escalated when he turned the key in the door with a sharp click. Elise sidestepped him when he would have backed her into a corner. The smell of oil, grease and rags gave the room a thick feel that the weak light from the small window did nothing to dispel.

"What do you want, Wil?" she asked.

"What do you think I want?"

Her gaze met his, and the air turned molten between them. "I think you want something you can't have," she said, her voice a breathy whisper. "If you think I was fooled by that charming little speech you gave on oil lubrication, you're wrong. I know exactly what you were trying to do to me."

"Did it work?" He took another step forward.

She ducked beneath his arm and retreated to the other side of the closet. "Stop trying to change the subject. This is not funny."

"Believe me, baby, I'm not changing the subject. I haven't thought about anything but the subject since last night."

He was standing so close to her now, she could smell his clean, intoxicating scent. Somehow it reached her through the stuffy confines of the small room. She still held her auction file, and her fingers clutched the thick sheaf of papers like a weapon as her temper kicked up a couple of notches. "You think this is all really amusing, don't you?"

"Oh, yeah. I think it's hilarious. I'm just about to die laughing that you've got me tied up in knots."

With an irritated huff, she moved toward him several paces. "Drop the sarcasm, Wil. It's not working. I know exactly what you're trying to do to me. I can't tell you how amused I was by that little stunt you pulled today. It ranked right up there with your lesson on premature ignition at the Art Institute fund-raiser. You're a real laugh a minute."

In the dim light, the angles of his face looked sharper, more pronounced. He looked predatory. And dangerous. She knew him well enough to know that his temper was nearing volcanic proportions. "At least I'm not the one denying what's going on here."

She glared at him. "I'm not denying anything."

"No? Then look me in the eye and tell me you've had one good night's sleep since last Tuesday."

"I haven't," she said, and was gratified by the shocked expression on his face.

"You haven't."

"No. I haven't been able to sleep, or think, or work, or even breathe right, since you kissed me Tuesday afternoon. Is that what you wanted to hear?"

This time, he was the one who retreated a step. "Elsa—"

She moved forward with measured precision until his back was pressed against one of the rickety bookshelves. "You want to know that you're making me miserable? You want to know that all I can think about is how much I used to love you? You want to know that my skin tingles every time I remember what it felt like to have your hands on me?"

He swore, softly and succinctly.

"Is that going to make it better for you?" she asked, closing the distance between them. "I wonder. Because it's making it hell for me."

"I didn't mean..."

At the idea that she'd managed to ruffle his normally unflappable calm, a heady power rushed through her. "You don't like not being in control, do you, Wil?"

"This isn't about control."

His eyes had taken on a wild look that both excited and terrified her. "No? You're the one who's always tossing around the innuendo. You're the one who wants to keep me off balance and confused. You're the one who makes all the

plans, creates all the strategy. Well, maybe I've had just
about all of that I'm going to take."

"What are you—?"

"Oh, shut up, Wil. For once in your life, just shut up."

She didn't give him time to react. If she'd given him time,
she'd have lost her nerve. Instead, she closed the remaining distance between them, then covered his mouth in a kiss
that lacked some of the ferocity, but none of the passion,
of the one they'd shared the night before. Momentarily he
went stiff with surprise, holding his mouth immobile under hers, but when she stroked his lower lip with her
tongue, he groaned and tunneled his fingers into her hair.

In a dim corner of her mind, she heard the heavy file she
carried drop to the concrete floor, and the skittering noise
of scattered papers. The feel of his fingers rubbing erotic
circles on her scalp quickly chased the thought away. One
of them gasped. She wasn't sure which.

He molded her mouth beneath his with expert precision,
giving and taking in equal measure. She'd started this to
teach him a lesson, but somehow, she'd lost the purpose.
Now, a deep, spiraling need to touch him was searing a path
to her hands, driving them upward to wend around his
neck. Her fingers threaded through the silken weight of his
hair. Her lips parted beneath the urgency of his tongue. She
couldn't get enough of him. Driven by a desire, a need, to
consume, she deepened the kiss, plundering his mouth until his lungs screamed for air and her body hummed with a
quickened energy that threatened to explode. Only when
the need to breathe overrode her need for the taste of him
did she manage to tear her mouth from his.

With a low moan, Elise dropped her head to his shoulder. Wil guided his mouth along the smooth skin of her
jaw, her neck. The pattern of his moist breath on her throat

made her shudder. He gripped her scalp, guiding her head to one side to allow himself better access.

When he found the spot at the base of her throat that memory must have told him had once been so sensitive to his touch, he laved it with his tongue. Elise sucked in a ragged breath at the shocking impact of the caress. Time had done nothing to lessen her sensitivity to his touch there. He pressed a gentle kiss to the shadowy hollow before trailing a wet path to the whorl of her ear.

When his tongue traced the delicate shell, Elise tugged slightly at his hair. "Wil, please."

"Please what?" He nipped her earlobe. "Please stop?" He pressed a hot kiss to the spot behind her ear. She shuddered. "Please don't stop?"

With a soft moan, she leaned her head away from him to whisper, "Please stop." Elise stepped hastily away from him, heedless of the papers beneath her feet.

As she struggled for breath, a conflict between a shocking sense of victory at having made him respond to her as he had and a deep mortification at her own lack of control warred in her spirit. Urgently she needed Wil to understand that just because the physical chemistry still burned between them, that didn't mean they weren't both responsible for how they reacted to it. She'd allowed him to goad her into losing control.

It must not happen again.

In vain she tried to control the irregular beat of her heart. The second she touched him, her pulse had shot through the roof. She pressed a protective hand to the base of her throat, where the feel of his lips still lingered. "Wil, I—"

Before she could finish, he shook his head. "Don't apologize," he said. His voice sounded ragged and harsh. "Whatever you do, don't apologize."

"I wasn't going to."

"Good."

Because she couldn't decipher the intense look on his face, she turned her attention to the scattered papers. "I—I wish you hadn't come today."

"Do you regret kissing me?"

She met his gaze again. "Of course."

"I sure as hell don't regret it." He raked a hand through his hair in an attempt to restore order to the unruly waves she'd mussed with her fingers. "It was like holding dynamite, Elsa. It's always been like that."

"And can't be that way again."

"Why not?"

"Because it can't. You chose, and I chose. It's that simple."

He muttered a curse. "I can't look at you without wanting you."

"Wil—"

"It's true. Every time I look at you—hell, every time I think about you—I want you." His jaw seemed to harden into a tight line, and the indentation she'd never had the nerve to call a dimple deepened at the side of his mouth. "In some ways it's like nothing has changed, and in other ways, everything has. I can't stop thinking about you. If you want to know the truth, I could strangle you for it."

Her mouth dropped open on an irritated huff. "It isn't my fault, you know! You're the one who keeps stirring it up. So I'm attracted to you. So what?"

"So what?" He looked outraged.

"So what? We're both adults, not hormone-crazy adolescents. We're both old enough to be responsible for our actions. I told you before, I didn't want to pursue this, but you just can't let it alone, can you? And now that you're angry because it isn't working out, which I *told* you it wouldn't, you want to blame me. Well, it isn't my fault."

His expression turned hard. She knew before he said the words that he was about to verbally strike at her. She'd long since come to recognize that as Wil's primary means of defense. In a way, she supposed, she deserved it, for goading him with the kiss.

"It became your fault the day you decided to lock yourself away in that ivory tower of yours."

Even knowing it **was** coming didn't dim the hurt his words caused. Elise conquered it with a burst of anger. "Just who elected you judge and jury of the universe?"

"The same person who made you think you were better than the rest of us."

She gasped. Once again, he'd zeroed in on her most vulnerable spot and struck like a rattlesnake. "You bastard. You cold, arrogant bastard."

Wil said nothing as she snatched at the scattered papers on the floor. Elise crammed them haphazardly back into the file folder, using the activity to calm her racing nerves. When she faced him again, his expression was hard as granite. Only the turmoil in his eyes belied the impassive look on his face.

"Look, Wil," she said, calling on her deepest reservoir of calm. "I don't know why you feel like you have to do this. The way I see it, you pretty much said every insulting thing you could think of to me ten years ago. I might have felt like I had to accept that from you then, but I sure as hell don't feel that way anymore."

She clutched the folder to her like a shield. "I think it would be best for both of us if I completed this deal with your father. I just can't take this anymore."

"I wasn't trying to be insulting."

"Oh, well, excuse me. I seemed to have missed that."

"Damn it, will you stop being so stubborn?"

"I'm not being stubborn. Every time I'm around you, you find a new way to insult me. Well, thanks, but no thanks." She gave him a bitter look. "I'm not going to let you do this to me again, Wil. Once was enough."

She shouldered her way past him toward the narrow door. "I think from now on, it would be best if I just did business with your father."

"Damn it, Elsa—"

"You have no idea what you did to me, do you?" The look in his eyes confirmed her suspicions. For years, he'd blamed her for what had happened between them. She'd have to be a lot stronger, and a lot more determined, to break down the wall he'd erected. Wil despised her. He'd never tried to disguise the fact. And she just couldn't stand the hurt of trying to reach him anymore. "I'm sorry. I'm really sorry. I'm just not strong enough."

Without waiting for his response, she fled the room.

Chapter Seven

At nine o'clock that night, Elise let herself into her apartment with a weary sigh. Rich Proliss had managed to monopolize most of her afternoon with details of the Collingham auction, and she'd had to work later than she planned to complete a contract for Alex Devonshire.

Unfortunately, the deluge of work hadn't kept her mind off Wil. Parker Conrad, she reminded herself, was all she'd ever wanted in a life partner. She respected him. She cared for him. She wanted to marry him, to have his children. What she felt for Wil was nothing more than the rekindled flame of a remembered infatuation. His reappearance in her life had forced her to think about old wounds and old battles she'd believed were behind her. It had been years since she'd allowed herself to grieve over the loss of her parents' closeness, years since she'd considered how much Wil's rejection had hurt. Dredging all that up from the past had taken its toll on her, and she reminded herself sharply that the sooner she forgot about him, the sooner she forced his memory back into the sealed inner closet where it belonged, the better.

Mentally and physically exhausted, she dropped her briefcase on the hall table, then headed for her room. Flannel pajamas had never been so appealing, she decided as she settled the soft fabric against her skin. Pulling her hair into a loose ponytail, she plodded back to the living room. When she finished going over the set of contracts Alex had sent her to review, she would go to bed.

Engrossed as she was in a particularly complicated clause, the sharp knock on her door startled her. With a frown, Elise glanced at the clock. It was after eleven-thirty. The only person who'd disturb her at this time of night was her landlord, and then only if there was some sort of problem with the apartment. Just what she needed, tonight: a late-night visit to fix rattling pipes.

The relentless knocking continued as she hurried across the living room carpet. If he wasn't careful, he'd wake the building. With an irritated huff, she jerked open the door. At the sight of Wil Larsen, his fist poised in midair, his features set in an angry scowl, she blinked. "Wil?"

When she jerked open the door, Wil shot a hasty glance at her elderly neighbor, Mrs. Fitzmartin, whose kerchiefed head peeked from the crack of her door. Shouldering past Elise into her apartment, he growled, "Don't you know better than to open the door without checking to see who it is first?"

The sight of her clad in those ridiculously oversize flannel pajamas sent his pulse racing. He suddenly felt like a fool for turning up on her doorstep in the middle of the night, but, God help him, he'd been going out of his mind since that afternoon. Several times that evening he'd tried calling her, but she hadn't been home. Now that he was here, he didn't know what to do. So he yelled at her. Great plan, Larsen, he thought.

While he studied her back, Elsa continued to stare into the hallway for several seconds. He had the distinct impression that she was trying in vain not to lose her temper. "Why don't you come in?" she told the empty doorway, her sarcasm unmistakable. Shutting the door with a distinct click, she turned to face him.

He paced a long path in the center of her living room. In the shadowy light, her expression was unreadable. Amid the soft greens and blues and tweeds of her apartment, he felt out of place, agitated. Now that he was here, he didn't know what to say to her. If he simply blurted out that he'd been feeling like a fool since he'd last seen her, he'd only make things worse.

"What are you doing here?" she asked him.

At his side, his hands flexed. He wasn't ready to answer that question yet. He didn't know what he was doing there. When she walked away from him in Chester Collingham's garage, he'd sworn to himself that he'd leave her alone. After hours of pretending, he'd driven to her apartment, without the first clue as to what he was going to do once got there. Now that he was here, he still didn't know. "You shouldn't have opened the door. You don't have a view glass. You didn't even ask who it was." He raked his gaze over her pajama-clad form. "Do you have any idea how vulnerable you are?"

"People don't generally bang on my door at all hours of the night. I was disoriented."

"Still—" he continued to pace "—you're smarter than this. It could have been anybody on the other side of that door." He didn't want to talk about anything as mundane as Elsa's security, or the lack thereof, but he had a cloying suspicion that the moment he changed the subject, he'd have to touch her again. If he did that, God only knew what would happen. With a brief flick of his wrist, he indicated the doorway. "I thought Nick was going to install a dead bolt for you."

His accusation seemed to shred what remained of her patience. "Stop it. I'm tired, and I want to go to bed. And I don't think you drove here in the middle of the night to shout at me about the locks on my door." She leaned back against the door with a quiet sigh. "He didn't have time to finish it this morning. He got called into the station."

At the tired note in her voice, he abruptly stopped pacing to stare at her. He didn't think he imagined the way she shrank back into the shadows. With only the moonlight illuminating her apartment, he couldn't see her face, but he still felt her discomfort.

"Why are you here?" she asked him.

"I tried to call you all evening. You weren't home."

"I worked late."

Long, anxious seconds ticked by. His body hummed with a pulsing energy, like a well-tuned engine. He hadn't noticed it before, had been too agitated, but as he watched her, he felt the heated blood running through him. The sensation was so strong, it should have vibrated across the plush carpet, through the floorboards, to the soles of her bare feet. Even from across the room he felt the warmth of her skin. He sensed the way her flesh prickled with awareness where the damp tendrils of her hair lay against her nape.

Indistinguishable emotions warred through her.

He absorbed them.

A skitter of anticipation raced along his flesh as memories of the feel, the exquisite sensation, of her pressed against him, her soft mouth under his, her scented flesh against his whiskers, washed over him like a rising tide. Another thread of his sanity withered and died.

"Wil?"

The catch in her voice undid him. For hours that had seemed liked years, thoughts of her, of touching her, had consumed him. Shuddering, unable to resist, he crossed the room in three quick strides to pull her into his arms, to bury his mouth in hers. "Damn you," he whispered. God, how he'd wanted to resist her. "Damn you."

Heat seared a path from her body to his. As his lips moved against hers with a blatant hunger, he felt her quiver. The same emotional power that had sent her fleeing that morning surged again. This time, Wil broke the kiss before it could consume them.

He stepped away from her so abruptly, she stumbled backward. He steadied her with his hands on her shoulders. "Sorry," he muttered. "I didn't mean—"

Elsa shrugged his hands from her shoulders. "This is becoming an annoying habit with you."

Cursing himself for being a thousand times a fool, Wil walked away from her. He yanked open the snaps on his leather jacket. From the corner of his eye, he saw her flinch. "I'm sorry," he told her again. "I didn't mean to pounce on you like that."

"No?"

"No." With his jacket hanging open, he wondered if she could see the way his heart was pounding beneath the faded denim of his shirt. It might have been a trick of the moonlight, but he'd have sworn he saw her shiver. "I just can't seem to keep my hands off you. A lot has changed, but I guess that hasn't."

"Evidently not."

At the bitter note in her voice, he winced. "I'm not going to apologize for wanting you, Elsa. Especially not when

I know it's a two-way street." Shrugging out of his jacket, he tossed it over the end of her couch. "Can we sit down? This could take a while."

She seemed to hesitate. "I'm really not up to this tonight. I've got a long day tomorrow."

The look she gave him made his gut clench. She had always had the power to turn him inside out with that look. "Elsa," he said, "I want to try and explain what's happening to me. I know I've been driving you crazy. If it's any consolation, I feel a little nuts myself." Without waiting for her permission, he dropped onto the couch.

Elsa lingered in the shadows. "You haven't been driving me crazy, Wil. I just don't understand why we're at each other's throat one minute, and trying to reclaim something from the past next."

He waited several heartbeats. "Please look at me."

Slowly she turned to face him. "Why are you doing this?"

"Because ten years ago, you meant the world to me. I tried, I swear to God I tried, but I can't pretend I'm not torn up over this," he admitted. "Now that I've seen you again, I found out that I need to know what happened to us. I need you to make me understand."

An agonizing few moments passed as she watched him. For long seconds, he was sure she'd refuse. If she asked him to leave now, he knew, things would really be over between them. He'd come here tonight in a desperate final effort. If Elsa wouldn't meet him at least partway, he'd be doomed to a lifetime of regret.

His heart kicked into double-time when slowly, as if compelled, she crossed the room to his side. He seized her hand and pressed it to his lips for a hungry, grateful kiss. He felt as if he'd been given a reprieve from the guillotine. A part of him screamed a warning that she shouldn't be this important, he shouldn't let her be this important, but he was powerless to stop the tide of relief flooding through him.

She sank into the overstuffed chair next to his seat on the couch. He doubted that she knew how appealing she looked with her feet bare and her hair curling in ever-loosening tendrils around her face. Her woman's curves had always been full enough to tempt him beyond reason, but outlined beneath the pajamas they seemed to beckon him. His palms tingled with the need to touch her. Had it not been for the slightly vulnerable look in her eyes, he might not have been able to restrain himself. But that look told him, without words, that Elsa was more than a little afraid of him. If he knew one thing about her, he knew she was fighting hard not to be vulnerable—not to anyone, and especially not to him.

In the years since he'd last seen her, he'd wanted to believe that she'd become a materialistic, *narcissistic* member of the very society he'd once lived in. Every time he spoke with her parents, heard her mother's pain at the separation that had rent their family, he'd resented Elsa for making it happen. Since Maks had been struck by a car and killed, Elsa's family had become his family. He still blamed her for the pain she'd caused them.

It had been easier to harbor his resentment by feeding it with visions of her living a too-fast life, filled with affluence and greed, a life in which nothing mattered but her wants and her desires. When he first saw her again, something in his heart had begun to crumble, like a great chunk of ice sliding into a tropical sea.

"Aina," he finally pleaded, using the once familiar endearment like a caress, "please let me explain."

He saw the look of pain that crossed her features and hated himself for it. "There's nothing to explain," she told him. "What happened between us was never really resolved. We were young, I was confused, you were angry. We shouldn't have let these wounds fester for so long. I guess it just seemed easier."

"No." His fingers tightened on hers. "I was twenty-eight years old. That's old enough to know what I was doing. I loved you, Elsa." At the look she gave him, he felt the band begin to tighten around his chest once more. "I loved you. The last thing I wanted was to hurt you. I haven't been the same man since the day you walked away from me. Whatever caused the argument with your father, I can't believe it was worth what this has done to both of us."

Elise turned her face to gaze out the window, not wanting him to see the pain his words caused. He still held her responsible for the way their relationship had ended, and that truth hurt her almost as much as the harsh words he'd said the day she left. Through the window, she watched as a shifting pattern of clouds raced across the surface of the moon. She felt cold, raw, despite the warmth of her apartment.

Instinctively rubbing her upper arms for warmth, she tried to ignore the way his gruff plea tugged at her, beckoned her, but couldn't. A part of her would always belong to this man, no matter how deeply she denied it. Turning slowly to face him, she felt her resolve disintegrate like a wave breaking against the rocks. "You will never know how much you hurt me, Wil. A part of me died that day."

"Tell me," he pleaded. "We'll start there and see where it takes us."

He wasn't going to be deterred, she realized. She would have to tell him, or he'd sit in her living room until he wore her down. With a deep sense of resignation, she leaned back in her chair. Carefully, lest they overwhelm her, she unlocked the secret door in her heart where she'd hidden the memories. "You know what it was like. You know how hard it was for Maks and Nikki and me. From the day we arrived in Chicago, we had no money, no family, no friends. We were the ragged little kids with the Russian-speaking parents and funny names. In case you forgot, Americans weren't particularly fond of Russians back then."

The callused pad of his thumb rubbed the top of her hand. Seeking his warmth, she tightened her fingers on his. "Pop couldn't find work in New York, so he and Mama decided to bring us to Chicago. He'd heard there were jobs here for men who'd work hard. Nobody told him that there weren't any jobs for men who worked hard and spoke Russian. If it hadn't been for your father, we'd have starved."

"You were very young. I'm not sure you remember things exactly the way they were."

"No? Some things I remember really well. Like how it felt to be bussed out to suburban schools where all the girls had nicer hair and nicer clothes and shoes that fit. I remember sitting in class and feeling stupid because I couldn't understand what we were reading, or what my teacher was saying. I remember being teased because my dresses had patches and my coat was made out of an old bedspread. After Maks's accident, things only got worse."

She drew a deep, shuddering breath. They'd been in Chicago less than a year when her brother Maks, three years her senior, was struck while crossing the street. Elise's school bus dropped her off at a particularly busy intersection, and her mother generally sent Maks to walk her home from school. The light had just changed, and Maks had started across the street toward her when a car raced through the intersection, striking him. The driver hadn't stopped, and Maks had never regained consciousness. After lingering in a coma for several weeks, he'd died. Her father, never an affectionate man, had become more withdrawn, more difficult. As her mother carried the grief on her own, Elise and Nikolai had been left to handle their brother's death any way they could.

"Pop criticized everything I did. We'd never gotten along well, but after Maks died, things seemed to explode. I couldn't replace Maks, but that's what Pop wanted. We weren't even allowed to talk about Maks around him." She met Wil's gaze. "Sometimes I wished I'd been the one who got killed."

"That's not—"

She shook her head to interrupt him. "You were the only one I could talk to about Maks, about how much I missed him, and how much my father hurt me. When I was twelve and you were fifteen, I kept thinking if I could just get you to love me, everything would finally be all right."

Wil flinched. "Elsa—"

"Let me finish. You wanted to know, so know. There I was, twelve years old, walking around with this horrible guilt, thinking I was responsible for my brother's death, and even my own father blamed me for what happened."

"He didn't blame you," Wil insisted. "It was an accident. He knew that. He just didn't know how to deal with the pain."

She ignored him. "I had to fight for everything. I had to fight for friends. I had to fight to fit in. I had to fight to graduate. I had to fight for grades. I fought for my scholarship, and my college degree, and to get into law school. And on top of all that, I had to fight for the love of my own father. Every day after school, I came home and swept out his butcher shop."

She brushed an errant lock of hair off her forehead. "You know, one of the only times I ever remember my father showing me anything but indifference or disdain was shortly after he bought the butcher shop. I'd come in from school, and before we did anything, he'd put a nickel in the jukebox so I could stand on his feet and learn how to dance."

At the memory, a wave of sadness caused tears to sting the backs of her eyes. "But that was before Maks died. Every day afterward, I walked out of one world and into another. Every day, the only thing I had that seemed real to me was you. When Maks was gone, you stepped into his shoes for me. I loved you, Wil. I always loved you."

She started to cry now, and she wiped the tears with the back of her hand. "By the time I was eighteen and you were twenty-one, I didn't think a part of me existed without you. You were a junior at Northwestern, and I had just gotten a scholarship to the University of Illinois. You kept telling me that things were going to turn out okay, and I kept believing you.

"You told me things would be different when I got to college. It wasn't supposed to be so hard anymore, but it was. I was still the Russian girl with the funny name and the parents who barely spoke English. I worked twenty hours a week and carried a full course load, and still couldn't make myself fit in. I got turned down for sororities. I had people send me nasty letters and accuse me of being a communist. I even got a couple of threats."

From the corner of her eye, she saw him tense. "You never told me."

"When I was with you, I didn't want to talk about any of that. You were the only person in the world that made me feel content. I was so busy, and working so hard, we only saw each other on breaks. I didn't want to spoil it by whining."

"I never imagined you weren't happy."

"With you, I was," she said quietly. "That's all that mattered. After you graduated, everything changed. That summer before you went to Harvard to get your M.B.A. — I'll never forget that. Having you love me was like having my world completed. I loved you so much. I didn't care what happened, or how long we had to wait. I was ready to go to the end of the world with you."

"Except to Massachusetts."

At his quip, she gave a halfhearted laugh. "Want to know something?"

"I'm not sure."

"The only reason I didn't marry you that summer was because of my scholarship. If I'd gone to Harvard with you, I'd have had to give up my scholarship. My whole life, I'd been somebody's financial burden. I didn't want that to happen to you and me."

"It wouldn't have been a burden, Elsa."

"To me it would have. I was terrified that you'd start to resent me the same way Pop did."

His mouth pressed into a tight line. "He never resented you."

"It felt like he did." She shook her head when he would have argued. "When you left for Massachusetts, I thought I was going to die. I did the only thing I knew to fill the void. I increased my course load, and my work load, and buried myself in schoolwork."

"That's why you graduated in three years."

"Yes. I went to summer school every year, just to avoid having to live at home. The first summer, you worked co-op in the city, and we didn't see each other much. The second year, you were offered that job, and we both decided you should stay in Boston."

"I still wanted to marry you."

"I know, but your career was taking off, and you needed time to concentrate on that."

His laugh was harsh. "I concentrated so hard, I practically let it kill me."

She ignored that. "Pop and I had grown even farther apart, and I couldn't stand being there with him. I kept holding on to the idea that soon I'd be with you, and none of it would matter. When I turned twenty-one, you gave me that Pierce-Arrow hood ornament."

"With that stupid card."

"It was a nice card. I still have it. How many women have a man tell them she's pierced his heart?"

"How many men are lovesick enough to put something like that in writing?"

"Not many. That's why I loved it. We'd become lovers the summer before, but the day you gave me that hood ornament, that's the day I let you have my soul. I'd never been happier in my life."

When Wil didn't respond, Elise continued. "For the first time, things seemed to be going my way. My relationship with Pop was still rocky, but he seemed proud that I was going to law school. He actually told me the day I left that he thought Maks would be happy for me.

"When I got to school, things were better," she told him. "Part of it was just maturity. I was older, and I was with older people. I was secure in our relationship, and I didn't feel the need to compete so hard anymore. I started to make new friends, to set goals. After almost twenty years, I felt like I'd found my niche." She stopped, feeling more than a little foolish for the way she'd rattled on. Once the words had begun, they'd tumbled out, one after the other, in an unstoppable flood. She felt vaguely like a sinner in confession.

"Is this where you tell me what happened that day at the butcher shop?" Wil prompted.

She nodded. "I got my notice that I'd passed the bar that day. It was a Friday afternoon, and you were on your way from Chicago. I had told you I was expecting the letter that weekend, and you were coming home to either celebrate or console me. I went by the garage first, but you hadn't arrived yet, so I went to tell Pop at the butcher shop. When I walked in, I went through the usual routine. I put on my apron and started sweeping out the back. He was with a couple of customers, and didn't come back to see me right away. When he got there, he made some comment about how pleased he was that his daughter, the soon-to-be-famous lawyer, still knew how to use a broom. I handed him the letter from my apron pocket and kept sweeping."

Elise paused, momentarily overcome by the force of the memory. Her father had glanced at the letter, at first not understanding what it meant, then finally realized that she'd passed the bar and was now eligible to practice law in Illinois. For the first time in years, he'd hugged her. It had felt so good, so right to be there and share that moment with him. Bellowing up the stairs, he'd called her mother down to look at the letter. Nikki had come racing into the shop.

Elise squeezed her eyes tight to keep the tears from falling, then continued with the story. "He read it, and once he understood what it meant, he was ecstatic. He called Mama downstairs, and started to read the letter out loud to her. That's when he noticed the name."

Wil's fingers tightened on hers. "The name?"

She glanced at him in surprise. "That's what started the argument. You don't know, do you?"

"I want to hear this from you first. I'll tell you the way I heard the story when you're done."

Frowning, she continued. "He got angry. Mama kept trying to calm him down, and I kept trying to tell him it didn't mean anything. He wanted to know why I couldn't be a Krestyanov and be a lawyer. He just kept yelling at me about how I'd turned my back on him, and on my family. And then he told me I'd betrayed Maks's memory."

She fought a brief war with a fresh surge of tears, and won. Barely. "That was the last straw, Wil. I was twenty-five years old, and I couldn't keep accepting responsibility for Maks's death. I was so upset. I didn't know what else to do. I ran all the way down the street, and I was so relieved when I saw your car parked in front of the garage."

"I had just gotten in," he remembered.

"And I needed you. I needed you so much. I was crying so hard, it took you twenty minutes to get the story out of me. By the time I finished explaining that Pop had practically thrown me out of the house, you were staring at me like I'd grown a second head."

Wil felt her hurt. His reaction that day had been rash and, to Elsa, irrational. She couldn't possibly know how the emotional turmoil he'd struggled with for the past five years had affected him that afternoon. Since the day he'd made love to Elsa, he'd walked around in stark terror that something was going to keep them apart. Knowing she loved him had seemed too good, too potent, to last. He'd been seized by an almost uncontrollable urge to bind her to him in every way imaginable. When she refused to marry him, wanted to wait, he'd spent five long years in terminal terror.

Always Maks's memory had hung over them, like the sword of Damocles.

By the time she passed the bar, Wil had begun to believe they could have a future. He'd convinced himself that he could carry the truth about Maks to his grave, if only he had Elsa to chase away the fear. When she forced him to choose between her parents and her, that hope had been destroyed.

He doubted she'd ever fully understand his rejection until he told her about Maks. The irony of it twisted his stomach into knots. Once again, Maks had left him helpless.

With a grim sigh, he realized that all he could do, all he would do, was try to explain that he hadn't been rejecting her that day. It had been the choices she'd made, the ones he'd feared making himself. "I'm going to try and explain something to you," he told her, "and I hope we've come far enough that you'll try and listen to me."

She turned to stare out the window once more. He saw her shoulders slump forward. The defeated gesture made his chest hurt. Slowly, lest he startle her, he pressed her hand to his chest. Elsa tensed, but didn't pull away. "My mother died when I was so young, and after Maks, well, your mother needed another kid to take care of. I became her son. She became my mother. You were my family. I couldn't choose between you."

"I never asked you to."

"I didn't feel like you'd left me any choice. I kept thinking I could fix it," he told her. "If I just worked hard enough at it, I could fix it. All I had to do was make you and your father see reason." Gently he tugged on her hand until she faced him. Tears had left streaks on her face, and he ached to pull her into his arms. "When I went to talk to your father the day you left, I'd never seen him so upset. He kept telling me how you'd betrayed him, how you'd told him you were ashamed of who you were, and what you'd come from. He told me you'd insisted that you wanted more out of life than he could ever give you, that he'd failed you."

Elsa gasped. "Wil, I never—"

He squeezed her hand to interrupt her. "I was angry, and frustrated, and the people around me were hurting."

"And you believed him," she said.

All too clearly he remembered the night Andrei had put away a bottle of vodka while telling Wil about Elise's actions and about how much he missed Maks. Dear, sainted Maks. Wil beat back a bitter wave of anger. Releasing a long breath, he said, "I kept telling myself that I didn't let anybody hurt my own people. I didn't want to believe him, Aina."

Elise's shoulders jerked with the force of a sob. "But you did."

"What was I supposed to think? You were barely speaking to me, and Andrei, he seemed so—defeated."

"I never said those things. I can't believe he told you that I did."

"He was drunk. He was devastated."

"And his command of English has never been that good. You shouldn't have taken his word so quickly, Wil. No wonder you turned on me."

He gave her a pained look. "So why don't you tell me exactly what you argued about?"

"You still don't know, do you?"

"No. Andrei never talks about you. Your mother, she and I have spoken about it, but not about the argument. Every time I brought it up, she said it was between you and your father."

Beside him, he heard Elsa draw a deep breath. "The day I got my notice that I'd passed the bar was the first time my father found out I'd legally changed my name from Elsa Krestyanov to Elise Christopher."

Wil glanced at her in sharp surprise. "What?"

She nodded. "It almost seems silly, doesn't it?"

"You changed your name? Legally?"

"Yes."

"Why?"

"I don't know. It just seemed easier that way."

"That's what the argument was about?"

"Yes. Believe me, you're not the only one who wants to know how something like that could cause an entire family to crumble."

"I can't believe he never told me." He fixed her with a hard look. "I can't believe you never told me."

"You didn't ask." He heard the bitter note in her voice.

"Your father's a very proud man, Elsa. Surely you knew something like this was going to hurt him."

"I don't know what I thought. I was young. I was ambitious. It wasn't a conscious thing on my part."

"If you'd known he would react the way he did, would you have done it?"

Elsa seemed to think it over. "I'm not sure," she admitted. "If I had it to do again, I don't know whether or not I'd make the same decisions."

"Why do you think your father told me what he did?"

"Because he knew you'd believe him," she said.

The harsh statement wounded him. "I don't think so. I think he was too ashamed to tell me the truth."

Elsa's eyes registered her hurt. "It's not like I went out and defamed my family honor, Wil."

"He thought you did."

"And I could never make him understand that I hadn't done it because I was ashamed, or embarrassed." With a soft groan, she buried her fingers in her hair. With her elbows braced on her knees, she looked weary, as if the weight of the memories had drained all the life from her spirit. "God, this is such a mess."

"Elsa," he said, laying a hand on her knee. "He's hurting, too."

She didn't try to deny it. "In fairness to him, I don't think Pop was reacting to the fact that I changed my name. I think he was reacting to the fact that we'd argued for almost twenty years. He'd never forgiven me for Maks's death, and I'd never forgiven him for wanting me to take Maks's place. The argument that day was the end result of a lot of bitterness and hurt."

Wil contemplated the information, thought about Andrei's harsh words, about his anger, and found the resentment he'd felt toward Elsa for so long begin to ebb away. In its place was a sickening sense of guilt, and the first bitter taste of anger toward the man who had misled him. He'd believed Elsa's father. When Andrei told him the story of the argument, he'd believed him. For years he'd respected the older man like a second father. At the time, Wil had been so frustrated with the way Elsa had virtually fled, he'd let his temper override his common sense. It was no wonder she felt like he betrayed her. How could he have been such a fool not to trust her? "I didn't know. My God, you have to believe me. I assumed— Oh, hell, I don't know what I thought, but I had no idea that's what happened."

She leaned back in her chair again, studying him with a contemplative gaze. "I felt so hurt that night. I needed you so much, and the few times I tried to talk to you, you were so angry."

He shook his head. "I was a fool." Warily he met her gaze. "And I hurt you, Elsa. I never wanted to."

She ignored the soft confession. "No wonder you were so surprised when you picked me up on Friday."

"Does my father know what happened?"

She shrugged. "He knew I'd changed my name. I'm not sure if he knows anything about the argument or not. Jan has a remarkable capacity for understanding."

At the bitterness in her voice, regret flooded his soul. "We wasted ten years, Aina."

"Time seemed to slide by while I wasn't watching," she said. "That first year, I kept trying to call, to send letters, anything to get Pop to talk to me, but he wouldn't. He'd completely withdrawn from me. It was like living through Maks's death all over again. After that, I gave up. I didn't know what else to do."

Because he didn't have answers, because both of them were worn out from the long-overdue conversation, they lapsed into silence. Wil leaned back against the couch with a weary sigh.

"We've really made a mess of things, haven't we?"

"I guess. But it's in the past now, Wil. There's nothing we can do about it."

"I don't want things to end like this."

"Wil, I—"

He couldn't stop himself from raising his hand to her face. "Aina, if you believe one thing I told you tonight, I want it to be that I never intended to hurt you."

"I know."

"But I did. Deeply. What would I have to do to make it right?"

"It's not a matter of making it right, it's just a matter of forgiveness." She glanced at her engagement ring. "I have a new life now. I've put the past behind me. It's time you did that, too."

"I don't think I can walk away from you again."

Elise felt a flutter of panic. "If you really care about me," she told him, "you will."

The defeated look in his eyes twisted her heart, but she held her ground. If she relented now, he'd win. And in winning, he'd destroy her.

Wil stared at her, studied her face with a close scrutiny that unsettled her. Finally he dropped his gaze. Picking up his jacket, he stood and faced her. "I'm sorry, Elsa," he said. "I never wanted it to be this way."

"Neither did I." She could at least give him that.

Again that defeated look. Elise forced herself to glance away.

"Take care of yourself, Aina."

Her apartment door closed behind him with a finality that left her feeling cold, inside and out. Unable to move from her chair, feeling deserted and alone, she stared at the winged-man hood ornament on her coffee table.

Wil had no right to make her remember these things. To reawaken the yawning ache she'd fought for so many years.

Before she had time to reconsider, she went to her bedroom and dug the cardboard box from the bottom of her cedar chest. In it were the memories. Cautiously, almost fearing her first glimpse of the contents, she removed the lid. Dried flowers, notes, photographs, ticket stubs and an assortment of other treasures met her gaze. One by one, she thumbed through them, remembering. There were pictures of Maks, pictures of her playing with Nikki, pictures of her father, of Wil. Each one brought a bittersweet pain of remembered joy, and never-forgotten sorrow.

How had she ever imagined that she could lock this part of herself away in a cardboard box? For a long time, she stared at a small, yellowed photograph of herself dancing on her father's feet. She'd been about nine when the photo was taken. The adoration on her face as she looked at him brought tears to her eyes.

This, this little girl with the bare feet and the disheveled hair, whose greatest joy had been learning to dance, this was who she was. This was the woman she'd lost.

Suddenly, she couldn't bear to look at the contents any longer. Wil had hurt her too deeply tonight. The pictures and cards were like salt on an open wound. Feeling a driving need to restore order to her world, she hastily crammed the contents back in the box, then thrust it into the chest. Scooping sweaters and jackets on top of it, she slammed the top shut. She turned the key. They belonged down there, safe, where they couldn't touch her. Feeling bitter and wounded, she crawled into bed to cry herself to sleep.

Chapter Eight

The next few days passed in a blur for Elise. As the date of the Collingham auction drew nearer, Roger Philpott grew crazier. Every member of the firm, from the receptionist to the senior partner, knew how important the Collingham account, and Collingham Industries, were to the firm's continued financial success. While the auction itself had seemed a mundane affair, the Collingham heirs had become more and more involved in its execution, elevating its importance to new levels of firm politics. It wouldn't have been so bad if she hadn't also been expected to continue carrying her normal caseload. Worse, Alex Devonshire picked that week to move ahead on a major merger that had Elise wrapped up in more red tape than a Christmas package.

Emotionally, she was a wreck. She hadn't spoken with Wil since that night at her apartment. On the rare occasions when business demanded that she phone the garage,

Jan always answered the phone. For days, she'd been telling herself how grateful she was for that small blessing.

But no matter how she avoided the issue, no matter how hard she tried to bury herself in work, she still had the lonely hours of the night to think about what seeing Wil again had done to her. He had forced her to rediscover a side of herself she'd fought long and hard to subdue. It was the side that lived with the terrible fear that she was a fraud; that at any moment, the world around her would see the gawky kid with the poor English and ill-fitting clothes; that with one slip from her, the world she'd struggled to build would crash around her ears.

It was the side that had once loved Wil Larsen, and had come dangerously close to loving him again.

By the time Roger Philpott finished grilling her late Thursday afternoon, she'd reached her wit's end. As if she didn't have enough to worry about in her personal life, Edgar Collingham and Rich Proliss had Roger in an uproar. It was her job to protect Brandy and her interest in the estate. Now that Rich Proliss was brandishing Wil's accounting ledger like a two-edged sword, Roger demanded that Elise run a second overview of the auction inventory, including the book value and estimated sale prices of all the cars. No matter how many times Elise cautioned Brandy against speaking directly with Edgar, the woman seemed determined to act as her own worst enemy.

Elise knew Brandy didn't really care about that money, that she merely wanted time to grieve, without Edgar's condemning looks and threatening comments. Still, in the long run, her interests needed protection, and Roger was convinced that Brandy must understand the gravity of Rich's threats in order to act on them properly.

The way Elise saw it, she had no choice but to ask Jan for a second report. When he ran the figures for Rich, Elise hadn't been the least concerned with the report's readability. As far as she was concerned, the more difficult it was to understand, the better. But this was different. Brandy needed to understand the kind of money involved, the stakes she was playing with. The only way she could make informed decisions was if she had detailed information. She needed a report that carefully inventoried the value of each item in the estate, and that would make vividly clear why Edgar had hired himself one of the sharpest lawyers in Chicago.

As she studied the half-written memo on her desk, Elise conceded that she could no longer handle the turmoil in her personal life while trying to keep her professional life in order. Her mind was in chaos, her concentration shot. In a few short days, Wil had managed to turn her world bottom to top. In the process, he'd almost convinced her that he shared none of her anxieties about the past, that he'd restored order to his life, and was complete.

Almost.

But a few times, once when he'd first picked her up in his pickup, again in Chester Collingham's garage, and then that night in her apartment, she'd seen an unguarded expression in his fog-colored eyes.

And its name was fear.

After his heart attack, Wil had given up the existence he'd carved for himself in the business world. Not for an instant did she believe that he missed the money or the power of trading on the Merc. It was the excitement he craved. The same thing that drew him to high-powered engines had drawn him to a world where fortunes were won and lost as quickly as the weather changed.

Though he claimed that he and Elise were different, she knew he was wrong. He feared being exposed as a fraud just as much as she did. Her solution had been to mask the fear. His had been to run from it.

When he turned his back on her ten years ago, he'd been running from his own fear of making the same choices. He'd left the Merc because he was too afraid of facing his former colleagues in the wake of his heart attack. And now, because he was afraid, he wanted to force her out of the world she'd built for herself.

When he came back into her life, he'd forced her to admit what she'd denied for ten years. He'd thrust her into a world where chaos ruled her thoughts, fears drove her decisions, anxiety plagued her nights. If she didn't soon set things right, she'd lose all that she'd worked for. It was time for Wil to realize that he couldn't use her to justify his own fears any longer. She had enough of her own without shouldering the burden of his.

With that thought in mind, she leaned back in her desk chair. As much as she'd resented Roger's insistence that she spend yet another fruitless afternoon working out details of the Collingham estate, in retrospect it seemed like a gift from God.

This was the weapon she needed to restore order to her world. With a sense of determination she hadn't felt in days, she tossed the memo into her briefcase, then headed for the door. Jan had told her where to find Wil. It was time to take control.

When Elise entered the Rack Room three hours later, Wil watched her measured approach toward the pool table with the sudden, sure knowledge that she was going to kill him. Maybe not today, maybe not this week, but eventually, Elise Christopher would be the death of him.

The Rack Room, with its wood-paneled walls, leather-padded bar, scarred walnut furniture and two pool tables, had the flavor and feel of an English pub. Rumor had it that, at one time or another, the bar had carried every brand of beer in the world. The current list boasted a selection of thirty-seven different brews, and by unspoken agreement the smoke-filled pub was a men-only kind of establishment. There was little in the way of ambience to attract a female clientele, and that suited the usual patrons just fine.

Wil paused in the process of chalking his cue to rapidly adjust his thinking. Women never entered the Rack Room. But if the way Elise's arrival affected the place was any indication, their presence was long overdue. Her tight jeans, scoop-necked white tank top and green flannel shirt knotted at the waist seemed innocent enough, but the combined effect made his mouth go dry. The jeans hugged curves he'd previously only remembered. The tank top teased him with shadows and ripples that made his palms sweat, and the flannel shirt seemed to ask him to slide his hands inside. The way her dark hair hung in loose waves around her shoulders made his body grow heavy and warm.

Every pair of eyes in the room followed her progress to the table, but if she was aware of the scrutiny, she didn't show it. Wil was forced to emit a warning kind of growl just to ward off the more lurid stares she received. Her gaze remained steadily on him. When she reached the table, she leaned her hip on its wooden shell. "Hello, Wil."

Something in the controlled sound of her voice warned him that her mood was reckless, maybe even a little dangerous. The thought made his blood pump faster. "Fancy meeting you here," he managed. To keep from reaching for her, he returned his concentration to the process of chalking his cue.

"Jan told me where to find you."

"Good old Pop." He reached for the frame so that he could rack the balls. "Is something wrong?"

"No." She pulled a folded piece of paper from her back pocket, then laid it on the edge of the table. "But I have something I need you to do."

One of the balls tumbled from his fingers to plunk on the table. He could think of any number of things he'd like to do with Elise, but had the distinct feeling that wasn't what she had in mind. Carefully he arranged the balls in the rack. "Do?"

"Paperwork. Roger wants Brandy Collingham to have a written analysis of the cars and their possible sale price. She doesn't seem to understand that Edgar is trying to cheat her."

"Isn't this the same report you had to do for Rich Proliss?"

"Similar, but not the same. Rich is putting pressure on Brandy, and she needs something to fight him with. For Rich, I wasn't too worried about making the numbers userfriendly. For Brandy, it's different. I want her to be able to justify every cent, so Edgar can't claim that she received more than her share."

"Those cars are worth every penny you say they are."

She pointed to the paper. "I know. And I know you think Edgar is as slimy as I do. That's why I have to have this by tomorrow afternoon."

"No problem. I'll get Pop to run it tomorrow." He'd finished racking the balls, so he forced himself to meet her gaze as he slid the folded piece of paper into his pocket. "I'm glad you came by."

"You are?" When she reached for a cue from the wall rack, the flannel shirt pulled tight against her full breasts.

Wil swallowed, still not sure how to read her mood. "Of course. I told you how much I like Brandy. I don't want to see Edgar get the better of her."

"Neither do I." Her fingers ran back and forth on the cue in a way that made him sweat.

Wil removed the frame from the racked balls. "You're in an odd mood."

"You think so?" She applied a liberal amount of chalk to the leather tip of her cue.

"Yeah. Is there a specific reason you decided to find me tonight?"

"I told you. I need the report."

"You could have faxed it to me."

"Probably. I just wanted to make sure you understood exactly what I wanted."

He stared at her for long seconds. "What do you want?"

"I think maybe we ought to talk about that." She had moved around to the end of the table, where she set the cue ball on its marker. "There is something I want to discuss with you."

"I see."

With a smirk, she centered her cue between her fingers. When she leaned forward over the table, Wil was afforded a generous glance right down the front of the tank top. A glistening bead of perspiration hovered between her breasts. His blood temperature neared dangerous levels. Belatedly he realized Elise was watching him watch her. He met her gaze, only to find her giving him a knowing look that almost knocked the breath from his lungs. He felt just as he had when she pinned him to the wall in Chester's closet. "You want to share a game?" she asked, lazily sliding her cue across the top of her hand.

"Game?"

"Of pool."

"Sure," he managed to say, seeking balance in a conversation heavily laden with multiple meanings. "You take the first shot."

Elise hit the ball with a long, firm stroke. When the cue ball scattered the arranged balls, the sound seemed jarringly loud in the charged atmosphere. Three balls dropped into the corner pockets. She gave him an enigmatic smile. "I'll take solids," she said.

He watched, riveted, as she caressed the end of her cue with the chalk square. The sight of her pink-nailed fingers rubbing the leather tip sent a bevy of erotic fantasies swirling through him. When she moved around to his side of the table and leaned over it, affording him an all too-tempting glimpse of her rounded fanny, he had to briefly close his eyes.

"Alex Devonshire called me today," she told him. "Six ball, corner pocket," she said.

The rattle of the balls, followed by the thump of the six ball into the pocket, recaptured his attention. "Alex Devonshire?"

"You remember." She paused to study the table. "You met him at that event at the Art Institute."

"Sure."

Elise had leaned a hip on the table and was stretched across it in an awkward position as she prepared for a shot. "Four ball, center pocket." The cue slid smoothly across her fingers. Wil estimated that the time of his death by unfulfilled sexual arousal would be within the hour.

The shot went a little wide. He moved hastily toward the other side of the table, needing whatever small measure of distance between them it could afford. "So what did Alex want?" He didn't bother to tell her he was aiming the nine ball for the corner pocket. Neither of them, he knew, was paying attention to the game.

"A reliable commodities broker," Elise supplied.

Wil sank the shot before meeting her gaze. He saw the unspoken challenge in her blue eyes. "Tell him to call Matthew Switcher," he said carefully. "He's the best I know."

"I told him to call you."

Wil straightened. "Then I'll tell him to call Matthew Switcher." He pointed to the thirteen ball with the end of his cue. "Center pocket," he said.

Elise shook her head. "I told him to call you about the broker spot, not for a referral."

He stroked the cue with unnecessary vigor, and the ball thudded against the lip of the pocket, then rebounded with a sharp bounce.

Silence hung between them in the cloud of cigarette smoke that permeated the bar. Wil met her gaze across the table. "Let's go," he finally said.

"Go?"

"Now."

She blinked. "Go where?"

He laid his cue on the green felt. "You want to talk about this, we'll talk. But not here." Quickly rounding the table, he pried her cue from her hand, and all but threw it back into the rack. He wasted no time dragging her from the smoky interior of the Rack Room onto the sidewalk, where the air was cooler and the lighting darker. He sensed another storm brewing between them, and knew he couldn't concentrate while she seduced him across a pool table.

"Where are we going?" she demanded as he pulled her around the corner of the building and headed for his car.

"Somewhere we can have this conversation without two dozen spectators."

"You don't have to drag me by the hair, you know. I just want to talk. That's all."

He stopped when they reached his car. In the faded glow of the streetlights, he discovered with alarm, she looked no less appealing than she had inside the bar. He rubbed his hands on his thighs, allowing the rough denim to assuage the itchy feeling he got every time he thought about touching her. "You want to talk, talk."

"Don't you want to go somewhere?" she asked. She didn't want to argue with him in the parking lot. "I could buy you a cup of coffee."

"Believe me, the last thing I need is more energy. If I had any more energy than I do at this moment, I might explode." The way her lips trembled all but begged him to kiss her. He recognized the slight movement as a show of vulnerability, and steeled himself not to give into it. "What are you trying to prove here?"

"I'm not sure. All I know is, ever since you walked back into my life, you've had me turned upside down."

"Join the club, Elsa. This street runs both ways."

"Wil, all I want to know is why you keep insisting that what happened between me and my family was some kind of personal betrayal." She waved a hand back and forth between them. "You and I made a lot of mistakes, I'll admit that. But I can't shake the feeling that you're holding what happened to you at the Merc against me. It's like you feel I'm personally responsible."

The breath left his body in a soft hiss. "So, that's what you think?"

"What other explanation is there?"

"A very long one." Dragging his hand through his hair, he waited while several Rack Room patrons made their way across the parking lot. "And you want to hear it, don't you?"

She pointed to the small diner across the street. "Let's go sit down. We can talk there."

He seemed to hesitate, then shrugged. "Sure, whatever you want."

They walked in silence across the narrow parking lot. The night air had grown cold, and Elise concentrated on the plume of her breath against the darkened sky. "It's chilly tonight," she told him, trying to break the tension.

The look he gave her spoke volumes. "Freezing." Without further comment, he pushed open the door to the diner. Blissfully, the place was empty. Only the waitress behind the counter would have to hear their conversation.

Neither of them spoke again until they were seated, each cradling a cup of coffee. Wil took a long sip of his decaf, then set the cup down on the table with a soft *plunk*. "Okay," he said. "Here's what happened. I was the number one broker in my firm two years in a row. I was pulling in over half a million a year in commissions alone, plus another quarter million or so in bonuses. In a couple of years, I was going to be top guy on the floor. Nobody could come close to me."

"That's what I heard."

"People were jockeying for a piece of my action. Every client in the world wanted me to broker for them. If Wil Larsen said it was a good gamble, it was. Period. No mistakes. No foul balls. Every at bat was a home run."

Layer by layer, the veneer of casual civility he wore like a suit of armor was beginning to fall away. He felt it happening, and couldn't seem to stop it. For days, all he'd thought about was the way Elise was tying his guts into knots.

"What happened?" she prodded, sounding darkly fascinated.

"I was handling too much, had too many clients to be paying proper attention. Before I knew it was happening, I started to get in over my head. I worked twenty-hour days.

I slept in my office. I carried a cell phone everywhere I went, so I'd be permanently linked in. A couple of times, I ruined a competitor just for the joy of the kill. I wasn't a man, I was a machine."

"Did you realize this before or after the heart attack?"

The question irritated him. She'd cut too close to the truth for his comfort. "After."

"So what caused you to collapse? What made you lose to the stress?"

"Killing the competition is part of the game. I was on my way to the top, and the guys at the top didn't want me there. Because of my account load, I didn't have time to track the money like I should. If a client told me he had funding, I believed him."

"And you got set up?"

"Yeah. One of my clients was dealing in insider trading. He had a source at the Department of Agriculture prepared to leak him a farm report. He was getting funding from non-U.S. sources."

"Which is highly illegal."

"Highly, and I should have gotten suspicious, but I didn't have time to think. Or maybe I didn't want to, I don't know. Next thing I knew, I was standing on the floor, about to ruin the lives of a farmers' cooperative so this guy and his backers could get rich. If I'd done it, and nobody caught us, I could have made the biggest profit of my career. If I'd done it and gotten caught, not only could I have been implicated in a criminal investigation, but I could have spent the rest of my life trying to live with the guilt of knowing I'd turned into some kind of profit-driven monster. If I didn't do it, I'd show my competition that I'd lost my nerve, and my instincts. That would have been deadly."

"And failure was so incomprehensible to you that you collapsed from the stress?"

Resenting her insight, hating the way she saw straight through him, he clenched his teeth. "It's not really as simple as it sounds."

"It isn't, is it?"

"What are you getting at?"

"I want to know the rest of the story."

He frowned. "There is no rest of the story."

"Sure there is. Why didn't you just tell the authorities what you suspected, then go back to the trading floor?"

"I couldn't handle the stress."

"I don't buy it."

"It damn near killed me, Elsa."

"Hmm. So why did you run from it?"

"I did not run." He hadn't meant to sound so harsh, but he couldn't seem to stop himself. Elise was treading on very dangerous territory. Perhaps this explained the slightly reckless look he'd identified in her eyes when she walked into the bar.

"No? Why don't you tell me about Celine Isaacs."

Reckless, he concluded, and dangerously out of control. "What do you know about Celine?"

"Just what Shelley Castelbrooke told me."

"Shelley?"

"Don't you remember? She came to see me about the inlaid armoire she wants from the Collingham estate. We talked."

"About Celine?"

"About a lot of things."

"But about Celine in particular?"

"Yes."

"I take it she wasn't very complimentary."

"No," she said, refusing to elaborate. She sensed Wil's agitation, knew she was pushing him harder than he normally allowed. If she wasn't careful, she could easily push too hard.

Shelley had been quite enlightening on the subject of Celine Isaacs. Elise had quickly gotten the picture of a typical society huntress. Celine had been interested in Wil as long as he was on his way to the top. Once he fell, she hadn't been able to get away from him quickly enough. He might pretend that he'd come out of the experience unscathed, but Elise didn't believe it. When Celine terminated their engagement, she'd forced Wil to confront the fear that no matter how hard he worked, how much he achieved, in the end he would be alone. "Did you decide to end your relationship with Celine before or after you decided to leave the Merc?"

"After." He cut off her next question with a wave of his hand. "Is this conversation going somewhere, or is its sole purpose to irritate me?"

"You don't like having the tables turned, do you, Wil?"

"What's that supposed to mean?"

"Only that I don't see why you think it's perfectly reasonable for you to grill me, but it doesn't work the other way."

"I don't grill you." She answered that with an arched eyebrow. Wil had the grace to back down. "At least not like this," he said.

Elise leaned back against the padded booth, sensing a subtle victory. "Not like this?"

"No." In obvious frustration, he dragged a hand over his face. "Look, all I've tried to do is understand you."

"And make me question myself, my life."

"That's not true."

"No? I'm supposed to believe that the barbed comments about my job, about Parker, about me, are just part of your learning curve?"

"Elsa—"

It was her turn to interrupt. "I think you've said enough. It's my turn to talk." She drew a deep breath. "You've done nothing but pressure me about my life. You keep telling me that I'm hiding, that I'm afraid of who I really am. Well, maybe that's true, Wil. Maybe I'm not as secure as you, or as certain of what I want, but if I know one thing, it's that I'd never do to you what you're trying to do to me."

To her horror, tears threatened to overwhelm her. This conversation was supposed to help her gain the upper hand in this strange duel of wills between them. If she lost control now, she'd have to admit defeat. Determined, she pressed ahead. "I didn't walk into your life and try to destroy you. You chose what you chose, and I left it alone. I can't make those choices for you, but since you've felt so free to tell me just what you think of me these last few days, I think it's time we turned the tables."

"I never—"

"Shut up," she snapped. The fragile rein she'd held on her patience was gone. In its place was a raw emotionalism she couldn't seem to control. "You've known exactly what you were doing to me. Don't think I don't know why you haven't spoken to me since Sunday. You wanted me to have every opportunity to sit around and agonize over what happened."

"That's not true."

"It is. You forced me to tell you what happened between me and my father, and then, just like you did ten years ago, you walked away from it. As far as you're concerned, *I'm* the spoiled little girl. *I'm* at fault. *I'm* stubborn and unreasonable. *I'm* scared. Well, let me tell you something. I'm not the only one around here who's scared, Wil Larsen. You're the one who can't face your past.

You're the one who turned your back on me ten years ago. You're the one who turned your back on the Merc. And you're the one who's turning your back now.''

"I'm not going anywhere.''

"No? Are you the same man who told me a few nights ago that I can't keep pretending to be someone I'm not?''

"Elsa—''

"Are you?''

"You're not being—''

"Are you?''

"Yes.''

"Why did you tell me that?''

"Because it's true.''

She shook her head. "You told me that because you wanted to give me an impossible choice. Well, you did it. You put me in a position where I have to choose between who I am and who you want me to be, and you know what? I chose me over you. You lost.''

He stared at her for several long, breathless seconds. "That's not what I meant.''

"Think about it, Wil. The one thing in this life you can't bring yourself to do is make an emotional commitment. You couldn't do it for me ten years ago, and you can't do it now.''

"I was the one who wanted to get married.''

"Sure. You were ready to commit to me physically, but not emotionally. When it got right down to it, the only way you wanted me was on your terms. God forbid you had to make a sacrifice. I was supposed to do all the changing. Now, the only way you know how to deal with it is to make me into a woman you can't abide. That's what you wanted, and you got it.''

"Elsa—''

"No." She summoned up what remained of her emotional energy. "Twice I've let you tear up my life. You're not going to do it anymore. Parker will be back in a few days. And when he gets here, I want you gone. This time, it's forever."

"This isn't going to work, Elsa."

"Yes, it is."

"Damn it, will you just—"

"For your information, I happen to like Elise Christopher, and if you don't, you can just go to hell."

He stared at her. She felt the weight of his intense gaze like a lead weight slowly squeezing the breath from her. "I'm going to leave you alone for now," he told her as he dug into his pocket for his keys, "but only because I don't think we're going to accomplish anything by shouting at each other."

Too drained to reply, she just waited.

Wil dragged in a ragged breath. "But I'm not through with this." When she still didn't answer, he levered himself out of the booth. "I'll talk to you later," he said as he tossed a couple of bills on the table. "I'll call you tomorrow."

Chapter Nine

Two hours later, Wil sat astride his 1957 Harley-Davidson XL Sportster, staring out into the dark, chilly night. After he left Elise in the diner, he'd needed the feel of the wind on his face, the freedom of the motorcycle, to sort through the tumult in his soul. Without being consciously aware of it, he'd allowed the road to take him to Half-Acre Field, a quiet stretch of land near the Salt River where he and Elise had often come to get away from the city, to share dreams. He'd given her her first driving lesson in Half-Acre Field. She'd sat in his lap and cried here the night Maks died. He'd brought her here for a picnic on her eighteenth birthday.

And it was here, in the back of his father's restored 1932 Cadillac, that they'd first made love.

The sensations drenched him.

That night had been like something from a dream, where nothing and no one could have told him that he'd live to regret what had happened here. Being here with Elsa had felt so right, so natural, it was still hard to believe that he'd let the treasure slip through his fingers.

From the moment she looked at him in his father's garage, during the silent drive to this spot, to the instant he'd slipped inside her for the first time, Wil would have sworn that nothing could ever destroy what he felt for her. But, he remembered, it hadn't been the first time that sealed her in his heart.

It had been the second. With the force of a broken dam, the memories assailed him, stealing his breath, making his chest hurt.

Under the starlit canopy, Elsa had leaned back against the side of the Cadillac. Wil had seen the wary look in her eyes and winced. "I hurt you," he'd said.

"No." She'd laid a hand on his sleeve. "No. I don't think you could hurt me."

When he finished adjusting his clothes, he shucked off his jacket. "Put this on. I don't want you to get cold." He tried not to notice the way her hair was mussed, or her lips were still slightly swollen and red.

"What about you? You've only got your T-shirt. Won't you get cold?"

The chances of that were a million to one. "I doubt it." His body was already stirring again, incredibly. He hadn't felt this way since he'd been a teenager. To be specific, he thought, keeping his gaze studiously trained on the back of the tan leather driver's seat, since the first time he'd seen Elsa leaning over the side of this car, running her fingers over the fine leather.

He heard the sharp twang of the zipper. "Wil?" She sounded wary, insecure.

"Yes?"

"Are you disappointed?"

He swung his head to look at her. "God, no." Shifting slightly in the seat, he reached for her hand. The same fingers that had moved in feather-light caresses over his skin now trembled in his grasp. "Elsa, I wasn't disappointed."

She didn't look convinced. "You're sure?"

"Hell, of course I'm sure. Couldn't you tell?"

"I don't know. You seem . . . upset."

He drew in a ragged breath. He'd been relatively sure she hadn't had much experience. Now he was positive she hadn't had any. She'd waited for him. And he'd pounced on her like a hormone-driven teenager, without thought or care for her satisfaction. Thank God he'd had enough presence of mind, barely, to use a condom. "I'm not upset, Aina," he told her. "I'm disappointed that I didn't please you."

She stared at him blankly for several long seconds. "You didn't?"

"No."

When she blinked, he saw a subtle understanding enter her expression. As if a curtain of mist had fallen, the look in her eyes altered to one of sensual understanding that seared a path straight to his heart. His entire body responded. Elsa slid across the seat to press against him, and the breath drained from his lungs. In seconds, he was rock-hard.

"How do you know you didn't please me?" she asked him.

Her face was turned to his, and her lips were so tempting, so close. He edged carefully away from her. Elsa followed. Soon, he was pressed back against the side of the car, blanketed by her warmth. "I just know," he said. "I'm twenty-three, not thirteen. After a while, a guy knows these things."

Her eyelids fluttered. "You mean it gets better?"

Wil swallowed. "Better?"

"Um-hmm." She pressed a kiss to the hollow of his throat, where the narrow strip of flesh was exposed above the line of his T-shirt. "You said you didn't please me. That must mean it gets better."

"Well, of course it gets—" With a gasp, he captured her hand where it had insinuated itself beneath the hem of his shirt. "Elsa, what are you doing?"

"Hold still. I want to try something."

If she tried something, she'd probably kill him. He was already on the verge of losing it. "Try what?"

"I want to see if I can make it get better."

"You don't— Ah, jeez—" His head dropped back against the car when her fingers found the waistband of his jeans.

With her other hand, she pushed his T-shirt up under his arms. Her warm mouth found his naked skin, and Wil felt his body contract into a tight knot of wanting. "Hang in there, grease monkey," she teased. "I'm just getting started."

Wil couldn't take any more. In a deft movement, he shifted her back against the seat so that he could cover her with his body. "Don't tease me," he warned her. "I can't take it."

"I'm not."

"You sure you want to do this again?"

An amused smile curved her mouth. "Are you kidding? I've been trying to think of a way to pounce on you for years."

Suddenly serious, Wil captured her face in his hands. "This is forever, Elsa. I mean it. Don't do this unless it's forever."

The humor left her eyes. "Wil?"

He pressed a hard kiss to her mouth. "Tell me it's forever."

Her arms wound around his neck. Her body arched against him. "Forever," she told him. "Forever and always."

With a low groan, Wil captured her mouth in a long, urgent kiss. How long, he wondered, had he wanted her like this? The feel of her beneath him ignited a consuming passion that stole his breath and threatened his sanity. Their first time had managed to take just enough of the edge off his driving need to give him some measure of control.

And he needed every ounce of it.

Elsa's hands were all over him. She skimmed his chest in butterfly caresses, following the slightly frantic touches with her mouth. When her lips found one of his nipples, he had to concentrate just to breathe. Mentally he calculated the torque ratio on his entire set of lug wrenches to prevent himself from exploding on the spot.

"Wil," she whispered against his collarbone. "I want to feel you touching me."

With trembling hands, he unzipped the jacket. Her body was warm and soft, and molded to his hands. He dipped his head so that he could work the buttons of her cotton blouse loose with his tongue.

Elsa moaned—a sexy, throaty noise that made his groin tighten. When her legs coiled around his, wedging his hardened, aching body against her pelvis, a shudder rippled along his limbs. This time, she seemed unwilling to simply let him make love to her. This time, she participated. And she enslaved him in the process.

She tugged at the hem of his T-shirt until he reluctantly raised his hands above his head. When she sent it sailing over the side of the car, he nipped her ear. "Cold yet?" she asked him.

His rumbling chuckle took him by surprise. He should have known that making love with Elsa would be unlike anything he'd ever experienced. He'd never had a partner he laughed with, wanted more. Her tongue found the whorl of his ear, and the laughter was forgotten. When she stabbed into the sensitive hollow with the moist tip, he couldn't wait any longer to taste her. He pulled open her shirt to bury his face in the hollow of her breasts.

Elsa squirmed against him. The feeling sent shock waves pulsing from his groin. "Kiss me," she told him. "There."

Wil took one satin-and-lace covered nipple between his lips. She clutched at his head. "Like that." Her voice was a throaty whisper that drove him wild. He laved at the nipple, suckling hard.

Her hands skimmed down his back to the waistband of his jeans. Soft fingers slipped beneath sweat-dampened denim to knead his buttocks. With a groan, he tore his mouth from her breast. "You're killing me."

The grin she gave him was wicked. "Really? You're pleasing me."

"God, Aina—"

Elise gave his nose a quick kiss. "Do it again," she told him. "Without the bra."

His fingers fumbled with the catch of her bra while she ran her hands over his hips, rubbed his thighs, skated over the line of his ribs, then delved deeper. When she pressed one hand against the hard ridge of his jeans, his body bucked in reaction. "You like this, don't you?" she asked.

Like he liked breathing. "Yes." His voice sounded guttural, harsh. Washed in a sea of moonlight, her face was flushed and beautiful.

"Will you like it if I touch you?" She ran one finger along the line of his zipper. His heart stopped beating. "Inside?"

At the question, his heart took off again, at a roaring gallop. "Yes," he told her. "Yes, I'll like it."

She didn't seem to need any further encouragement. She eased the zipper down in a slowly torturous movement that spiked his temperature up several notches. When his legs shifted to give her better access, he found his feet wedged between the driver's seat and the car door. "Damn," he muttered. Each time he tried to free his feet, his aching shaft pressed into the soft warmth of her hand. The sensation was simultaneously heaven and hell.

"You're so hot," she said. "Is it always this hot?"

"With you it is."

"Hmm..." Elsa rubbed her lips across his chest. "I like it."

"It likes you, too."

She laughed, then pressed a kiss to his neck. Her fingers were running up and down the length of him, massaging him through the thin cotton of his briefs. "Can I touch you inside?" she asked.

He shivered. "You can do anything you want," he told her. "I'm yours. All of me."

With a sigh of pleasure, she pushed her fingers beneath the flap of his undershorts. All the blood in his body seemed to surge to the place where her hand pressed against him.

"Aina..." he groaned. He cupped both her breasts in his palms, rubbing the hardened tips with the pads of his thumb. "You're tearing me apart."

"Tell me how it feels," she said.

"I'll show you instead." With one hand, he found the button of her jeans. Elsa's fingers tightened on him in a guileless response. He captured her mouth in a possessive kiss while he pulled at her zipper. When he slid his hand down the smooth skin of her belly, threaded it through the fine hairs, then found the moistened folds of her core, she shrieked in his ear.

"Oh, Wil," she breathed, clutching at him. "It really does get better."

He smiled against the curve of her throat. "Lots better."

With tender passion, he caressed the place where he'd recently stolen her innocence. The crisp night breeze brushed through his hair, bringing with it the scents and sounds of Half-Acre Field. But nothing compared to the heady scent of their passion, the feel of her desire in his hands, the sound of her sexy moans and throaty demands.

His thumb found all the places that sent her blood singing and her heart pounding, and while her hands skimmed over his body, pushed at his clothes, rubbed his skin, he deliberately took her to new peaks.

He knew the instant her body toppled over the edge. One minute, her fingers were plucking at his nipples. The next, she was arching into him, calling his name, with her head back and her eyes closed. He raised his head to watch, enthralled by the sight of his Elsa finding magic in his arms.

"Wil," she whispered. Fine tremors still skittered along her flesh. He felt them beneath his fingers. "Oh, Wil."

"I told you it gets better."

"I want to feel you inside of me." Her hands moved to caress him again, to support the heavy weight of his arousal. "I want to be closer."

Wil hesitated. He still had another condom. Protection wasn't a problem, but he didn't want her to feel obligated. "We don't have to, Elsa. I did this for you."

Her head moved back and forth in mute denial. "I want to. Please, Wil. I need you."

Tenderly he removed the rest of her clothes. His body ached with the need for release. Twice he had to set her hands aside lest he spill himself. "Easy, Aina. I can't take much more."

When she took the condom from him to roll it onto his length, the pain in his groin tightened with razor-sharp intensity.

"Now, Wil," she whispered. "I want you now."

His gaze found and held hers in the near darkness of the moonlit night. "Forever, Elsa," he said.

She nodded. "Forever."

He slipped inside of her, found his release, and lost his soul for eternity.

Wil dragged his thoughts back from the memory. With an aching sense of loss, he realized that the pain in his body couldn't compare to the pain in his heart. That night, he'd meant what he said. It was supposed to have been forever.

But Elise had been right. He'd given her a physical commitment, but he hadn't been willing to offer her the emotional commitment to go with it. He'd loved her. He knew he had. But he'd always held a part of himself in reserve. When she needed him most, when she had nowhere else to turn, he'd still refused to give her that piece. She'd said he was afraid. He balked at the idea. What he'd done, he'd done to protect her. If he'd let her get too close to him, she'd have demanded that he give her everything, even the truth about Maks.

So he'd refused to let her have that final part of his heart. And now, because of it, he'd probably lost her forever.

At seven o'clock Friday evening, Elise glanced sharply at the door of her apartment. With a sickening sense of dread, she knew exactly who that firm knock belonged to.

She contemplated ignoring it, but the second knock confirmed her worst suspicions. He wasn't going away. Padding to the door in her bare feet, she checked the view glass—newly installed, compliments of Nikki. Wil's stony expression sent a flutter of panic to the soles of her feet. Once again, he'd turned up on her doorstep, uninvited and unwanted. The set of his jaw told her she had as much chance of making him leave as she had of persuading Edgar Collingham to respect his stepmother.

"Let me in, Elsa," he said, his voice implacable.

"Go away."

"No. I'm going to stand here all night if I have to."

She didn't doubt that for a second. Bracing herself for battle, she pulled open the door. "Thanks so much for calling," she sarcastically told him. "I'm really glad you bothered to find out if this was a convenient time."

"You would have hung up on me if I'd called."

"So you just barged into my apartment instead."

At her stormy expression, he frowned. "What's wrong with you tonight?"

She gaped at him. "What's wrong?"

His gaze swept across the living room of her apartment, resting briefly on the stack of paperwork she'd piled on the coffee table, before returning to study her face. "What's wrong?"

"What do you mean, what's wrong? Even you're not that stupid."

"You don't think so?"

"No."

When she made no move to let him in, he shouldered his way into the apartment. "Sometimes I wonder," he said cryptically. He laid a thick computer printout on her couch. "This is the report you wanted."

"I suppose I should thank you."

Shedding his jacket, he faced her. "No need. You look frazzled."

"Gee, thanks." To her acute irritation, Elise was again struck by how "right" it seemed to have him in her apartment. Parker had always looked strangely out of place amid her eclectic belongings, comfortable furniture and homey atmosphere. In jeans and a denim shirt, Wil could almost be the "do" example in a magazine article about how to appropriately dress for an occasion. He looked perfect. And tempting. Too tempting.

"Look at you," he said. "Your hair looks like a chrysanthemum run amok. Your eyes are red. You look like you haven't had a decent meal in two days."

"You really know how to flatter a girl, don't you?"

"Just stating the obvious. You going to stand by the door all night, or are you going to come back in?"

"I was going out," she lied, more because she needed to stall for time than because she expected him to believe it.

His gaze traveled over her loose-fitting pajamas. "Just where were you planning to go in your pajamas at seven o'clock at night?" The question was deliberately evocative.

"None of your business." She was starting to feel ridiculous. Wil knew she was lying, and she felt like a fool for letting him manipulate her.

He held up his hand. "I'm not trying to pick a fight. I just want to know what's wrong."

"What's wrong is that you've obviously completely disregarded everything I said to you last night."

"I haven't," he said. "I came here to talk to you."

For long seconds, she studied the look in his eyes. Pain, and something else, lurked beneath the surface. Her resolve began to melt, but she wasn't quite ready to concede. "I'm on my way to the movies," she said. "If I don't leave now, I'll miss the trailers. That's my favorite part." Still wary, she waited for his reaction.

With a slight smile, he touched the collar of her pajamas. "I don't think so."

At the vulnerable look he gave her, Elise knew she was lost. When he pushed her, she found it easy to resist him, but never, not once in her entire life, had she been able to resist that pleading look.

"Aina," he whispered, and the word carried with it a world of hurt.

Much as she wanted to, she couldn't turn away from him. Unless she missed her guess, she'd wounded, and perhaps even frightened, him yesterday. If he needed solace half as much as she did, she couldn't make herself refuse him. Because she wasn't ready to confront him, she deliberately made light of the situation. "I'll have you know," she said, trying very hard to concentrate while his finger traced a path along the neckline of her pajama top, "that I used to wear my pajamas to the movies all the time."

He seemed to sense the softening of her mood. Some of the tension left him. "Is that a fact?"

She nodded. "When I was a kid, Pop would take us to the drive-in for special occasions. Mama would dress us in our pajamas to make it easier if we fell asleep in the movie. Pop would come home and just carry us to bed." Her voice trailed off on the last word as she immediately recognized her mistake.

A flash of heat registered in his gaze. She'd come to recognize that look. It was the same one that had flared in his eyes Wednesday night, just before his parting shot. Slowly his eyes traveled the length of her body. "Elsa," he said, his voice just above a whisper, "when I carry you to bed, it isn't going to have anything to do with sleeping."

Elise shivered. Wil's fingers tightened on her elbow. "You look as tight as a rubber band, and I don't think it has much to do with the fact that you and I have been stringing each other out lately. I know that look. I used to see it in my mirror every morning."

What remained of her resolve evaporated at the soft confession. It still disturbed her to think of Wil, a man she'd always imagined as invincible, lying in a hospital bed, fighting for his life. "It's been a rough week," she told him. "Nothing I can't handle. I'm just a little bogged down in details."

Not relinquishing his grip on her elbow, he guided her toward the sofa. "And the fact that I've been acting like an insufferable bastard hasn't helped."

"That, too," she admitted.

With a firm hand on her shoulder, he settled her on the couch. "Talk."

Elise hesitated. They'd rarely discussed anything about her work beyond Wil's involvement with the auction. Somehow, she wasn't prepared to tell him the more intimate details of her frustrations with her job. From the beginning, she'd sensed what she believed was his disapproval of her career and her dedication to it. Whether deliberately or not, she'd avoided the subject rather than face his scrutiny. Yet yesterday she'd accused him of being afraid of commitment, of intimacy.

If she refused him now, she realized, she'd be just as guilty as he. Whatever was between them, no matter how forbidden it seemed to her, they'd started down this road together. She owed it to him to see it through—even, she thought with a sinking sense of dread, if it destroyed her.

Reluctantly she picked up the four-inch file on Alex Devonshire's merger with SYNTEC. "The closer we get to the auction, the more Roger drives me crazy. Edgar is watching every penny we spend preparing the items. Proliss wants detailed reports on all the collections, the arrangements for sale, the invited buyers, everything.

Collingham Industries is one of our firm's largest clients, and Roger knows there's a lot riding on this. We don't want to alienate Edgar, but our first obligation is to carry out Chester's will. He wanted Brandy taken care of, and that's what we aim to do."

"I thought he dumped the auction on you because he expected it to be some relatively mundane event."

"He did, but—typical Roger—he didn't bother to think it through to its logical conclusion. Chester Collingham was a major client until his death. We were on retainer for both him and his firm. When he died, he left his estate to his wife and five children, *including* his controlling interest in Collingham Industries. As in most major estate cases, the heirs are all jockeying to see who comes out in the strongest position."

"Vultures, aren't they?"

"Unfortunately, that's fairly normal." She dropped back against the couch with a sigh of resignation. "It doesn't help any that the IRS is going to get almost thirty-seven percent of Chester's estate, despite everything I did to protect his children from the inheritance tax." With a sigh, she wiped a hand through her tangled hair. "Isn't that the most obscene thing you've ever heard? Fortunately, Brandy doesn't have to pay taxes on her share. Spouses are exempt."

"How generous."

Elise snorted. "But everybody else gets hit with this enormous estate tax for everything over the six-hundred-thousand-dollar limit. If you ask me, that's criminal. I mean, why should a guy like Chester work hard all his life, then have to fork over a huge chunk of his money to the government just because he dies? Do you know, if I hadn't shuffled some things around into tax shelters, Edgar's tax burden would be over fifty percent? Fifty percent! So after I spent all that time trying to protect his money, he's still determined to make my life hell." She knew she was rambling, but the mundane conversation seemed to calm her nerves.

Wil gave her an amused look. "Sounds sticky."

"Like glue."

"So now that Roger Philpott has finally figured this out," Wil said, "he's driving you crazy with the details of the auction. Am I right?"

"Yes."

"So what's that?" he asked, pointing to the thick file in her hand.

She rolled her eyes. "Alex Devonshire picked this week to launch a major merger with SYNTEC. If the deal doesn't go through by Wednesday, it probably won't go through at all."

Wil let out a low whistle. Because of his days at the Merc, Elise knew he understood the complications the merger presented, and why it had thrown her schedule into chaos. "And on top of that, I've been running you through the emotional wringer for the last two weeks."

"Something like that."

Wiping a hand over his face, he pulled in a ragged breath. "I think we should make a deal here."

"Another one?"

At her quip, he offered her a brief smile. "I think we both need a break from the pressure we're putting on ourselves. You need to get some work done, and I don't need to be standing in your way. I sure as hell don't need to be making your life miserable."

Wary, she studied his expression. "Are you sure you're not just avoiding the conversation?"

"I wouldn't go to the bank on it. I'd be lying if I didn't confess that I'd rather not get into all that with you right now, but the way I see it, you've got other things to worry about for the moment.''

"So what's this deal you had in mind?"

"Kind of like Cinderella."

Dubious, she narrowed her gaze. "Cinderella?"

"Yeah. We'll work until midnight, then we'll talk."

"I don't know, Wil—"

With a sweep of his hand, he indicated the stack of files. "It doesn't make you less of a person to ask for help, you know?"

"Did you learn that in post-heart attack therapy?" she asked before she could stop herself.

"As a matter of fact, I did."

The blatant honesty of the comment surprised her. "I didn't mean—"

"It's all right. I can still take a joke."

"I wasn't trying to make light of it."

"I know. I spent a year trying to come to grips with what had happened to me. When you're thirty-five years old and wake up to find yourself in intensive care, it tends to radically adjust how you view yourself. For months afterward, I was useless. I didn't want to leave the house, because I was afraid I'd keel over dead."

Without thinking, she pressed her palm to his heart. Beneath his faded denim shirt, she felt the steady beat. "Is it all right now?"

"It is if I treat it right." He covered her fingers with his. "I learned an important lesson that day. It made me realize that everything we have in this life can be snatched away in less than a couple of heartbeats. The only thing that really matters is the people we care about."

Cautiously she met his gaze. "Wil—"

He shook his head to interrupt her. "Not now," he said, raising her hand to his lips to press a kiss on the palm.

"Soon we'll get into it, but not now. You need to work, and I need some time. It's going to take me a couple of hours to psych myself up for this. Okay?"

Hesitating, she tried to read the indecipherable look in his eyes. She couldn't tell whether he was being deliberately facetious. Somehow she doubted it. Finally, she nodded. "All right."

Wil dropped her hand. "Now, you got a file on this auction?"

"A file?"

"Sure. You're the most organized woman I know." He began shuffling papers on the coffee table. "I can't believe you don't have a file."

She pulled a manila folder from the bottom of the pile. "It's here."

"Great." He accepted it, then began thumbing through the contents. "Is there a list of things to do?"

"First through third pages," she mumbled.

Wil removed the sheets, glanced at them, then looked at her computer. It sat on a small desk in the corner of her living room. "Do I need a password to get into that thing?"

"No." She frowned. "What are you doing?"

"Helping you." He strolled to the computer and flipped it on. "You work on the merger, I'll work on the auction."

"But—"

"I can handle this," he assured her. "Most of what you've got on this list is memos and letters to family and buyers. I'll rough everything in for you, then leave the blanks for you to fill. You can look over Devonshire's contracts while I find—" he checked the list "—a caterer and a security company."

"I don't expect you to do this," she told him.

"Piece of cake. I once helped a guy corner the market on goat by-products in less than three hours."

"Lovely."

With a slight wink, he said, "I think I can handle Chester Collingham's yard sale."

Chapter Ten

At eleven-thirty, Wil glanced up from the computer to see Elise lean back against the sofa with a quiet moan of exhaustion. As it had when he walked through her door, relief coursed through him in a heated rush. Elise still wanted him. He'd known it from the way she met his gaze with that wary hunger he found so addictive.

Had he not insisted on delaying the inevitable conversation, he probably would have fallen at her feet and begged her forgiveness. Which, in retrospect, might not be such a bad idea.

She looked more than a little run down, and he blamed himself, entirely, for what he'd done to her. He'd been so absorbed in proving to himself that he could live without her that he'd put her through hell. The stress she felt now was his fault, due to his selfishness and, as she'd so aptly pointed out to him the day before, his fear.

The four-and-a-half-hour reprieve she'd given him had only served to heighten his guilt. They'd worked in companionable silence. Despite the challenge of offices closed during nonbusiness hours, he'd managed to reach a reputable caterer, arrange for event security, inventory and list most of the Collingham collection and write Roger Philpott two twenty-page memos detailing Elise's plans for the event. He'd been particularly eloquent on the topic of Larsen Restorations, and the outstanding bargain they were giving the firm. Somewhere in all the confusion, he'd even managed to order Chinese takeout for their dinner.

The only thing he hadn't managed to do was keep his gaze from straying in her direction. From the second he walked through her door, a strange sort of fever had begun building inside him. His body throbbed with awareness. Like the rise of high tide, the inner pressure had built until it took every ounce of reserve he had to keep from touching her.

Elise seemed to sense his scrutiny. Her eyes drifted open. "Sorry," she mumbled. "I think I fell asleep."

Determined, he punched a few buttons to save the inventory list he'd been working on, then moved toward her with a measured sense of purpose. "Turn around," he prompted.

Something, maybe panic, flared in her eyes. "What?"

"Turn around." When she still didn't seem to understand, he said, "I want to rub your shoulders."

Elise's gaze searched his before she hesitantly turned her back to him. When his hands settled at the base of her neck, he felt the shudder that ran through her. In response, his heart beat an erratic rhythm. Slowly he began to knead the tight muscles in her shoulders. "You're tense," he told her, working her skin through her flannel pajama top.

Elise moaned in luxurious response. "God, that's wonderful."

He found a stubborn knot and worked it with his thumb. "You shouldn't work so hard."

"Ummm..."

Wil slid his hands along the line of her collarbone, over her shoulders. When his fingers settled in the warm vee of flesh at her throat where the flannel gaped open, he felt her go momentarily stiff. The feather-light caress of his callused fingertips left a trail of goose bumps in its wake. Wil flicked open the top button of her pajamas.

Her hand pressed to his, stilling his relentless pursuit of the next button. "What are you doing?"

He brushed her hair aside with his free hand, then pressed a kiss to her nape. "Relax. I can do a better job of this if I'm not hindered by your shirt."

"Why do I think this has nothing to do with my tension and everything to do with seduction?"

He didn't answer. Instead, he wriggled his fingers free of hers so that he could flick open the second button.

"Wil, stop."

"I'm not going to take it off," he assured her. "I'm just going to lower it so I can rub your shoulders." He was glad she couldn't see his face. Surely she'd notice the glistening beads of perspiration on his forehead, the way his lips had tightened into a thin line, the fever he knew burned in his gaze. He drew a calming breath as he lowered the blue-and-red flannel to expose her shoulders.

The top slid to rest on the full upper curves of her breasts, where it provided the unexpected benefit of pinning her arms to her sides. The blood rang in his ears as his vision momentarily blurred. On the edges of his sanity, he felt a mad rush of need begin to tear at his restraint.

She seemed to notice his hesitation. "Wil?"

His breath came in fits and starts as he studied the smooth lines of her shoulders. With a trembling hand, he brushed her hair over one shoulder, completely baring the other to his view. Without stopping to consider the consequences, he pressed his lips to the spot where her neck became her collarbone. She shuddered, and might have moved away from him, had he not captured her breasts in his palms. Elise gasped when he pressed her against his chest. "God, Aina. I need you."

Without waiting for her response, he thrust his hands beneath her flannel top. The warm curves of her breasts filled his palms, tormented him with visions of her, flushed and ready, spread beneath him. Like a man possessed, he rubbed his mouth over her skin, tasting, licking the tender flesh.

He palmed her breasts, rotating the nipples until they beaded and pulsed against his hands. When he took each rosy peak between a thumb and forefinger, Elise moaned—a feline, throaty sound that stripped away his remaining layers of civility. With a guttural growl, he flipped her beneath him, pressing her into the cushions, covering her with the length of his aroused body.

Elise's eyes widened at the heated look in his eyes. The languor had left his body, only to be replaced with a crackling tension that made the hairs on her arms stand at attention. In the shadowy light of her living room, his blond hair gleamed a burnished copper. He looked, she thought on a rare flight of fancy, every inch a Viking prepared to conquer whatever stood in his path.

The tenderness was gone. The gentle lover she remembered had been replaced by this driven, urgent man whose eyes gleamed with seductive promise and need.

Her mouth went dry at the sight.

He murmured something in Swedish, something hot and suggestive, seconds before he captured her mouth in a kiss that threatened to pull the soul from her body.

There was nothing civil about the kiss. It bore no resemblance to the seductive caresses they'd shared before. This one rocked her to her toes. Its raw power excited. Its bare need awakened an answering hunger. With her hands still pinned to her sides, while his large hands kneaded her breasts, she felt unbearably wanted.

Needing his closeness, she wrapped her legs around his to wedge the hard heat of him firmly against her pulsing center. Wil tore his mouth from her with a low groan. Again, the softly spoken Swedish, the feral look in his eyes as his mouth lowered to take the aching peak of her breast between his lips. The scratch of his late-day whiskers sent erotic pulses singing through her blood. They'd leave marks on her, she was sure of it, and she welcomed the tender savagery.

He sipped and tugged at her areola with his hot mouth. When his teeth grazed the taut peak, a cry ripped from her lungs.

The sound seemed to galvanize him as his hands tugged at the remaining buttons of her shirt. Baring her to the waist, he trailed a wet path to her navel. "Aina." He whispered against her sensitized flesh, "I want to touch you. Let me touch you."

Elise wriggled her hands free from the confining sleeves of her pajama top. Swiftly she moved her fingers to the buttons of his denim shirt. She found that her urgency matched his, the pressing need, the gnawing hunger. "I want to touch you, too," she told him. Caught in the web of his desire, she ruthlessly pushed aside the warnings that screamed through her mind.

One after another she flicked open the buttons, only to find her progress frustrated by his white cotton T-shirt. She was so intent on tugging the T-shirt from his jeans, she almost failed to notice when his hands plunged beneath the elastic waist of her pants to cup her bottom. Hard, he pulled her against his mouth.

His teeth skimmed the line of her waistband, once, twice. Her back arched to give the marauding, insistent pressure of his tongue better access. He nipped her navel, then lifted her bottom in his hard hands so that he could place a kiss, shockingly intimate, scaldingly possessive, on the most intimate part of her. Even through the satin of her panties, and the flannel of her pajama bottoms, his mouth seared her. The rough texture of his whiskers seemed to brand her inner thighs. Moist heat to moist heat, the sensation sent the spiraling energy out of control.

The drenching rush of sensation was on her like a sudden storm, breaking and ravaging whatever lay in its path. Her head dropped back against the sofa as a low cry tore from her throat.

Between her legs, Wil held as still as a mountain pool on a breezeless day. Watching. The feel of his gaze, now charcoal-black, skimming her features, taking in the damp sheen on her flushed skin, the breathless parting of her lips, the goose bumps that peppered her flesh, the quivers and shudders that traveled through her, seemed to carry the sensations to unbearable heights.

Elise sank into the sofa cushions with an exhausted gasp when the final wave had passed.

Wil continued to watch. Seconds passed, and her languor changed to unease. "Wil?"

Slowly he reached for her left hand. His fingers twined with hers as he pressed her palm to her belly. "What about this, Elsa?"

Her gaze found her diamond engagement ring. Guilt, anger, frustration, raced through her with mind-numbing speed. Suddenly she felt open and exposed. With her pajama top spread wide, her body still feeling weakened, she felt raw. Pushing him away with an angry burst of energy, she clutched the lapels of her shirt together. "How dare you!"

Wil took his time levering himself off the couch. "How dare I what? Stop before we made love? Refuse to sleep with another man's fiancée?"

"You did this on purpose."

"Come on, Elsa. You think I like walking around in an unfulfilled state of arousal? I'd tell you that you're the one making this hard—" he paused, as if to let the double meaning sink in "—but that would be the understatement of the century."

To her horror, Elise found herself fighting tears. "So you set out to humiliate me? Is that what you wanted?"

"No. You were the one hurling around accusations the other night. I just don't think we should complicate matters any further by falling into bed." He took two steps forward.

Elise backed away from him. "Everything I said to you was true. You're afraid."

"Cut the crap, Elsa. This isn't about me."

"No? Then you explain why you felt like you had to get even with me tonight."

"Damn it—I was not getting even." He advanced two more steps.

"Not getting even?" She couldn't contain her outrage. "Who are you kidding? You were furious with me last night, because I cut too close to the truth." When he would have spoken, she shook her head. "Don't even try to deny it. You were. Nikki told me."

"The bastard."

"That's what brothers are for."

"I thought you said he didn't want to get involved in this."

"Maybe he changed his mind. *You* were the one that called *him*. How the hell should I know why he decided to stick his nose in this?"

She saw the flash of annoyance in his eyes. "For the record, I called Nick because I knew you were upset."

"Oh, spare me." She quickly buttoned her pajama top. "That male-pride crap isn't going to work with me. You were angry because I figured you out. Every time you tell me I'm running away from my problems, it's because the same finger is pointing right at you."

"At least I'm not the one sleeping around on my fiancé."

The remark was deliberately cruel, and he knew it. Elise fixed him with a hard glare. Once again, he'd retreated behind a verbal attack. "Get out."

"If I walk out this time, Elsa, I'm not coming back."

"Well, I just can't tell you how much that thought terrifies me."

"You're acting like a shrew."

"And you're an arrogant SOB. How dare you do this to me! What gives you the right?"

His gaze flicked over her. The look on his face would have been impenetrable, had it not been for the anger in that gaze. "Contrary to what you seem to think, I didn't come here tonight to argue with you."

"Then why are you here, Wil?" She pointed to the couch. "Why did you do that?"

Long seconds passed. The only sounds in the quiet apartment were the hum of the radiator and the relentless ticking of the hall clock. Wil stared at her, his face a hard mask. At his sides, his hands clenched and unclenched, as if the monotonous motion gave him an odd sort of focus. "Don't let it end like this, Elsa."

She resisted the urge to turn her back on him. "We've both been fooling ourselves," she told him. "It ended a long time ago."

The words hung between them like a death knell. Elise felt their cold impact to the darkest place in her soul. Shivers that started on the inside, chilled her blood, then reached her skin, began to tear at her heart like ice-coated talons.

A flicker of pain flared in his eyes. His mouth pressed into a taut line. The planes of his face seemed to sharpen as he studied her in the dim light. Lips parted, she sensed his denial before he uttered it.

"I want you to leave, Wil," she told him before he could speak. "Right now. And I don't want you to come back."

With a defeated look that threatened to tear her heart out, he reached for his jacket.

The shrill ring of the telephone sliced through the thick air like a fencer's blade.

Elise started, then glanced toward the insistent noise.

"Are you going to answer it?" Wil asked.

"It's probably Parker."

He jerked on his jacket. "Then, by all means, don't let me stop you."

Because it was easier than watching him walk out her door, she reached for the phone.

"Hello?"

"Elise?" She didn't recognize the voice.

Something in the grim sound sent fear sluicing across her already sensitized nerve endings. Wil must have seen it reflected on her face. He paused, his hand on the doorknob.

Elise clutched the receiver in suddenly numb fingers. "Yes?"

"Elise, this is Bill Garrison. I'm afraid I have some bad news."

Bill Garrison, she knew, was Nikki's partner. The fear in her gut turned to terror. "Bill, what's wrong. Is Nikki all right?"

"He's been shot."

"Oh, my God." She dropped onto the couch. Wil hurried across the room to squat in front of her. His hands rested on her knees. The anger had left his expression, and concerned eyes met and captured her gaze.

"He's in surgery now," Bill was saying. "He took a bullet in the thigh and two to the chest."

"Oh, my God." Her fingers gripped the receiver so tightly, the blood drained from them.

"I don't have any news yet, but he's tough, Elise. He's going to make it."

The determination in Bill's voice reached her, comforted her. "Where is he?" she asked.

"Northwestern Memorial."

"I can be there in an hour."

"I don't think you should drive," he said. "Do you want me to send someone to pick you up?"

She'd started to shake. "No. It'll take too long. I have to get there."

"Elise," he said, his voice stern, "don't drive. You're too upset."

He sounded so much like Nikki in that moment that she felt her insides start to crumble. "I won't."

"Promise me."

She looked at Wil. "I—I have a ride. Don't worry."

"He's going to be in surgery for a while. There's no need to rush."

"I understand."

"You're sure you're going to be all right?"

"Yes." Lord, no, she wasn't going to be all right. She was going to fall to pieces any minute. "I'll be there soon, Bill."

"All right. He's going to make it," Bill told her again. "Just keep remembering that."

"I will."

Elise all but threw the receiver into its cradle.

Wil covered her hand with his. "Honey, what's wrong?"

The tension of the previous hour gave way to the wave of horror that swept through her. Despite her anger, despite the way he'd hurt her, she needed Wil's familiar presence. She couldn't bear to face this alone.

Like a beacon, the picture of her and Maks, the one in the cardboard box buried beneath the pile of sweaters and jackets in her cedar chest, flashed into her mind. With stricken eyes, she met Wil's gaze. Dear God, she'd lost one brother—she couldn't lose the other. "It's Nikki," she whispered. "He's been shot."

Panic, wicked and alive, shot through him. He knew, *knew*, she was going out of her mind. She'd been there when Maks died. She couldn't live through it again.

He crushed her to him in a desperate embrace while self-recriminations washed through him. He'd been so close, so damned close, to walking away from her again. Twice he'd let pride destroy him. If he'd left, he knew, she would never have called him, shared this with him. She needed someone, urgently. And he'd come within seconds of not being here for her. "Shh, baby, hush." She began to sob against him. "Everything's going to be all right. I'm here."

"He can't die," she sobbed. "He can't."

"I know." He fought a wave of panic as he cradled her to him. The scent of their recent passion still clung to her skin. Recriminations flooded him as he realized what he'd nearly done to her. "I know."

"I have to get there."

"We're going." He combed his fingers through her still-mussed hair. "I want you to go in your room and put on some clothes and shoes. Okay?" She didn't loosen her grip. "Elsa?" Her shoulders continued to shake, so Wil picked her up and carried her to the bedroom.

He sat on the bed while she hurried into the bathroom to change. With his face buried in his hands, he sent up a quick prayer that Nikki would live. He wasn't sure Elise could survive if she lost him. Surely this family had suffered more than their share.

When she came out of the bathroom, he gave her what he hoped was a reassuring look. She'd pulled her hair into a loose ponytail that seemed to emphasize the redness of her tear-laden eyes. "Let's go," she told him.

"Do you want anything. Coffee, some tea?"

"No, I just want to get there."

Her cold fingers closed on his offered hand in a bruising grip.

They were headed into the city before Wil coaxed her into speaking again. In a halting voice, she told him what Nikolai's partner had told her. "That's all I know," she said. He heard the fresh surge of tears in her voice. With a stricken look that threatened to shatter his heart into a million pieces, she turned to him. "He has to be all right, Wil. He has to."

The car's heater was turned so high that Wil felt the sweat running down his body, but he could hear Elise's teeth chattering. He tightened his grip on her hand. "It's going to be okay. Whatever happens, you're going to make it."

"What if he dies?"

"Don't think about it," he warned her. "If you start thinking about it, you're going to drive yourself crazy."

Her fingers trembled in his. In the glow of the oncoming headlights, he saw her pale face, streaked with tears. Her lips trembled. "Aina." He rubbed one knuckle against her cheek. "Listen to me. Nick's tough. He's going to be okay."

"You can't promise me that."

No, he couldn't, but he wanted to, wanted to do anything that would ease the look of stark terror that seemed to have permanently settled on her face. "He's in God's hands," Wil told her. "Just hold on to that."

By the time they reached the hospital, Elise seemed to have fallen into a state of emotional exhaustion. He almost preferred her near hysterics to the unbearable silence, the look of tortured hurt in her eyes. They hadn't spoken for the second half of the trip, and, except for the death grip she'd maintained on his hand, she appeared almost lifeless. He found a parking space outside the emergency room, then leaned across the car to press a gentle kiss to her trembling mouth. "Let's go inside," he told her. "We'll see how he is."

Wordlessly she nodded.

Wil guided her through the emergency room traffic until he found the information desk. He got the name of Nikolai's surgeon and the floor number from the duty nurse. Elise made it to the elevator with him before she fell against his chest.

"Wil." His name was a breathless whisper.

Gently he stroked her hair, supported her with his arms at her waist. "Shh . . . It's going to be all right, Aina. Everything's going to be all right."

God, he wished he had something else to say, anything to comfort her with. He'd stood with her once and watched a brother die. He wasn't sure he could go through this again. He knew she couldn't go through it. Her hands clutched at his shoulders. Her face pressed into his chest. She seemed to be trying to climb inside of him, be absorbed by him. He was powerless. And he hated it.

They stepped off the elevator into the relative calm of the fourth floor. Compared to the emergency room, the place seemed deserted, lifeless. The antiseptic smell burned his nostrils. Like a mortuary, he thought, in grim realization that the drawn faces and huddled figures in the hallway were all there for the same reason. Each kept a watch between life and death.

A burly man in rumpled clothes met them in the hallway. His graying hair was disheveled, his face slightly pale, but he had a comforting look in his hazel eyes. "Elise," he said. "How are you doing?"

Elise stepped from the circle of Wil's arms to hug Bill Garrison. "Hi, Bill."

"How are you doing?" he asked again.

Elise shook her head. "I'm all right," she lied. "How's Nikki?"

"No news." Bill stuck out his hand to Wil. "I'm Bill Garrison. Nick's partner."

"Wil Larsen." Bill's handshake was firm, and oddly reassuring. Wil reached for Elise again, not yet ready to relinquish contact with her. He needed her warmth just as he knew that she needed his. Pulling her against his side with a slight tug, he asked Bill, "Can you tell us anything more than what you told Elise on the phone?"

Bill shook his head. "Not really. We were moving in on a warehouse. We've been working this case on interstate contraband for about six months now. Nick got a tip that a shipment was coming in tonight."

"A trap?" Wil asked.

"Yeah. They were waiting for us. The minute we started approaching the building, they started shooting. Nick and I were on the back side." Bill paused to clear his throat. "He was furious that we'd been set up. When he saw Steven Mitchell go down, he started screaming orders to pull back. All our guys had already taken refuge behind the cars, but Steven was lying out there, exposed. Nick went after him."

Elise pressed her hands to her mouth. "Oh, God."

"We covered him as best we could, but they put three bullets in him. He took one in the thigh and two in the chest." Bill shuddered, as if the memory were too much for him. "He managed to drag Steven to safety before he collapsed."

"How is he?" Wil asked.

"Steve? He's going to be all right. He was shot in the stomach. His surgery went okay. He's got a young wife and two kids."

"Did you—?" Elise shivered. "The men, did you—?"

"Yeah," Bill said. "We got 'em. After Nick went down, all hell broke loose. There were eight of them inside the warehouse. Two are dead, four wounded, and we got the other two trying to escape through the loading dock."

"I'm glad," she said.

"Yeah." Bill's eyes had taken on a bitter look. "Me too. I've never seen anything like what Nick did today, Elise. In twenty-seven years, I've never had a partner I admired as much as I do your brother."

"Thanks, Bill."

He accepted her statement with a solemn nod. "If you two want some coffee, my wife brought a couple of thermoses. They're in the waiting room."

Wil glanced at the clock in the hall. "Any word on how long the surgery might take?"

"No. This part is hell," Bill told him. "You just pace and worry." He gave Elise's arm a slight squeeze. "Why don't you go on in the waiting room and make yourself comfortable? It's going to be a long night."

"All right."

"And, Elise?"

She met Bill's gaze. "Yes?"

"He's going to make it. I know he is."

"Thanks, Bill."

With a slight jerk of his head, he indicated the waiting room. "Go on in," he said. "Your parents are waiting."

Chapter Eleven

The floor dropped out of her world. Elise gave Wil a helpless look. "I can't go in there."

His palm felt warm, reassuring, at the small of her back. "Aina, they need you now." With the slightest of pressure, he guided her toward the waiting-room door. "They're scared, too."

She shook her head. "I can't. I can't go in there."

With a look so tender it stole her breath, he gathered her into his arms. "You're the strongest woman I know," he told her. "They need you. They're afraid of losing another child, and they need you."

She drew several deep breaths, but nothing seemed to keep the panic at bay. "Go with me," she whispered.

"Anywhere."

Her gaze met his in the glare of the fluorescent lighting. For a moment, she allowed herself to believe that all would be well, that as long as she held on to Wil she could face the coming demons and escape whole. In his eyes she saw the tenderness, the warmth, she'd once craved from him. Drawing from his strength, she took his hand and walked toward the waiting room.

Neither of her parents looked up when she entered the room. Her mother sat on the green vinyl couch, a Bible clutched in her wrinkled hands. Always a plump woman, Anna Krestyanov had a crown of silver curls framing a broad face. The usual ready smile that made her features so appealing was gone. In its place were lines of worry and fear. Her lips moved in a silent litany of prayer.

Andrei faced out the window, his wide shoulders slightly hunched, his head tipped against the glass.

The breath slowly drained from Elise's body. A clawlike sensation began to relentlessly squeeze her chest until her heart ached from the pressure. She glanced from Anna to Andrei and back again. Her mother had begun a slow rocking motion. Behind her, Elise felt Wil's hands settle on her shoulders, offering reassuring warmth. She had to try twice before she found her voice. "Mama?"

With a startled gasp, Anna raised her head. A surge of tears wrinkled her face like a woolen blanket as she rushed forward to enfold Elise in a comforting embrace. "Elsa," she whispered. She raised her plump hand to cradle Elise's head. "My Elsa." Gently rocking her back and forth, Anna began to cry.

The impact of her mother's embrace caused a shattering deep in Elise's soul. Uncontrollable shudders swept through her as tears long suppressed rushed forth in a torrent. She sobbed against Anna's shoulder, clinging to her like a small child.

Feeling torn, slightly battered, Wil took his gaze from the heart-wrenching scene and sought Andrei's figure across the room.

He remained as he had been, facing the window. A stiffness had altered the curve of his shoulders. In the glass, Wil saw the reflection of his face. The expression made his blood run cold. Andrei's features were impassive, except for his eyes. Even from his distance across the room, Wil could see the bleakness in his eyes. Slowly he made his way to the window.

"Andrei," he said, laying a hand on the man's shoulder. "I'm sorry about Nikolai."

"Wilem." Despite the brief acknowledgment, Andrei didn't move.

The soft sound of weeping was the only respite to the oppressive stillness of the room. Wil gave Elise and her mother an anxious glance, then turned to face Andrei once more. "She needs you, Andrei," he said. "She's lost one brother. She's afraid of losing two."

Elise's father didn't answer. Wil fought back a surge of anger at the old man's stubbornness. All he could think about was the pain he'd seen on Elise's face when she told him about the quarrel with her father. He felt that pain as surely as if it were his own. He could only imagine what she'd gone through in the wake of his accusations. To make matters worse, Wil had turned on her, too. The thought made him feel slightly sick. And he lashed out at its cause. "Is it worth it?" he asked Andrei. "Has resenting her all this time made you happy? Is this what you wanted? You lost one son. You might lose another. Do you want to lose your daughter, too?"

"She is not my daughter."

Rage exploded in him. "Damn it, Andrei, why are you doing this?"

"She is not my daughter," he repeated.

"Pop?" Elise's voice was soft, distraught. Wil turned in surprise to find her standing just behind them. He hadn't realized she'd crossed the room. "Pop, please talk to me."

Andrei remained silent. Anna came to him, laid her hand on his arm. "Andrei," she said. "Please."

Andrei pulled his arm away from his wife's grasp. "I have nothing to say."

"Pop—" Elise's voice broke on a sob. Wil no longer resisted the urge to hold her. From behind, he wrapped his arms around her waist, so that she could lean against him. "What do I have to say to you to make you listen to me?" she asked Andrei.

"I don't know you," he said, still staring out the window. "There was a time when you didn't want to know me. Now, I don't know you."

"Andrei!" Anna's voice had grown sharp. "It is time to end this."

Andrei raised his head. Wil saw him meet Elise's gaze in the reflection. At the look in his eyes, Elise shrank back against Wil with a soft gasp. He tightened his hold on her. Andrei held her gaze for long seconds, then shook his head. "She is not my daughter," he said. At the finality in his voice, Wil felt Elise's body shudder. With a soft cry, she broke free of his embrace and fled the room.

Wil struggled for control as he stared at Andrei's back. Beside him, he heard Anna's soft sobs. Fighting a desperate battle with the cloying anger and frustration that threatened to engulf him, he thought about how much he'd loved these people. Once, they'd been like family to him. The bitter realization that because of Andrei he'd driven Elise from him filled him with rage. His insides clenched into a tight ball. His hands fisted at his sides. He felt the quaking frustration tear at his gut, pound through his blood, until he tasted it on his tongue. "Why?" he finally managed to ask.

Andrei turned on him like an animal caged. "I have told you why. She chose. I did not."

"No," Wil said, his voice lethally calm. "No, she did not choose. You both chose." He narrowed his eyes on the hard face of the man he'd once loved like a father. "And you both chose wrong. At least she admits it."

Anger flared in the other man's eyes. "She is not my daughter. You were Maks's friend. You know what we suffered. My daughter would not have betrayed me, have betrayed Maks."

Anna reached for his arm once more. "Andrei, no."

"Maks," Wil said, unable to keep the scorn from his voice. "All of this because of Maks. He died, Andrei. It's time you let him go. You're punishing your whole family because you can't let Maks go."

"Elsa made her choice," Andrei said. "She is no longer my child."

"And you're an old fool," Wil told him. He gave Anna an apologetic look. "I'm sorry, Anna." Tears streamed down her face. His heart broke at the pleading look she gave him. "I'm sorry," he said again, then strode from the room to find Elise.

She leaned against the cool wall of the chapel. Why? Why had she let him do this to her again? For ten years she had struggled to find herself amid the ruins her father had created in her heart. For ten years she'd forced herself to see her value, to believe in her abilities, to believe he couldn't hurt her again. In a few short sentences, he'd managed to crush her.

Now, when she needed them, needed to be with the people who loved Nikki most, her father had deliberately and cruelly hurt her. She dropped her head into her hands with a sob. God, what would she do if she lost her brother, too? She'd have nothing, no one. Her whole life, she'd been afraid. Afraid of moving from New York. Afraid of her new school. Afraid of losing another person the way she'd lost Maks. Now those fears seemed to swamp her, overwhelm her.

For years she'd managed to isolate herself from caring too deeply, loving too freely. But Wil had changed that. He'd opened her heart, found her secrets, shared her pain. Would he condemn her now, as he had before, because Andrei had turned on her? Would she be left without him, without Nikki, with no one?

"Aina." She heard Wil's voice from the door of the chapel, but didn't raise her head. At the soft endearment, she found a measure of strength. If he was going to reject her, he wouldn't call her that wonderful name in that tender voice. "Aina." He hunched down in front of her. "Look at me."

Elise slowly lifted her head. Wil took both her hands in his, pressed a kiss to each palm, then cradled them in his warm grasp. "I'm sorry," he told her. His voice carried a wealth of emotion.

She felt a fresh surge of tears. "Oh, Wil . . ." Wrapping her arms around his neck, she leaned into him. He shifted to sit beside her on the bench, then pulled her into his lap. Cradling her like a child, he pressed his lips to her temple. "I'm so sorry."

"Why?" she sobbed. "Why did this happen?"

"I don't know." Gently, he rocked her. "I don't know."

They sat that way for a long time. She drew strength from his heat, while he drew solace from her touch. When she finally raised her head, she felt completely and utterly drained. The emotional turmoil of the past few hours had dragged the spirit from her soul. The look he gave her carried with it a host of emotions. She pressed a soft kiss to his lips, to tell him that she understood, that words weren't necessary. "We should go check on Nikki."

"I told Bill Garrison where to find us. We can stay here awhile." He shifted her in his arms. "I'm sorry he did this to you," he told her, referring to her father.

"He's hurting."

"So are you."

Slowly, she nodded. "Yes." She buried her head in the crook of his neck. "Thank you for staying with me."

"I'm not leaving."

The words sounded like a vow. "Wil?"

"Yes?"

"I'm sorry about tonight."

A shudder coursed through him. She felt it as his arms tightened around her. "I'm glad I could be here for you."

"No. I mean earlier."

"I'm sorry, too. Not for what we shared, for why we shared it. I didn't want to hurt you, Aina." His voice was gruff.

"That word," she said, deliberately steering the subject to safer territory. "What does it mean?"

"What word?" he asked, pressing a tender kiss to her forehead.

"Aina. Every time I asked, you told me it lost something in the translation."

"It doesn't translate exactly," he confessed, "but I can give you a close approximation."

Brushing the damp tendrils of hair from her forehead, he held her gaze for long, meaning-filled seconds. In his fog-colored eyes was a look that stole her breath, and somehow began to mend her soul. "It means 'joy,' Aina. You were always my joy."

* * *

Wil had no idea how long they sat in the chapel, waiting for some word on Nikki's condition. Holding Elise in his arms he stroked her hair, breathed her scent. And over and over again, in his mind, he replayed the words of their conversation in her apartment. Calling himself a thousand kinds of fool, he found comfort in the way she clung to him. A few hours ago, he'd threatened to walk out of her life forever—not that he figured he had a snowball's chance in hell of sticking to that threat. Something about Elise always drew him back. The thought that a few seconds later and she would have faced this crisis alone was enough to send him to his knees in front of her.

Everything she said to him that night at the Rack Room had been right. He'd been too angry, too *arrogant,* to admit it, but she'd been right. He'd lost her once, but even then he'd been the one to withhold himself emotionally. He'd been so afraid of losing her that he pushed her away.

Hiding behind Maks's memory, he'd tried to drive her away from him. Twice. Why in heaven he should have been given another chance, especially when he'd managed to thoroughly screw up the first two, he didn't know, but he cherished her closeness, protected it deep in his heart, where it completely filled the yawning void that he'd tried so long to ignore. She fit against him, and with him, as if she'd been made especially for that purpose. Her spirit linked with his to bring him a joy he'd never known. He clung to it like a fragile new flower, understanding how easily it could be crushed.

For the first time in ten years, he fully realized the extent of the wrong he'd done her. Andrei's anger had been like a palpable thing tonight. Wil had realized, too late, that his resentment had been misdirected, that he'd been so quick to judge Elise by his standards, never willing to trust her when she told him her side of the story.

When he thought of Maks, sorrow flooded through him. It was past time he quit protecting himself and began thinking about Elise's needs before his. She needed to be free from the terrible guilt she'd carried so long. He needed to free her from it. With a certainty born the minute he'd seen the cold look in her father's eyes, he knew he couldn't wait any longer. It was time to tell Elise about Maks. Even if he lost her, he'd know that he'd set her free to heal. As soon as they had news about Nikolai, he vowed, he would give her the truth. If it helped heal the resentment, the bitterness, between her and Andrei, it would have to be enough for him.

"Elise?" Bill Garrison's voice sounded from the doorway.

Both of them started. "Bill," Elise said, scrambling from Wil's lap. "What's happened?"

"Nick is coming out of surgery. His doctor should be out in a minute."

Wil rose from the bench, gathered Elise's hand in his, then headed for the door. "Let's go."

When they joined Andrei and Anna in the waiting room, Anna hurried to them. Elise hugged her. "It's going to be all right, Mama. Everything is going to be all right."

Andrei turned back to the window, but this time Elise ignored him. She sat with her mother, holding her hand, waiting out the awful long minutes that ticked by. Bill paced anxiously around the room, and Wil did his best to keep from losing his sanity.

Finally the surgeon joined them. The compassion in her gaze told Wil the news was not good, but neither was it devastating. Her scrubs were splattered with blood, her eyes tired, her face drawn. "I'm Karen English. I'm sorry you've had to wait so long," she told the small group. "We removed all three bullets. The last one was lodged very near to his heart, and it took us a while to get to it."

"How is he?" Elise asked.

"He's resting. He sustained quite a bit of internal damage, and his condition is still critical." She glanced around the room. "Nikolai seems to have an extraordinary will to live," she said. "Once, we almost lost him." With a slight smile, she pulled the green cap from her head. "But he wasn't ready to go yet. The next few days will tell, but I'd set his chances at better than fifty percent."

Anna buried her face in her hands with a soft cry. Bill's breath left his body in an audible *whoosh*. Elise wrapped her arm around her mother's shoulders. "Can we see him?" she asked.

"One at a time," Dr. English said. "And please don't upset him. His condition is still very serious. Because I think it's good for him, I'm going to authorize for one of you to be with him around the clock. You can take shifts if you want, but I think it will do him good to hear you. I want you to talk to him."

"We will," Elise said. "Thank you."

Dr. English turned to go. "I really believe he's going to make it," she said. "He's a very lucky man."

Nikki looked strange lying in the hospital bed, his dark hair rumpled against the pillows, his face drawn. Tubes jutted out from his nose and arms, while machines blipped and hummed around him.

Slowly Elise approached the bed. When she folded his large hand in both of hers, she was surprised at its warmth. Somehow, she'd expected his skin to be cool to the touch. Life seemed to pulse through him, and in that instant, she found hope. "Oh, Nikki..."

She pressed his hand against her face. "You promised you wouldn't scare me like this." It might have been a trick of the light, but she was almost certain she saw his mouth twitch. "And it's nothing to laugh about, either," she told him. "I could have lost you."

For countless moments, she simply stared at him, absorbed the blessed feel of life from his hand. "I love you," she said. "You'll never know how much I love you." She might have imagined it, but the lines in his face seemed to soften.

Brushing a lock of his thick hair off his forehead, she pressed a kiss there. "I have to go now. Mama's going to sit here with you. I'll come tomorrow, and we'll talk," she promised. Gently she laid his hand back on the sheets. "Get well, Nikki," she whispered. "I need you to get well." With a final look at his pale, sleeping form, she left the room.

Wil was waiting for her just outside the door. She stepped into his embrace. "Thank you for bringing me," she told him. "For being here."

He rubbed his chin on the top of her head. "Thank you for asking." Tipping her away, he studied her face. "You all right?"

"I will be." With a deep shuddering sigh, she felt the tension drain from her. In its wake was a bone-deep exhaustion. "He's going to be all right, Wil."

"Yes."

"Take me home? I'm exhausted."

She fell asleep the instant she sank into the passenger seat of his car. He buckled her seat belt, brushed her hair from her face, lingered to press a soft kiss to her forehead. "Sleep, Aina," he whispered. "I'll take care of you."

On the long drive back to her apartment, he had plenty of time to think about all that had happened. Like daggers to his heart, he recalled the angry words she'd hurled at him in her apartment in the minutes before Bill's call. He was ashamed that it had taken a nearly fatal tragedy to make him realize the magnitude of his mistake.

Elise was right. Every time she got close, he pushed her away.

Once, he'd barely survived losing her. That was when his feelings for her had been the pure, uncomplicated longings of a young man. What he felt for her now bore no resemblance to that simpler time. Everything about the way he felt toward Elise was complex and frightening. He wasn't sure he'd survive losing her again. The way she'd clung to him tonight in the chapel, the way she'd turned to him for comfort during the long hours of the night—he needed those things the way he needed oxygen. God help him, he'd allowed himself to love her again.

His anger at Andrei still had not subsided. Nor, if he was honest, had his anger at Maks.

Because he needed to touch her, he took her hand and rested it on his thigh. In her sleep, she turned her head toward him. The moonlight cast shadows on her face, emphasizing the exhausted lines around her eyes and mouth. The confrontation with her father, he knew, had taken its toll. Emotionally battered, she'd been on the verge of collapse by the time she left her brother's room. It amazed him that she'd made it to the car under her own steam.

Unfortunately, he feared, the storm had not yet ended. Casting a quick glance at her, he couldn't prevent the warm feeling that seeped through him. For tonight, he vowed, he would allow himself to be in love with her again. There'd be time enough for the problems tomorrow.

By the time they reached her apartment, it was almost dawn. Elise was sleeping soundly. Wil didn't have the heart to wake her. He dug through her purse until he found her

keys, then lifted her from the car to carry her the short way
to her door. She didn't stir until he set her on the bed. As
he straightened, he felt her fingers curl into his jacket.
"Don't leave," she mumbled. "Please."

"I'm not leaving. I'll sleep on the couch."

"No." She didn't open her eyes. "Here. With me."

"Elise—"

She tugged at his jacket. "Please."

He couldn't resist her. Carefully he removed her shoes so
that he could settle her beneath the covers. He quickly shed
his jacket and shoes, then crawled in beside her. She curled
into his arms with a contented sigh. "Thank you."

"You're welcome, Elise."

She pressed a sleepy kiss to his jaw. "And thank you for
calling me, Elise."

He fell asleep, feeling content for the first time in ten
years.

Chapter Twelve

Disoriented, Wil concentrated on the sound. It seemed to reach him through a long tunnel of fog. Pounding. Someone was pounding on the door.

He opened his eyes, and memory assailed him. Elise still lay curled against him, her face pressed to the curve of his throat. Dark circles smudged her eyes, and tired lines still etched her face. She'd probably have to sleep for the next twenty-four hours before her body rejuvenated itself both emotionally and physically.

Casting a quick glance at the clock, he realized it was nearly three in the afternoon. Gingerly, careful not to disturb her, he slipped from the bed. The cool air met his skin like an arctic breeze. Elise had awakened hours before, cold and shivering. Delayed shock had begun to set in. Wil remembered pulling the comforter on her bed around them, then needing to shed his chambray shirt, as he'd begun to sweat. Even the heat hadn't been incentive enough for him move away from Elise, who clung to him in sleep as if he were the only thing that kept her from drowning.

His temples throbbed from the tension and stress of the previous night, and as the pounding on her door continued, he shook his head to clear it. Stepping over his shirt, he walked, barefoot and bare-chested to the door. Dragging a hand through his disheveled hair in a fruitless attempt to restore order, he pulled open the door.

And found himself eye-to-eye with Parker Conrad.

Parker blinked. "Larsen."

"Hello, Parker." The other man stared at him. Wil felt last night's contentment begin to ebb away. "When did you get in from Bangkok?"

"Earlier than you expected, evidently."

Frustrated, Wil shrugged off his lingering exhaustion and motioned Parker into the apartment. "I'd appreciate it if you'd keep your voice down. Elise is still asleep."

"Oh?" He raised a dark eyebrow.

"This isn't what you think. Not what it looks like."

"I don't doubt that," he said. "Elise wouldn't betray me like this."

Despite his determination not to like the man, Wil's opinion of him rose several notches. At least he had the good sense to respect Elise. "No. She wouldn't."

Parker set his briefcase down on the hall table. "I was able to get back earlier than expected. When I went by the office this morning, Carrie told me about Elise's brother. When I couldn't reach Elise by phone, I was worried."

"I called Carrie this morning, then unplugged the phone. Elise is worn out. She needs to rest."

"Thank you for taking care of her." The statement seemed genuine, free of hidden meaning. He'd followed Wil to the kitchen, where Wil scrounged about for coffee filters and coffee.

"Do you know where the filters are?" he asked Parker.

"Third cabinet, bottom shelf."

Wil tried not to feel irritated at the intimate knowledge of Elise's kitchen cupboards. "Thanks." He started the coffee maker before speaking to Parker again. "Like I said, this isn't what it looks like."

"I suppose I should be glad that you don't know where the coffee filters are."

Wil shook his head. "She needed someone last night. It was rough."

"I can imagine."

"I think she needs sleep more than anything."

"How is Nikolai?"

"Still critical, but he seems to be doing all right." Parker sat in one of the oak chairs. Wil leaned his hip against the counter. "The next few days are going to be touch and go."

"She must have been terrified."

"Yeah."

A tense silence fell between them. When the coffeepot began to gurgle, Parker asked, "Were her parents there?"

"Yes."

"I see."

"You think so?"

The other man frowned. "Of course. Elise and I have discussed the situation in detail. It must have been quite difficult for her."

"It was."

"And you were there to pick up the pieces."

Wil ignored the sarcasm in the statement. He could just imagine how he'd feel if he came home to find another man asleep in his fiancée's apartment. Turning to pour two cups of coffee, he said, "Elise couldn't have handled being alone last night. I was just glad I could be here for her."

After a long pause, Parker cleared his throat. "I am, too."

Wil handed him a mug. "I think things are going to be pretty hard on her until after Nick gets out of the hospital. She's going to have to deal with her parents a lot, and Andrei isn't exactly the forgiving type."

"So I understand." Parker sipped his coffee. "How long have you known Elise, Wil?"

Wil glanced at him in surprise. "Almost thirty years."

"Hmm." He seemed to ponder the situation. "Have you ever known her to do something impulsive, for no reason at all?"

"Sure. Lots of times."

"Hmm," he said again. "I haven't."

Wil frowned. "What do you mean?"

Parker considered him for several long moments as he sipped his coffee. "I'm not sure," he said at last. "I just think Elise and I need to talk about it."

Wil opened his mouth to speak, but just then the door of Elise's bedroom opened. With her flannel pajama top half unbuttoned, her hair mussed and her eyes heavy-lidded with sleep, she looked more like fifteen than thirty-five. With a sinking sense of dread, he felt the full weight of responsibility bear down on him. The contentment he'd felt last night had come to an end. They were back in the storm.

Elise glanced from Wil to Parker, then back again. "What's going on? What time is it?"

Parker stood to press a kiss to her forehead. Wil's fingers tightened on his coffee cup. "It's after three," he told her.

"In the afternoon."

"Yes, darling." Parker brushed the hair off her forehead. "You must be exhausted."

She stared at him, still visibly disoriented. "You're home."

"Yes. I finished earlier than I expected. When I heard about Nikki, I came straight over."

"Nikki." The mist cleared from her eyes. "I need to call the hospital."

Wil glanced at Parker. He was watching Elise with a hungry expression in his eyes that made Wil's chest hurt. With measured precision, he set his coffee mug down on the counter. "I think maybe I should go, now," he said. Looking at Elise, he added, "You'll call me if you need anything?"

She stared at him for several seconds, then slowly nodded. "Yes. Yes, I will."

"All right." He went into the bedroom to collect his shirt and jacket. When he returned, dressed, Elise was on the phone with the hospital. Wil extended his hand to Parker. "Take care of her," he said.

The other man seemed to understand the implied message. He took Wil's hand in a firm grip. "I will. Thank you."

Elise was still on the phone, so Wil pressed a kiss to her forehead, mouthed, "Goodbye," then left the apartment.

She hung up the phone with a soft click. Nikki's condition hadn't changed. Cautiously she glanced at Parker. He was studying her with an indecipherable expression on his face.

She sat down, reached for his hand, then exhaled a long breath. "Welcome home."

"I'm glad to be home."

"I guess we should talk."

"So," Parker said, after long seconds had passed, "what do you want to talk about?"

Elise gave him a slight smile. "You're a nice man, Parker."

"I try."

She stared at her mug of coffee. "That's why I can't keep doing this to you."

He took her hand in his and waited until she looked at him. "Why don't you let me go first?"

"Because I'm the one who should be doing all the talking."

"Yeah, well, I'm more used to having my own way."

With a self-deprecating smile, she said, "I don't deserve you, you know."

"That's true." He leaned back in his chair, his eyes twinkling despite the grim tone of the conversation. "I've always been too good for you."

"And you're modest, too."

"Incredibly humble. Did I tell you about the book I'm writing. I'm going to call it *Humility, and How I Attained It.*"

Elise laughed. "Sure to be a bestseller."

"Elise," he said, his expression turning serious, "I think I know what you're going to say."

"You do?"

"Yes. I'd have to be a fool not to notice the way Wil Larsen looks at you. The way you look at him. I saw it first at the garage, then that night of Alex Devonshire's charity benefit at the Art Institute."

Elise felt her skin flush. "Parker—"

He held out his hand. "I think I was aware of it long before you were. When I left for Bangkok, I knew something was wrong. Each time I've spoken with you over the last couple of weeks, you've been edgy and distracted."

"I'm sorry."

"The heart has a way of doing that to a person."

"Still, I didn't mean to hurt you." Elise leaned forward to cover his hand with her own. "Please believe that. If you don't believe anything else, believe that I never meant to hurt you."

"I know you didn't. And the truth is, I think I always knew we weren't going to make it down the aisle."

"You did?" Her eyes widened.

"Yes. I wanted to believe we could work it out, but somehow, I knew you had doubts."

"I wanted to marry you, Parker."

"I know you think you did, but you didn't love me." Before she could protest, he said, "It's all right, Elise. I can be a little hard to love."

"That's not true."

"Thanks for the defense."

"It isn't. You're a wonderful person. If I had half a brain in my head, I'd have fallen for you like a ton of bricks."

"Even if my parents are obnoxious."

She smiled. "Even if."

"But you didn't, did you?"

Elise winced. "No," she admitted. "I didn't."

"You can't choose who you're going to fall in love with, Elise. If you could, I'd have picked Georgette Duvet."

With a slight laugh, Elise said, "Never trust a woman named after a bedspread—that's what I always say."

"Nevertheless, her father could have done wonders for my career."

"So instead of poor Georgette, you picked me."

"That's right. I fell in love with you, Elise. I fell harder and faster than I've ever fallen in my life."

"Oh, Parker..."

"But you didn't love me back."

"I wanted to."

"That means a lot to me."

"It's true. I— If it hadn't been for Wil, I would have married you. I would have made it work."

Parker shook his head. "Elise, I don't want the woman I marry to feel like she has to work at our relationship. I want her to love me as much as I love her. You couldn't give me that."

She felt the tears begin to sting her eyes. "I'm so sorry," she told him again. "I'm just so sorry."

With a gentle smile, Parker reached for her left hand. "You know," he said, "I never liked this ring."

"You didn't?"

He rubbed his thumb on the surface of the large diamond. "Nope. Too splashy. It wasn't really your style at all. You didn't like it, either, did you?"

"I never said that."

"But you didn't."

"I might have picked something smaller."

He grinned at her. "And less ostentatious."

"Maybe."

"Definitely. In fact, I think it makes your hand look wrinkled."

"Parker." She frowned at him.

Ignoring her, he continued to study the ring. "You should have had a white diamond and not a yellow one." He pointed to her knuckle. "See how it makes your skin look sallow."

"It does *not* make my skin look sallow."

"Hmm . . . Still, I think you'd be better off without it." He finally met her gaze. "Don't you?"

Her heart warmed at the light in his eyes. "I guess you're right."

Slowly he removed his ring from her finger. He slipped it into his jacket pocket, then reached up to caress her face. "Elise, don't let him get away from you this time."

"I'm not sure I have him to begin with."

"You do. I can tell."

"You don't understand. There are things—"

"I understand more than you think I do. I know that until you face and deal with the rift with your father, you're always going to be guarding your heart. He hurt you very much, just like you hurt him."

"I didn't—"

"Elise," he said, his voice insistent, "let me say this. It's time you realized that you can't walk around keeping people at arm's length so they can't hurt you. That's a very lonely way to live."

"I don't do that."

"Yes, you do. You lost Maks. You lost your dad. You lost Wil. You're scared to death of losing anyone else. It's no wonder you're wiped out today. I'm sure the thought of losing Nikolai was terrifying for you."

"He almost died. Anyone would have been upset."

"Of course. But were you angry at him, too?"

She looked at him, stunned. How could he know? Understanding showed in his intent gaze. "You know," she said.

"I know. You were angry because you thought he was going to leave you. It's all right to feel that way. Nobody can tell you what to feel. You just need to learn that if you're going to keep anyone from getting close to you, you're going to be lonely for the rest of your life."

The tears began to fall. "This is going to sound like a really obnoxious thing to say, but that's amazingly astute for a man."

His gruff laugh pleased her. Parker rarely laughed. She was glad she could give him that. "One thing about growing up with wealthy parents, you get to spend a lot of time in therapy."

She sniffled. "You're one of the most psychologically healthy people I know," she told him. "God knows you've got me beat hands down."

"I just know that falling in love with you gave me some insight into how you think." He stuffed a napkin into her hand. "Now, do you want me to give you a ride to the hospital, or would you rather I drop you off in Valdona on the way?"

She managed a watery smile. "Don't I get to drive myself?"

"Absolutely not. You're too tired to drive, and besides, this is my last act of proprietary dating."

"And you have the better car."

Again he laughed. "And I have the better car."

She pushed her hair back from her face as she stood. "You know," she told him, "if I don't have much else to be proud of, at least I had the good sense to get engaged to you."

"You have a lot to be proud of. I hope you're going to recognize that one day."

With a watery smile, she said, "Let me just change my clothes."

"Take your time. I'm not going in to work until the day after tomorrow."

"I don't think it will take me that long."

With a brief shake of his head, Parker waved her toward her bedroom. "Just promise me one thing, okay, sweetheart?"

"Name it."

"Invite me to the wedding. I need an excuse to ask Georgette for a date."

Wil scraped vigorously at the stained varnish on the tulipwood Hispano-Suiza roadster, using the physical exertion to take his mind off his growing frustration. After two attempts to get him to talk, Jan had finally given up and disappeared into the small office that flanked the garage.

The radio was pumping out big-band music, but today Wil barely heard the normally calming instrumentals. Instead, he kept thinking about Elise holding on to him.

Images of what it had felt like to touch her, to kiss her, of her wonderful, intoxicating textures, filled his mind. He recalled the husky sound of her laugh, the same one that curled his toes. He remembered what she'd looked like when he danced with her. How she'd smiled at him. How she'd cried in his arms.

The expression in her eyes when she'd seen Parker Conrad sitting in her kitchen.

His scraping tool slid over his knuckles and tore the skin. "Ow! Damn it!" He popped the knuckle into his mouth to suck the blood from the cut.

"Careful, grease monkey," came a soft voice from the door. "You might need that hand later."

Wil jerked his head up to see Elise standing in the garage. As if in slow motion, he pulled his finger from his mouth. "Elise." His voice was a breathy sigh of disbelief.

"Hi."

"Hi."

She seemed nervous. She glanced at the roadster. "Is this a bad time? Because if it is, I could—"

"No." Wil dropped the paint scraper into his toolbox. "It's not a bad time. I just wasn't expecting you."

"Oh."

A nerve-racking ten seconds passed while he stared at her. He knew he should say something, but couldn't seem to make his brain function. He'd assumed that she'd spend the day at home, then go in to the hospital, and that he wouldn't have to confront his demons until he had time to adjust. Caught off guard, he wasn't sure what to do. "Where's Parker?" he asked, as if he cared.

"Home. He dropped me off."

"I see."

Elise began to fidget with the hood strings of her cotton windbreaker. "I, uh, just wanted to stop by and thank you again for everything you did last night."

"No problem." Move, you idiot, his brain warned him. His feet remained glued to the floor.

"You didn't have to do that. I know it couldn't have been easy for you, seeing my parents and all. Not after... Well, it just couldn't have been easy—"

When her voice broke on the last word, Wil finally snapped out of his trance. "Ah, Elise," he said as he walked across the floor to hold her. "It wasn't particularly easy for you, either. Was it?"

With a muffled cry, she sagged against him. "No."

"I'm sorry."

"I'm sorry, too."

"You know, we say that an awful lot," he said. "You think we're going to spend the rest of our lives saying we're sorry to each other?"

"We are if we keep acting so stupid."

A warmth like a rising sun spread through him. Wil continued to hold her, not yet willing to relinquish the exquisite feel of her in his arms. When she moved to break the embrace, he tightened his hold. "Not yet, Aina. I'm not through."

Her arms closed around his waist. "I'm glad. I'm not really through, either."

With a sad smile born of the realization that the time had come to talk about Maks, Wil rubbed his face against her hair. "Are you on your way to the hospital?"

"I told Mama I'd relieve her tonight. I don't have to be there until seven."

His eyes darted to the wall clock. It was after five. He couldn't delay it any longer. With a reluctant sigh, he draped his arm across her shoulders, then led her to the door. "Come on. Why don't you come home with me until it's time to leave?"

Neither of them spoke during the short walk to Wil's house. Both of them seemed to know that the air was too clouded to allow for any idle chatter.

With a strange sense of detachment, he led her through the front door. He'd resisted bringing Elise here, knowing that he'd find it difficult to handle the ghosts that would remain long after she left, but now he realized that the ache in his soul would persist with or without the physical memory of Elise's presence.

When she was seated at the kitchen table, he said, "Do you want anything? A soda or something?"

Elise shook her head. "I'm all right."

"Have you eaten today?"

"Parker made me eat a sandwich before he brought me over here."

"Good. I know you don't feel like eating, but you'll be glad you did later."

He pulled a bottle of root beer from the refrigerator, then took the seat across from her. "Elise," he said, "I have some things I need to tell you, things I'm not sure you want to hear, and—"

"Look, Wil," she said, interrupting him with an agitated flick of her wrist, "if it's about what happened last night, I don't want you to worry about it. We both went a little crazy. No explanations are required."

"That's crazy, and you know it. I owe you a whole hell of a lot more than an explanation."

"I just don't want you to feel that you're obligated in any way, because you're not. I know this is awkward for you. I know how you feel about my parents, and I realize that you can't possibly..."

"Elise..."

She ignored him, continuing on with her tirade. "...be expected to take sides. It wouldn't be fair if I..."

"Elise." His voice was more firm.

"...tried to manipulate you into something you weren't comfortable with. And I certainly don't feel that you ought to—"

"Jeez, Elise, will you shut up for a minute?"

Stunned, she stared at him. "What?"

"Shut up. Are you going to let me get a word in edgewise, or are you just going to explain to me how I feel?"

"I wasn't trying to do that."

He winced at the slightly stung expression on her face. "Aina," he said, his lips curving into a hint of a smile, "it's okay. Sometimes I think you do a better job of explaining to me how I feel than I do of explaining it to myself."

"You do?"

"Yeah. Everything you said to me at the Rack Room the other night was true. I'm the one that pushed you away."

"You were?"

"Yes. I had to. I know you don't understand that, but I had to. I did then, and I do now."

Her gaze dropped quickly, too quickly. He suspected she'd shifted her focus to the tabletop so that he couldn't read her hurt. "I broke my engagement with Parker this morning."

"Oh?"

"I— After last night, I thought—"

"Don't say it, Elise. It'll make it worse."

"Make what worse?"

"What I have to tell you."

"You're scaring me."

Not nearly as much, he thought, as he was scaring himself. Slowly he allowed the memories to take control. "The day I met you, you were six years old, and you were crying."

"Maks had broken my doll carriage."

"I fixed it."

"I remember."

"You gave me this adoring look, like I'd just found the secret to world peace."

"Sibling peace, anyway."

"And I wanted you to keep giving me that look. It was weird. I wanted you to look up to me more than I'd ever wanted anything in my life. I don't think I knew then how lonely I was. My mother died when I was so young. It was just Pop and me."

"I never did stop looking up to you."

"I know."

"I never even went through the same phases my friends went through. I never noticed other boys, because I never stopped looking at you."

"I knew that, too. For a while, I tried to pretend that I thought you were a pest. Maks liked it better that way."

"You were very convincing."

He laughed. The warm chuckle warmed a part of her soul. "Maybe part of me did think of you that way. I was uncomfortable, and embarrassed about how I felt for you. I didn't want to tell Maks that I wanted you to idolize me."

"Don't all men want women to idolize them?" she quipped.

"Not when the men are fifteen and the girls are twelve, they don't."

"I guess not."

"So I kept it to myself. It was fairly easy then. I really thought of you like my younger sister, someone I wanted to protect. When Maks died, it seemed so natural for me to step into that role."

"I thought you were stuck there forever."

"Sometimes I thought so, too." Pausing, he studied the neck of his root beer bottle. "I especially thought so around the time you turned sixteen, and I found out I couldn't look at you like a brother anymore."

Frowning, she thought back to the time in her life. She'd been unhappy then, struggling to find her place in the world, more interested in books than in boys, self-conscious about the way her body had developed faster than her friends', a fact that her ill-fitting clothes only emphasized. Wil had seemed a safe haven. In his garage, in his home, she'd felt comforted. She'd belonged. "If I'd known," she confessed, "I'd have been all over you."

"I thought about that. Actually, I thought about you being all over me so much, it's amazing I didn't lose my mind."

"Does this explain why you got so surly with me?"

"Yeah. Every time you walked into the garage, I started having the fantasies."

"Really?" The notion made her avidly curious. And more than a little heated.

"Really. I had this one continuing fantasy about what you and I could do in the back seat of that 1932 Cadillac my father was restoring."

"I had quite a few of those myself," she admitted.

"I doubt yours and mine had much in common." He downed another sip of the root beer. "Mine had all the lurid markings of a nineteen-year-old male in heat."

Elise couldn't prevent the mischievous smile that curved her lips. "Wil, I'm so amazed."

"Yeah, well, I wasn't amazed. I was about to go stark raving mad. If my hormones had been running any hotter, I'd have combusted." He shook his head. "Damn, Elise. The way you filled out those dresses gave me the sweats."

"I can't believe you waited until I was twenty to make love to me. You know I would have fallen at your feet if you'd asked me sooner."

"I knew. But I wanted you to see me, not Maks's best friend. I wanted you to look at me and want me the way I wanted you."

"That night in the garage."

"Yeah, that night. I saw it in your eyes that night. Even you were amazed."

"For the first time, what I wanted from you had nothing to do with cuddling."

He gave her a rueful smile. "It's a good thing. I'm surprised I didn't shock you."

"You couldn't have shocked me. I wanted you so desperately."

"I don't remember it being very pleasant for you the first time."

"Want to know a secret?" she asked.

"Sure."

"It knocked my socks off that you wanted me so much you lost control like that. I didn't have any experience, you know."

"I know. The minute I discovered that, I lost any shreds of restraint I had."

"But I knew enough to know that a man your age wouldn't normally go wild like that."

"Not unless he wanted the woman so much he couldn't help himself."

She smiled at him. "That's pretty much how I saw it. I have to tell you, it was really flattering to have you paw me that way."

"If I'd known, I wouldn't have been so thorough the second time."

"Don't get me wrong. I've got no complaints about our sex life. You were incredible."

"We were incredible together," he told her. "That's what we need to talk about."

"Wil?"

"This isn't going to be pleasant."

She felt the warmth drain from her heart. "What's the matter?"

After a long pause, he dropped the front legs of his chair back to the floor with a dull thud, then rose to walk to the window. "What you said the other night, about how I pushed you away—didn't you ever wonder why?"

"Of course. I think I was too blind to see it at the time. You wanted to marry me. I wanted that, too. I always figured the rest would work itself out."

He braced one hand on the window frame. "I didn't want to do it, Elise. God knows, I was petrified of losing you, but I just didn't see how I could love you the way you wanted and not tell you the truth. You weren't going to let me keep any secrets."

"The truth?"

"About Maks."

Ah. Elise felt a warm kind of relief seep through her. She'd always wondered if these demons haunted Wil the way they haunted her. This, she knew how to handle—she'd dealt with it herself. All she needed to do was let him talk it through. It made her sad, an aching kind of sad, to realize that he'd carried this pain for so long. She wanted to go to him, to heal his hurt. His tense posture told her how much of a strain the burden had been, and Elise had to re-strain herself from crossing the room to wrap her arms around his waist. Even from her distance across the room, she could feel the anguish in him. "What about Maks?" she gently prodded.

"You were so young when he died, Elise. You idolized him."

"You think so?"

"I knew it. He was the oldest in your family, and all of you, from Andrei to Nikolai, believed in Maks."

"I loved him very much."

The inarticulate sound that tore from his throat seemed a cross between a laugh and a groan. "You all did. I did, too."

"I know."

"Maks was my friend. I loved him like he was my own brother. In fact, I loved him so damned much that I never told anybody, not you, not your parents, not anybody, what I knew."

"What did you know, Wil?" she prompted, wishing she could spare him this, knowing she couldn't.

"Elise," his voice was harsh, "Maks's accident wasn't an accident."

"It wasn't?"

"No. About three years before it happened, he'd started getting involved with things he had no business doing. He was drinking regularly by the time we were thirteen. I'd say he was an alcoholic by his fourteenth birthday, maybe sooner. At fourteen, he started doing drugs, and by fifteen, he was dealing."

Wil turned from the window to face her, his face a ravaged mask of longing. Elise bit back a sob. She'd give any-thing to spare him this. Wil scrubbed a hand over his face. "Back then fifteen-year-olds did not deal drugs. It's horrible now, but then, it was unspeakable. I didn't know what to do. I knew he was handling for this guy on the East Side named Gino Scartoni. I also knew that Maks didn't want to fool around with the kind of guys Gino worked with."

"Mafia?"

"Yeah. Big in the trucking industry. Union thugs. Pop and I had talked about it, about the influence they had in the neighborhood. He always believed that I couldn't make good decisions if I didn't know what was going on."

"Smart man, your father."

"Like most of the ethnic areas in the city, we had mostly blue-collar workers—unionists."

She nodded. "And men like Scartoni knew that they needed our fathers if they wanted to stay in power."

"That's right. I kept warning Maks, telling him not to get involved. I pleaded with him. When he started selling that crap, I hated him for it. One of the reasons I spent so much time with him is because I thought I could keep him straight."

Elise swallowed the tight knot in her throat. Honest, decent, caring Wil. He'd given up so much for her, for all of them. "But you couldn't?"

He shook his head. "The day of the accident, he'd confessed to me that morning that he'd started stealing money from the guy he handled for. He'd taken almost a thousand dollars by then, a nickel and a dime at a time, and was using it to buy his own stock. He wanted to set himself up as a dealer, without running interference for somebody else."

"And the dealer found out?" Elise asked.

"He found out. Maks was run down deliberately."

"Oh, Wil."

"I didn't know what to do," he said. "Maks was so important to you, to your family. I didn't think I could tell the truth and hurt you more."

At the pained expression on his face, Elise wanted to gather him into her arms. But she knew he'd have to face the demons his own way. Wil turned to the window once more. "Every time your father said something about Maks's memory, I got a little sick inside. At fifteen, I was just scared to death. I was afraid that if I said anything, Scartoni would get to all of you. As I got older, and I saw what Maks's death had done to you, how your relationship with Andrei had started to disintegrate, I was terrified to get close to you. I was caught in a trap between loving you and needing to protect you."

"Didn't you think I'd understand if you told me the truth?"

"I don't know what I thought, but I knew I couldn't be with you, love you, and not do something to ease the guilt and grief you felt over Maks's death." He turned to stare at her again. "If I told you the truth, I knew how much it would hurt you. I couldn't destroy you like that."

The look on his face sent her running to him. Elise wrapped her arms, tight, around his middle, and tried to absorb his pain. Wil seemed stunned by her embrace. For long seconds, his arms hung by his side, then slowly came around her shoulders. "Oh, Wil," she said, pressing a kiss to the hollow of his throat. "How can two people as smart as we are be so stupid?"

She felt him tense. "What are you talking about?"

"I knew," she told him. "I always knew. I was twelve years old. I wasn't blind. I didn't know the depth of what was going on, but I knew the substance. I'd seen him drinking. I'd even covered for him a time or two. I knew what he was doing, and I couldn't make him stop. That's one of the reasons I resented my father so much after Maks died."

With a soft groan, Wil dropped his head back against the window. "My God," he breathed. "What have I done?"

"Wil—" she laid her hand against his bearded cheek "—we were kids. We didn't know better. Maybe if we'd been older, we could have handled it, but the whole time you were protecting me from the truth, I was protecting you."

"Aina." He rubbed his lips across her forehead. "There was a time when I would have given ten years off my life for you."

"I felt the same way."

"The day you argued with your father, I had an engagement ring in my pocket. I was going to propose to you that weekend. I can't believe we got that close, and then I threw it all away."

"It wasn't your fault." Raining kisses along his jaw, she cradled his face in both her hands. "It wasn't."

"I couldn't fight it anymore. I needed you. My soul needed you."

"I needed you, too."

"Then you argued with your father."

She relaxed against him, then went easily into the vee of his thighs when he seated himself on the wide window ledge. Wil's hands rested on her waist as he gazed up at her. Elise threaded her fingers into his thick hair. "No wonder you were so hurt," she said. "If you were carrying around all that guilt over Maks, I understand, now, why you felt like I'd betrayed my father. The way you saw it, you'd done everything including hiding what you knew about Maks in order to protect my family. When my father told you I'd turned my back on them, you must have felt like all your hard work had been in vain. Am I right?"

"You're right. I would have done anything for Maks. Keeping your family together was so important to your father. When I realized I'd carried around that burden for so long—and it didn't seem to matter to you—I just exploded. It was like setting off a time bomb."

They spent several minutes finding solace in each other. Wil finally found the courage to finish the conversation. "Elise?"

She seemed to sense his mood change. "Yes?"

"I want you to know something about last night."

"What?"

"The reason I didn't make love to you had nothing to do with the fact that you were still wearing Parker's ring."

She leaned back so she could see his face. "It didn't?"

"No. I'm not that honorable." He studied her serious expression in the waning afternoon light. "I didn't because I couldn't give you what you wanted."

"What do you mean?"

"Ten years ago, we were lovers. You were right about what you said. I was ready to give you a physical commitment, but not an emotional one. If I'd made love to you last night, we'd have been right back where we started."

With a wary expression he had come to recognize as a storm warning, she slipped away from him. "Well, that's just great, Wil. It's perfectly all right for you to tell me how you were forced to do everything you did because of how *you* felt, what *you* needed. But that's as far as it goes, isn't it?"

"What's that supposed to mean?"

"As soon as the emotional stakes get too high, as soon as you might, just maybe, have to admit that you acted like a self-impressed, arrogant fool, then you have to duck out the back door."

"That is not true. I told you I was sorry for what happened."

"You told me you were sorry for the way things turned out. It's not the same thing."

"You're being ridiculous."

"Oh, yeah? So look me in the eye and tell me you were wrong."

"Hold on a minute—"

"You can't do it, can you?"

"You're not—"

"I didn't think so. So since you can't admit that you were wrong, I'm supposed to take all the blame. Again. Well, I'm not doing it this time."

"Aina, listen to me."

"I can't believe that after you saw what happened last night with my father, you still think that this is my fault. I can't make him accept me."

"It's not about him. It's about you."

"I've done everything I can do," she insisted. "What do you expect? Do you want me to grovel to him?"

"No." Struggling for patience, Wil drew several calming breaths.

"I've dealt with it, Wil. That's the best I can do."

"Damn it. Don't you want this to work out?"

Her laugh was bitter, more like a groan. "Nobody wants this to work out more than I do. But wishing doesn't make it so." She retrieved her jacket from where it lay across the back of a chair. "So here we are," she said. "Back where we started. You resent me, and I resent you."

"That's not true."

Ignoring the comment, she shrugged into the jacket. "Only trouble is, Wil, you had to go and turn my life upside down again." The eyes that met his had a chill in them that threatened to freeze his soul. "I hope you're pleased."

Without waiting for an answer, she headed for the door.
Wil levered away from the window. "Elise, wait."
"Sorry, Wil. It's time for me to move on."
Before he could stop her, she walked out of his house.

Chapter Thirteen

Elise stroked Nikki's hand with her fingertips. Relief had flooded her when she'd found Bill Garrison in Nikki's room instead of her mother. After she left Wil's house, Jan had insisted on driving her home to pick up her car. By the time she reached the hospital, she'd been too drained for another emotional confrontation. Bill had explained that he'd dropped by the hospital to see Nikki and found Anna, exhausted, asleep in the chair by her son's bed. Firmly he'd sent her home, promising to wait until Elise arrived.

He'd informed her that Nikki's condition had been upgraded from critical to serious, and that Dr. English seemed to be very optimistic about his recovery. With a shuddering sense of gratitude, Elise had settled in by his bed to talk, and wait.

She'd made it through the first hour by talking about trivialities. Still stinging from her confrontation with Wil, she'd needed something, anything, to keep her mind off him. She'd read Nikki the sports page and the op-ed section of the *Tribune*. Soon, however, she'd run out of small talk.

Before she knew it, she'd been telling Nikki about the events of the past few weeks. At first, she'd felt strange confessing the long story to her silent brother, but soon, the more she talked, the more she'd found she was able to reason things out in her mind.

Beside her, he lay still, his warm hand clasped in her fingers. The only noise in the room was the raspy sound of his breathing and the buzz of the monitors.

"So that's the whole story, Nikki," she told him. "And now, I don't know what I'm going to do. Wil keeps telling me that I've allowed myself to be governed by what I think I should do and what I think I want, but you know how Pop feels about this. You know I can't change his mind." A fresh surge of tears brimmed over in her eyes. She was beginning to feel as if she'd done nothing but cry for three weeks. "He expects me to confront Pop, and I can't do it. I just can't. I was so scared last night that I was going to lose you. When Pop couldn't face me, not even then, I knew there just wasn't any hope." Pressing her face to his hand, she kissed the tanned flesh. "I'm so glad you're all right, Nikki."

One of her tears plopped onto his skin. She kissed it away. "I don't know what I'd have done if I lost you." Was it just a trick of her imagination, or did his fingers flutter in her hand?

With a quick breath, Elise glanced at his face. "Nikki?" Had he moved? "Nikki, can you hear me?"

Again his fingers seemed to flutter. Tightening her grip on them, she leaned over him to brush his hair off his forehead. "Are you awake?" she asked him. "Did you squeeze my fingers?"

A soft gust of air broke from his parted lips. Elise laid her hand on his face. "Don't push yourself. You don't need to say anything." This time, she was certain she felt him tug on her hand. She leaned closer to his face. "What is it?"

Slowly, with what appeared to be a supreme effort, Nikki's eyes fluttered open. Elise stared into the amber-colored depths, seeing recognition, seeing a sparkle that made her want to weep with relief. "Oh, Nikki..."

He parted his lips to speak, wet them with his tongue, then tried again. "So," he finally said, his voice a rusty whisper so quiet she had to practically press her ear to his mouth to hear him. "Is he going to marry you, or do I have to beat the hell out of him?"

Three days later, Elise returned to work. She hadn't heard from Wil, although she knew from Nikki that he'd stopped by the hospital several times. With the auction just a week away, her days were filled with almost enough details and crises to keep her mind off her problems.

It was the nights that were agonizing, long, sleepless and miserable. She began to fear the hours she'd spend alone in her apartment with nothing to do but think about him. Once, her home had been like a safe haven, free from the rush and pressure of the city. But now, she saw him in every room.

Over and over, she studied the picture of herself dancing with her father. This was where she'd come from, who she'd been. How had she allowed herself to lose that person along the way, and how could she get her back? In the long hours of the night, the answers began to take form.

And she knew, knew with a surety she hadn't felt for years, that she had just one hope of happiness. It lay with Elsa Krestyanov.

When Kate English allowed Nikki's discharge a week later, with the strictest possible orders that he had to keep still, rest and not allow anything to hinder his recovery, Anna and Andrei took him home with them.

Without even the reassuring visits with her brother, Elise felt more bereft, more alone, than she had in her life. A part of her resented Wil for doing this to her. Before he unsettled her life, she'd been satisfied, if not content. Things in her life had been simple. Choices few. Decisions easy.

In a few short weeks, Wil had taken her peace of mind and turned it into chaos. Worse, he'd made her love him again. And he'd left her exactly as he had before. Hurt and deserted.

The days passed in relentless succession as she struggled with herself, with the choices that lay before her. Twice she nearly lost her temper with Roger Philpott. The day before the auction, she had agreed to take delivery of the cars from Jan Larsen. It never occurred to her that Wil would oversee the vehicles' transport himself. That must be the reason, she decided, why her heart lodged itself in her throat the moment she saw him standing in the auction house, a clipboard in his hand, waiting for her. She'd deliberately chosen this auction facility for its large storage area. It had enough space to display the cars in. But now she almost regretted the rural location. She would have felt less trapped if she hadn't been forced to see Wil again in the relative solitude of the glorified barn.

Her heels clicked on the concrete floor as she slowly moved toward him. She'd chosen this particular location for the auction because of the wide, barnlike doors, which provided ease of access for the antique cars, and its large space. Today, it seemed cavernous.

"Hello, Elise." Lines of fatigue marred his handsome face. He looked much as he had when she first saw him a couple of weeks ago, except for the slightly haunted look in his eyes.

She swallowed. "Hi. I was expecting Jan."

"He refused to come."

The air between them seemed to thicken as she took the clipboard from him. "Still playing matchmaker?"

"Something like that."

The heat from his body seemed to envelop her. Elise pushed a tendril of hair behind her ear as she studied the clipboard. "Everything looks fine," she told him. "Where do I sign?"

"Don't you want to inspect first?"

Quickly she glanced at the collection of twenty vehicles, parked in neat rows, their paint and chrome gleaming in the artificial light. "No," she said, forcing herself to meet his gaze. "I trust you implicitly."

For long, tense seconds, he stared at her. "Aina—"

"Where do I sign?" An urgent need to flee the auction house, his presence, began to build within her.

With a muttered curse, Wil flipped a page on the clipboard. "Here."

She scrawled her signature, then handed the paperwork to him. "You'll invoice me within thirty days?"

"Per our agreement."

"Per our agreement."

They stared at each other. Neither seemed willing to walk away. "I've been meaning to call you," he said, as if that explained the silence of the past few days, "but Pop and I have been busy finishing the work on the cars."

"Of course." She wouldn't give him an inch.

"It's not that I didn't want to, Elise."

"Whatever you say."

"Damn it, you aren't going to make this easy, are you?"

"Why should I?"

"Why indeed?" He exhaled a long breath, then changed the subject. "So how are things coming for the auction?"

"All right." The neutral conversation gave her time to collect her wits. Grateful, she seized on it. "I've already sold most of the items to various museums and private collectors. Tomorrow all we have to auction are the cars, a few odds and ends, some art pieces, and the wedding dresses."

"Wedding dresses?"

She nodded. "Chester Collingham had a fetish. There are seven dresses from different eras. Each has some type of historical significance. One belonged to Princess Claire." She was babbling, but couldn't seem to stop. If she stopped, he'd leave.

"Fascinating."

At his quip, she ended the inane conversation. "Sorry. I'm sure you have work to do." She would have left then, but Wil's hand closed on her elbow.

Through the linen fabric of her suit jacket, his fingers felt warm, like heated steel. "Elise, wait."

Several seconds passed before she could make herself look at him. "What do you want, Wil?"

"You." His voice broke on the word. "I want you. Aina, I'm miserable."

Despite herself, she swayed toward him ever so slightly. "I can't do this."

"Tell me you've slept more than eight hours since the last time I saw you."

"I haven't."

"Then why are we doing this to ourselves?"

"Because you want something from me I can't give you." She almost choked on the words.

"Can't or won't?"

Something inside her started to crumble. "There's no point in having this conversation," she told him.

"How long are you going to let yourself be ruled by your head, Elise. What's it going to take to let your heart make a few of the choices?"

Because the question echoed the one she'd asked herself so many times over the past few days, she couldn't answer it. "We've said everything there is to be said."

His fingers remained on her elbow, but the grip loosened, became a caress. "Have you seen Nick since he went home?" he asked.

"You know I haven't."

"He's doing much better. He misses you."

"He called me."

Another nerve-racking pause. "Do you want to see him?"

Elise knew all too well that Wil wasn't asking her to see Nikki. He was asking her to face her father once more. "I'm not welcome there."

"I'll drive you. I'll stay with you."

"I can't go there, Wil." Unable to hold his gaze, she glanced away. "I'm not strong enough."

"Aina." Wil pulled her into his arms. "I'm dying without you."

The soft fleece of his sweatshirt pressed against her face like a comforting blanket. "I'm miserable, too," she confessed.

"Please." His hand cupped the back of her head. "Please."

For long moments, she enjoyed the feeling of holding him again, of being held. His nearness comforted her, like a balm to her weary heart. With Wil, she had the strength to do what she couldn't on her own. "Promise you'll stay till it's over."

He sucked in a ragged breath. "Elise?"

"If you promise to stay, I'll go with you."

For long, breathless moments, Elise stared at the butcher shop, and the small apartment above it, that had been her home for nearly twenty years. Little had changed on the bustling street in West Chicago.

Children on bicycles laughed as they played in the street. A lively game of baseball occupied the vacant corner sandlot. A sumptuous display of pastries still decorated the front window of Otto Korlov's bakery. Stands of fresh fruit still sat in front of the corner market. A wooden sign, cut in the shape of a suit jacket, still hung in front of Martin Bernstein's tailor shop.

And the window of her father's butcher shop still read Krestyanov Sons.

Beside her, Wil took her hand. "You okay?"

"No." She continued to stare at the building.

"It's going to be all right, Aina."

"What makes you think so?"

Wil nudged her chin until she faced him. "Because you're here. Because I have faith in you."

"What happens after today?" she asked.

He rubbed his thumb across the curve of her mouth. "We'll take this one step at a time. All right?"

After a brief hesitation, she nodded. "All right."

In silent mutual agreement, they stepped out of the car into the warm afternoon. Elise felt oddly out of place, like an intruder in a world where she didn't belong. Her gray linen-weave suit seemed inappropriate, her upswept hair a bit too formal.

And her feet hurt.

She glanced down at her gray pumps in amazement. She'd grown up wearing shoes that didn't fit. Always she'd had hand-me-downs from Maks, until his feet had stopped growing. Then she'd shared shoes with Anna, despite her mother's smaller foot size. As an adult, she conscientiously sought shoes for their comfort. She spent a fortune on the best-made, most expensive shoes she could own. The pair she wore had never hurt before, but being here seemed to arouse the remembered pain.

Wil's hand settled at the small of her back. "Ready?"

No. She'd never be ready for this. She'd run from this moment for ten years. Through the window of the shop, she saw her father laughing with several customers. Countless times she'd walked down this street to that very sight. Now it all seemed to be happening in slow-motion, as if her memories were overlaying the reality. "The back door," she whispered. "I want to use the back door."

Wordlessly Wil followed her down the narrow alley to the back of the butcher shop. The narrow iron staircase that led to the upstairs apartment was lined, as always, with fresh linens. Anna put them out to dry every afternoon. Elise picked up one of the cotton aprons and slipped it over her head.

The worn cotton was butter-soft against her hands, testimony to the hours Anna had spent scrubbing the stains from its front. She fumbled briefly with the strings, adjusting the apron until it tied at her waist. Without looking at Wil, she stepped into the back of the shop and picked up the push broom.

Andrei's laughter boomed from the front of the store. He was in the middle of telling a story about Nikki's accident, one Elise suspected he shared with every customer, when she stepped into the brief hallway that separated the back storage room from the shop. Andrei didn't look up. Elise continued to sweep.

Several long minutes passed while she pushed the broom in the remembered ritual. When finally the bell on the front door rang, signaling the customers' departure, the shop fell silent.

"Benjamin," Andrei called toward the back of the shop, "is that you? You're late today."

Elise stepped from the shadows of the back room into the small corridor that separated the storage area from the butcher shop. Andrei was facing away from her. "It's been a good day, Benjamin," he said. "Mrs. Weischman, she's having a party. She bought three racks of lamb." Elise's throat went dry. "Why were you late? Did you get held up at school?"

Late. Why was she ten years late doing what should have been done long ago? "I'm late because I was too stubborn to listen to my father—" she said. Her voice broke on the last word.

Andrei spun around. His wide shoulders partially blocked the sunlight from the front window, and an eerie shadow settled on the interior of the shop. Eyes so very much like her own met her gaze. In them, she saw an indecipherable emotion that frightened her. Squelching a growing sense of panic, she resisted the urge to flee to Wil, where he still stood, in the shadows of the storeroom.

She indicated the broom in her hand instead. "I see you're training a new boy?" Andrei still didn't answer. "He doesn't get the corners, just like I used to." She pointed to the small pile of dust she'd swept from the storeroom. "And the cobwebs." Pointing to the ceiling, she continued. "You probably have to remind him to brush down the cobwebs. You know how Mrs. Weischman is. If she sees cobwebs, she'll complain." She choked out the last word as she saw her father's expression slowly begin to crack.

The implacable mask was gone. In its place was a fierce anger that made her insides tremble. "Why are you here?" he demanded.

Elise shivered. "Because I can't do this anymore." She set the broom aside. "I can't pretend it doesn't matter to me that I hurt you." Slowly, she walked toward him, encouraged when he didn't back away. "I never wanted to hurt you, Pop."

"You chose this way. You no longer wanted to be my daughter. This, it is not my fault."

She shook her head. "That's not true. That's not what I wanted." Two more steps. "I wanted to make you proud of me. Everything I did, I did because I wanted you to be proud of me."

"You gave away your name because you wanted my respect?" he asked.

The bitterness in his tone made her cringe. "I gave away my name because I was foolish," she said. "And I was young. Pop..." She walked the remaining steps between them. "I needed to know that you loved me. Maybe I did it to see how hard I could push you. I don't know. I just know that I'd lived in Maks's shadow so long, and the day I felt like I stepped from it, you rejected me."

"Maks." He said the name with a wealth of passion and sorrow. "You don't know what you say, Elsa."

"I do." She barely resisted the urge to clutch his apron front. "All I ever wanted was to be close to you. After Maks, I couldn't make myself forgive you for loving him more than you loved me." A tear plopped onto her cheek. Followed by another. And another. "And you never forgave me for not dying in his place."

Andrei's big body shook. Elise glanced at him in surprise when his large hands settled on her upper arms. "This is not true."

"It was, Pop. But we can't change that. I know how much you loved Maks, and I'm sorry I couldn't replace him for you. But I love you. I need you."

"Elsa." He said her name with such sorrow, that tears clogged in her throat.

"At the hospital—" she shook her head "—I needed you. I was so scared of losing Nikki, and I needed you. Why did you turn on me like that? What did I do to make you hate me that much?"

For long, unsettling moments, he stared at her. Elise began to wonder if he would even answer her. "I do not hate you," he said.

"Then why? Why, Pop?"

He drew a deep breath. "*Kynìeza,* what have I done?"

Startled, Elise met his gaze. He dropped his hands, then turned from her to walk to the window. Bracing his arms on the large jukebox, the same one he'd used when he taught her to dance, he hung his head forward. "Pop?"

He seemed not to hear her. "Elsa—" his voice sounded ragged, as if he'd swallowed gravel "—I am an old fool. What will I have to do for you to forgive an old fool?" She didn't dare answer. She was in serious danger of melting into the floor if she did. After several minutes, Andrei dragged in a weary breath and asked, "I have never told you about the day you were born, no?"

"No." Her voice was little more than a whisper.

"You do not know, then."

"Know what, Pop?" Elise's hands fisted at her sides as she watched him struggle.

"Maks, he was a good boy. I was glad to have a son, but your mama, she wanted a girl."

"You didn't?"

"In New York, I thought the boys, they would have a better chance at life."

"Oh." The knowledge that even then, long before the tragedy of Maks's death, he hadn't wanted her, wounded her.

"But then you were born," he continued. "From the first time I saw you, I lost myself. There has never been a baby more beautiful than you."

Elise sucked in a shallow breath as she tried to prevent a fresh flood of tears. Andrei continued to stare out the window. "You wrapped your fingers on my hand, and I lost myself," he said again. "It was for you we moved here. The boys, they would have survived, but I could not bear to see you there in New York.

"Maks, he died because he had no strength. He was weak, my Maks. I knew that. But you, you were my *Kynieza,* my princess."

"Pop?"

He seemed not to hear her. "I wanted to give everything to you. After Maks died, sadness filled our house. I didn't know how to find you in that sadness. If I pushed you from me, it is my biggest sorrow." He mumbled several phrases in Russian. Phrases she recognized as bitter self-recriminations. "I was angry that you blamed yourself for Maks's death. I was angry at my son for doing that to you. I loved Maks, but I never wanted him more than you. Never."

The raw feeling in Elise's throat eased as the sobs she'd withheld shook her shoulders. How could she have been so foolish? In their grief, they'd both pushed away the one thing they most wanted. "I'm so sorry."

Still Andrei didn't face her. "When you came here that day, when you told me you no longer were a Krestyanov, I lost my temper. I have regretted those words for ten years, *drouska.* You are not the stubborn one. It is me." He straightened his shoulders then, as if the weight had suddenly been lifted from them. "It is me," he said again. "I pushed you from me. In my sorrow for Maks's death, I pushed you from me."

"Then why did you tell Wil that I said all those horrible things?"

He shuddered. "I was ashamed."

"I never meant to shame you."

"Not of you," he said. "Of me. Of how I acted. I didn't want to admit to him that I'd pushed you from me. I couldn't tell him the truth. At the hospital—" he shook his head "—I was afraid. I couldn't think that I could lose you and Nikki the same night, so I turned you away from me. I hope you can forgive me for that."

She wiped her hand across her eyes, mopping at the tears that now flowed freely down her face. "There's nothing to forgive. I just want you to love me again," she whispered.

Reaching to the small shelf on the wall, he picked up a nickel. Elise watched, a glimmer of hope beginning to build in her wounded soul, as he dropped the nickel into the old jukebox and punched a few buttons.

Slowly he turned to face her. "Come, *Kynìeza,* stand on my feet. I will teach you to dance."

With a sob, Elise raced across the room and flung herself into his large arms.

In the shadows of the storeroom, Wil wiped a hand across his eyes. It wasn't every day that a man witnessed a miracle. He'd never loved Elise more than he did at that moment. What she'd done had taken more courage, more love, than he'd ever felt in his life. He knew in that instant that he could offer her no less. She owned his soul. Now he merely had to find a way to give it to her.

Then, because he felt the moment too private, too tender, to be witnessed by outside eyes, he turned and left the butcher shop.

Chapter Fourteen

"I look ridiculous." Elise tugged at the full skirt of the Princess Claire wedding dress. "I can't believe I agreed to wear this."

Parker, elegantly clad in white tie and tails, brushed her hands aside. He straightened the skirt with a few efficient swipes. "To be honest, I can't, either." He smiled at her. "It's not your normal style."

Elise frowned. "I'm starting to wonder if I have a normal style anymore. I've turned into a schizophrenic."

"Of course you do, darling." He attached the veil to her hair with a bobby pin. "It's a little odd, but it's yours."

His quip helped lighten her mood. Standing behind the screen that separated the staging area at the auction, she listened to the drone of the auctioneer's voice. Auction day had finally arrived, and Elise was practically a basket case. To make matters worse, one of her models for the wedding dresses had canceled at the last minute. If it hadn't been for

Parker's offer to help, she might have gone crazy. His call the night before had been like a godsend. With his usual efficiency, he'd helped her smooth over the last of the problems. It had taken more than a little prodding, but Parker had finally convinced her to wear the gown herself. In a way, she was grateful for the diversion. She'd spent the past couple of days with her parents, and while they still had a long way to go, they'd talked a lot, listened even more, and been able to go a long way toward mending the hurts of the past.

But she hadn't heard from Wil.

At first, she'd hardly noticed his absence. Her family had needed the time. There had been so much to discuss. Just being together had been crucial. By nightfall, however, she'd begun to wonder where Wil had gone. When she phoned Jan, he'd told her Wil had not yet returned to the garage. The following day, he'd called her, but even then he'd been almost deliberately vague. He'd seemed to be in a hurry to get her off the phone. Sternly she'd reminded herself that their last conversation had hardly given her a reason to expect anything more from him.

Parker seemed not to notice her distress as he finished adjusting her veil. "I suppose this is as close as we'll get to a wedding," he said.

Elise met his gaze. "I'm sorry, Parker. I know this is uncomfortable for you."

He covered her hand with his gloved one. "I told you before, I want what's best for you. If you're happy, I'll be happy."

Why, she wondered, couldn't she have loved this man? Impulsively she went up on tiptoe and kissed his cheek. "You're a very nice man, and I know some woman who's a lot smarter than I am is going to figure that out someday."

He grinned at her as the model whose dress had just been sold was escorted from the stage by her makeshift groom. "Ready, darling?" Parker said.

Elise nodded. "Wait for the auctioneer to do his spiel. I'm expecting this dress to be the top seller." She smoothed her fingers over the luxurious satin as she listened to the auctioneer's explanation.

"This next dress," his voice boomed, "is a gem. Princess Claire of Caldonia wore this in 1943. It's not only a gorgeous gown, it's a collectible for its contribution to silver-screen history."

"Now," Elise told Parker.

An appreciative applause greeted their entrance. Though she'd promised herself she wouldn't, Elise couldn't help scanning the crowd for a glimpse of Wil. As she'd suspected, he wasn't present. She squelched her disappointment with an overly bright smile at an astounded Roger Philpott.

"Well," the auctioneer was saying, "this is a pleasant surprise." He pointed to Elise. "This entire event owes itself to the woman in this dress. This, ladies and gentlemen, is the Elise Christopher who's been running you all in circles so she can take your money."

The crowd laughed, then applauded again. Elise managed a cheery wave, despite her sinking spirits. Jan stood by the back door. If Wil had planned to come to the auction, he'd have been with his father. She refused to consider what his absence might mean. There'd be plenty of time for misery when she wasn't standing in front of two hundred people.

Parker seemed to sense her distress. He gave her hand a reassuring squeeze. "Don't lose heart," he told her in a low whisper. "Sometimes things work out the way you least expect them to."

She gave him a surprised look. "What are you talking about?" Parker's eyes sparkled with an unusual twinkle. "You're up to something," she said.

"Perhaps." He inclined his head toward the photographer at the foot of the stage. "Smile for the camera, darling."

Elise groaned. She'd forgotten that a photographer from the *Tribune* was covering the event. This was just what she needed. A full-color picture of her and Parker Conrad in full wedding regalia sprawled across the front page of the paper.

After the pictures were snapped, the bidding began. As Elise had expected, it was fast and furious. The fact that Claire Davis had worn the gown gave it a considerably higher popular appeal than any of the other pieces. The bidding seemed to stall at four thousand dollars when a tremendous noise from the back of the auction house interrupted the auctioneer.

Elise frowned. Dear God, now what? It sounded like the roof was caving in.

Her frown quickly turned to a gasp of shock when she saw Wil, looking impossibly attractive clad in jeans, a white T-shirt and a suede jacket, riding toward her on a red 1957 Harley-Davidson XL Sportster. Roger Philpott appeared on the verge of apoplexy. Completely undisturbed by the reaction of the crowd, Wil rode the bike down the center aisle, stopped at the foot of the stage and fixed Elise with the sexiest smile she'd ever seen.

A tiny bubble of hope, along with the insane urge to laugh, found its way into her heart. "What are you doing?" she shouted above the idling engine.

"Showing you that I'm not a coward," he said. He indicated the crowd with a sweep of his arm. "You told me you didn't think I wanted to make a commitment to you."

"You didn't."

"Maybe not." He regarded her with a sexy go-to-hell look that made her toes tingle. "You also told me I wasn't willing to admit I was wrong."

"You weren't."

"Maybe not that, either."

His gaze turned serious. "But I got to tell you something, Elise."

"Here?"

"Here. You were right about everything. I pushed you away. I misjudged you. I was wrong. I was a fool."

"Oh, Wil."

"So Parker and I talked it over."

Elise frowned at Parker. "You knew?"

Parker nodded. "I didn't plan the gown, though. That was just nature's way of blessing this little fiasco."

Wil revved the motorcycle engine to get her attention. "We decided that you weren't ever going to trust me unless I was willing to really make a fool out of myself for you." His gaze scanned the audience until they landed on the newspaper reporter. "That's Larsen," he said to the astonished woman. "With an *e.*"

Elise couldn't stifle a laugh. Wil's gaze found hers again. "Parker and I decided," he continued, "that what you needed from me was a grand gesture. So I'm doing it in front of all these people." The flash of the photographer's camera made him smile. "In front of the media." His gaze turned suddenly serious. There was a raw hunger in his eyes that made her heart soar. "Because, my God, Aina, I'm going to die if I don't have you."

With a laugh of pure, undiluted joy, Elise pressed her hand to her mouth. Roger, she noticed too late, had risen from his seat and was stalking toward the stage. "Elise—"

he hoisted his considerable bulk onto the elevated platform ''—you've got to put a stop to this.''

''Oh, stuff it, Roger.'' Indicating the crowd with a flick of her wrist, she said, ''They're loving it.''

He was so aghast, his double chin dropped to his chest. Elise took the opportunity to push her bouquet into his hand. ''Everything's running like clockwork. You're going to make a mint for Brandy off this little event, and I don't even care if you take credit for it.''

''Elise . . .''

Ignoring him, she turned to Parker. ''Would you help me down?'' she asked.

Parker led her to the side of the stage, leaped down, then lifted her the two feet to the ground. Wil still studied her with that intent look on his face, the one that made her heart accelerate. With a soft smile, she put her hands on his shoulders. ''So tell me, grease monkey, is this a proposal, or what?''

To the applause of the crowd, he pulled her into his arms for a hot, satisfying kiss. When he lifted his head, he grinned at her, that funny lopsided grin that stole her breath. ''Am I acting like a big enough fool to suit you?''

''Yes.'' She laughed. ''Oh, yes.''

And before she could draw her next breath, he said the words she'd longed for. ''I love you, Elise.''

''I love you, too, you big idiot,'' she told him.

In seconds, the kiss flowered, ran hot and urgent and out of control. Wil pressed her to him with a ferocity that made her shiver. When he swept his tongue into her mouth, she clutched at his head. Nothing, but nothing, had ever felt as right as holding this man.

Wil's mouth was slanting over hers to deepen the kiss when Parker tapped him on the shoulder. Reluctantly Wil lifted his head. The befuddled look on Elise's face sent a jolt of pure adrenaline rushing through him. He almost told Parker to go to hell so that he could kiss her again.

Parker cleared his throat. "Listen, pal, I think this conversation would be best continued outside."

Wil grinned at him. "You know, I never expected to like you."

"Yes, well—" Parker assisted Elise onto the back of the motorcycle "—the feeling was mutual."

She laid her hand on Parker's face. "Thank you," she said.

With a brief laugh, he kissed her fingers, then laid them on Wil's shoulder. "Thank you, Elise. You taught me what it means to love an extraordinary woman."

Wil waited for her to wrap her arms around his waist before revving the engine once more. At the back of the crowd, Elise saw her father and Jan slapping each other on the back as if they'd just pulled off the coup of the century. With a happy laugh, she pressed her face into Wil's shoulder.

As he rode the motorcycle out of the auction hall, she heard Roger Philpott call after her on the microphone, "But... who is going to pay for that dress?"

With a happy laugh, Elise tossed her veil over her shoulder as Wil headed for the road.

And then, one by one, as if she were shedding shackles from the past as they moved toward their future, she left her white satin shoes lying in the dirt.

*   *   *   *   *

WELCOME TO SILVER CREEK COUNTY

A place full of small-town Texas charm, where
everybody knows your name and falling
in love is all in a day's work!

Award-winning author **SHARON DE VITA** has
spun several delightful stories full of matchmaking
kids, lonely lawmen, single parents and humorous
townsfolk! Watch for the first two books,
THE LONE RANGER
(Special Edition #1078, 1/97)
and
THE LADY AND THE SHERIFF
(Special Edition #1103, 5/97).
And there are many more heartwarming
tales to come!

So come on down to Silver Creek and make
a few friends—you'll be glad you did!

Bestselling Author

MAGGIE
SHAYNE

Continues the twelve-book series—FORTUNE'S CHILDREN—
in **January 1997** with Book Seven

A HUSBAND IN TIME

Jane Fortune was wary of the stranger with amnesia who
came to her—seemingly out of nowhere. She couldn't deny
the passion between them, but there was something
mysterious—almost dangerous—about this compelling
man...and Jane knew she'd better watch her step....

MEET THE FORTUNES—a family whose legacy is greater than
riches. Because where there's a will...there's a *wedding!*

FC-7

If you're looking for irresistible
heroes, the search is over....

Joan Elliott Pickart's

FAMILY MEN

Tux, Bram and Blue Bishop and their pal,
Gibson McKinley, are four unforgettable men...on a
wife hunt. Discover the women who steal their
Texas-size hearts in this enchanting four-book series,
which alternates between Silhouette Desire
and Special Edition:

In February 1997, fall in love with Tux, Desire's
Man of the Month, in **TEXAS MOON,** #1051.

In May 1997, Blue meets his match in **TEXAS DAWN,**
Special Edition #1100.

In August 1997, don't miss Bram's romance in
TEXAS GLORY—coming to you from Desire.

And in December 1997, Gib takes more than marriage
vows in **TEXAS BABY,** Special Edition's
That's My Baby! title.
You won't be able to resist
Joan Elliott Pickart's **TEXAS BABY.**

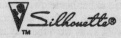

COMING NEXT MONTH